I0688306

Erasmus W. Jones

Gold Tinsel and Trash

Stories of country and city

Erasmus W. Jones

Gold Tinsel and Trash
Stories of country and city

ISBN/EAN: 9783744751100

Printed in Europe, USA, Canada, Australia, Japan

Cover: Foto ©Andreas Hilbeck / pixelio.de

More available books at **www.hansebooks.com**

GOLD ·TINSEL AND TRASH

STORIES

OF

COUNTRY AND CITY

BY REV. ERASMUS W. JONES

AUTHOR OF

*The Captive Youths of Judah, The Adopted Son of the Princess Llangobaith:
A Story of North Wales,* etc

———————•—•—◆—•—•———————

NEW YORK: HUNT & EATON
CINCINNATI: CRANSTON & STOWE
1890

PREFACE.

SOME of these stories have appeared as short serials in the *Northern Christian Advocate*. I have been often requested to publish them in book form. In looking them over it was found that they would make but a small volume, and "Gold, Tinsel and Trash," "The Conspiracy," and "I Took You with Guile," were added to the number. While in the main they bear particularly on Methodist usages, they are designed to interest and benefit all the branches of Zion, and check, in a measure, the rising tendency among professed Christians to indulge in worldly and unholy amusements.

E. W. J.

Utica, N. Y., 1889.

CONTENTS.

GOLD, TINSEL AND TRASH.

OTHER STORIES OF COUNTRY AND CITY.

GOLD, TINSEL AND TRASH.

CHAPTER I.

"DUST TO DUST," AND A COWARDLY PLOT.

THE fever had subsided, and reason had resumed the throne from which it had been banished for more than three weeks. But such had been the severity of the attack that there was hardly any hope that nature would rally. Dr. Thomas, a physician of wide repute, had faithfully attended to the sick man, and nothing which skill and personal friendship could accomplish had been wanting. Some two days after the fever had turned the sufferer expressed a wish to be left alone with the doctor for a few minutes, and the attendants left the room.

"Well, doctor," said Mr. Trevor, in a very faint voice and with a pleasant smile, " I understand the situation perfectly. I am about to emigrate, and I am fully prepared for the voyage. My mind is calm and my spirit tranquil. That religion which I embraced in my early youth sustains me now. I am very happy, and perfectly reconciled to the will divine. I simply wished to tell you this, and nothing more."

"Gordon," said the doctor, "the providence that takes you away in the midst of your days and in the height of your influence is mysterious; but in the light of heaven we shall clearly understand it. The grace so richly bestowed upon the husband and father will grandly sustain the wife and children. I must now leave. I will call again in the morning." The physician left, and the attendants re-entered the sick chamber.

The next day, after the departure of the doctor, the sick man spoke to his wife, who, with his hand in her own, was close to his pillow.

"Jennie, while I have yet a bit of strength I would like to have once more family prayer. Let Arthur and Alice be called in."

In a few moments, accompanied by their pastor, the children came into the room, and, sobbing, they stood by the side of their father's dying bed.

He cast upon them a loving smile and said: "My sweet, loved ones, your papa is about to leave you. You have been very good children, and in the bright hereafter we shall all meet again. We will pray together once more. Kneel down where I can put my hand on your heads."

The mother and children fell on their knees close together, within the reach of the father's right hand. All others in the room bowed before the Lord, while in faint accents and with a face illumined that good man offered his last prayer. When it was over he affectionately kissed his wife and children, and bade them farewell. He sank into a quiet slumber, and in the afternoon, without a struggle or a groan, the happy spirit passed away to the " Bright Forever."

Marvindale at the time of our story, thirty years ago, had reached a population of three thousand, and was noted for its many attractive features. It stood on both sides of a river which, owing to a large number of tributary springs, never became low. Its water privileges were very fine, and many of its citizens were engaged in milling. Within a mile of the place there was a small lake, surrounded by delightful groves, which rendered the vicinity in the summer season a favorite resort. There were in the village quite a number of stores, the most prominent of which was owned and conducted by Hon. James Mason.

Gordon Trevor until his sudden sickness had been a man of great business energy. But his strict attention to worldly matters did not retard his religious activity. He was one of the most efficient and liberal official members in the village Methodist church. His death spread a deep gloom over the whole vicinity, and his funeral was the largest ever witnessed in Marvindale.

Mrs. Trevor was an accomplished, amiable, and pious lady. Arthur was a splendid specimen of young humanity in body and mind, sixteen years of age. Alice, two years younger, was fair in person, kind in disposition, sprightly, and, with her brother, already a member of the Christian Church.

Although Mr. Trevor in his milling enterprise was a successful man of business he was by no means rich. At the widow's request his friends sold the mill property for a sum which, after paying all indebtedness, left the family in moderately comfortable circumstances.

Fortunately for the bereaved household there was in the village a very excellent academy, into which Arthur had entered some months before his father's death, while Alice preferred to remain awhile longer in the district school, under the training of a very superior teacher. The academy had flourished for years under the good management of Professor Lewis.

After Mr. Trevor's death Arthur, with a thoughtfulness and piety seldom found in a boy of his years, solemnly vowed to his heavenly Father that in all his movements at school and elsewhere he would aim to comfort his mother and protect his sister. With this holy pledge stamped upon his memory and graven upon his heart the boy took hold of the various branches of study with renewed energy.

Attending the academy at this time was a boy about one year older than Arthur, by the name of Mark Floyd. His father was a wealthy brewer residing in C——, about fifty miles from Marvindale. Floyd was a good scholar, but selfish beyond measure, and in order to accomplish his ends would often resort to deception and falsehood. He was domineering and arbitrary. His money, which seemed to be abundant, he freely shared with those boys who flattered his vanity and put up with his selfishness. In this way he found a few in his own class that were ready to run at his bidding. His love of being admired was immoderate, and this, more than any thing else, had urged him onward in his studies. The success of others filled his mind with jealousy. There were many in the school who did not know the depth of this youth's depravity, and among them was Arthur Trevor.

Mark was aware that Arthur was mastering his studies with astonishing rapidity, and that his own superiority in his class was in some danger. Such a disaster would be terrible. And so, from a low motive, he applied himself to his studies with increased vigor. In his recitations he appeared to good advantage, and more than one of the teachers in well-chosen words had bestowed praise upon the manner he and Arthur mastered their lessons. This did not at all please Mark. The equal praise bestowed upon Trevor made him wretched, and his countenance denoted displeasure. How widely different Arthur felt! He was delighted with the praise bestowed upon his young friend, and thought all the more of him for his perseverance and industry. One afternoon after having received the praise above mentioned, when the school had been dismissed, Arthur, noticing a frown upon Mark's face, addressed him in the most pleasant manner.

" Floyd, after those high compliments from your teacher I cannot account for your displeased appearance."

" If I am displeased," was the curt reply, " it is simply my own business. I presume you think that to be put on an equality with yourself is a great compliment."

"Mark, your words are unkind and uncivil," said Arthur, with some feeling. "It gave me pleasure to hear your perfect lessons, and I embrace the first opportunity to congratulate you."

"And in doing this you congratulate yourself," said Mark.

"Not at all," said Arthur; "I would rather be praised by my schoolmate."

"I am not in that mood just now," said Mark, "and a fellow that is so wonderfully delighted by a little praise from his teacher doesn't stand in need of any more praise on the same day."

"I am sorry to find you in such an unfriendly spirit," said Arthur. "Can it be possible that you are displeased because my lessons have been praised as well as your own? Mark, I cannot afford to have imperfect recitations in order to please you or any one else. I am going to do my very best, and so are you. If you leave me behind I shall rejoice in your victory. If you find yourself behind, which is not probable, can't you rejoice in mine?"

To the relief of Mark a number of the boys joined them, and Arthur Trevor in a thoughtful mood left the room and slowly walked toward home.

Floyd well knew that his treatment of Arthur was not at all in harmony with polite usages, and did not feel quite easy. But his selfishness outweighed his better judgment, and very unworthy and degrading purposes were readily admitted into his ungenerous soul. Trevor, who had never showed him that deference which some other boys had, must not be permitted to remain his equal.

The more Arthur reflected upon the brief conversation between himself and Floyd, the more that student fell in his estimation. His amiability and loving disposition did not at all interfere with his moral courage, decision of character, and keen sensitiveness to an insult. Therefore it will not be wondered at that after calm reflection on the situation he became more determined than ever to apply himself diligently to his books, and strive in a fair and honorable manner to reach a high mark in his studies.

The Hon. Judge Mason was considered by far the wealthiest man in Marvindale. When young he had studied law, and graduated with high honors in that department. He had been repeatedly elected to the Legislature, and subsequently to the State Senate. He had also served for some years as county judge. He might have easily reached higher distinction if he had permitted his friends to present his claims. He chose, however, in the midst of his popularity, to retire from politics and devote himself to the interests of his mercantile business. He was highly popular with the masses. With this his brilliant talents had much to do; but his kind heart, his wonderful benevolence, and his unblemished public record weighed more than his fine abilities. He was ever ready " for every good word and work." He was a devoted member of the Methodist Episcopal Church in the village and of its Quarterly Conference. He took deep interest in all educational measures.   He was specially interested in the Marvindale Academy, and to him much of its success was justly attributed. There was one annual " Mason prize," twenty dollars in gold, to a gentleman of the graduating class, for the best original oration in composition and delivery, with a ten-dollar prize for the best original essay from one of the lady graduates.   In addition to this he would often surprise other classes with irregular prizes, given for their encouragement and advancement.   His family consisted of a wife and one daughter, a young lady then in her twentieth year.

On the morning following Mark Floyd's ill-natured remarks to his young classmate Professor Lewis, at the close of recitations, addressed the class of the second year as follows:

"I am happy to inform you that as an incentive to study, and for the encouragement of faithful scholars, Hon. Judge Mason, with his usual liberality, has put in my hands two valuable prizes, to be competed for by members of this class at a time to be mentioned hereafter: ten dollars for the best original oration, in composition and delivery, and five dollars for the second best.   The competition is confined to young gentlemen.   This will make a lively entertainment aside from our usual exercises at the close of the term.   Those who will take a part in this contest will please hand in their names within a week from to-day.   The names will not be made public until the evening of the competition.   It is not expected that the orations will be equal in merit to those of gentlemen of riper years. Remember that they must be *original.* You may be tempted to borrow. Trample on the temptation and be honest. You may now retire."

This caused lively a talk among the members of the class. All the boys were at home in declaiming, but an original oration was something they had never undertaken. Some shook their heads and declared that it was beyond their ability. Mark was silent, and from his behavior it was impossible to understand his purpose. He most earnestly coveted the prize, but there were obstacles in the way, and how could they be removed? He well knew that in showing his ill-feeling toward Arthur he had seriously blundered and had injured his own chances. He saw that he must use different tactics or fail. On this day, after school in the afternoon, he met his young schoolmate, and in a very polite manner asked him to go with him to his room for a few minutes. Arthur readily complied, and they were soon seated in a well-furnished apartment.

" Trevor," said Mark, " yesterday my head ached badly. Under that bad feeling I felt cross and used language that I would not have used under other circumstances. I hardly knew what I was saying. I hope you will let that pass and say nothing about it."

" I will do that most gladly," said Arthur. " You ought to be thankful that in spite of headache you can get such splendid lessons."

" O," said Mark, wondering whether there was

any sarcasm in Arthur's reply, " I had mastered my lessons before the headache came on."

" That was fortunate," said Arthur, smiling, "and I would advise you to master your temper as well before you get another attack."

" That is good advice," said Mark, hiding a rising resentment. " But what do you think of Mason's new notion ? "

" I think it is very kind in him," was the reply; " but to ask an original oration from fellows of our ages is something new."

" And I should say perfectly unreasonable," said Mark, in a sneering tone.

" That cannot be," answered Trevor; " Judge Mason and Professor Lewis would not propose any thing unreasonable."

" This time I think they have," said Floyd. " What can boys of seventeen and eighteen produce in the shape of an original oration ? They will be laughed at. And will not such wretched failures discourage the class instead of advancing it ? I will have nothing to do with it, and I am informed that this is the feeling of the whole class."

" I can hardly believe that you have been correctly informed," said Arthur. " Professor Lewis knows what the class can do, and I am not going to despise his judgment."

" You may do as you please," said Mark. " I say again that I believe the boys will follow my example and that there will be no competition."

Here the conversation was brought to a close by

the coming in of two members of the class, and Arthur quietly departed.

" Well, boys, you are here a little sooner than I expected," said Mark, " and it doesn't look much as if I was to entertain my friends. To-day it must be on a small scale, hoping for something better in the future."

He then opened a cupboard, and placing before them a good supply of oranges, nuts, candies, and cakes, asked them to help themselves and to feel at home; which request, to all appearance, was cheerfully complied with.

" Baker, did you ask Tom Jones and Fred Williams to come?" asked Floyd.

" I did," was the reply, " but they declined in terms that you would not consider complimentary."

" Just as I expected," said Mark. " Those two chaps and Arthur Trevor are jealous of my standing in the school, and they would be glad to injure me if they could do it on the sly."

" They can't do it!" cried Thompson, inspired by a plentiful supply of oranges. " Hurrah for Mark Floyd! He is our leader, and we are ready to follow."

" You pay me too much honor, gentlemen," said Mark, " but I thank you for your cheering words."

" By the way," asked Baker, " what does Arthur think of this original oration business?"

" He thinks the job is too heavy for the class," said Floyd, "and in this I agree with him. Since his name is mentioned I will give you the nature of a good round joke which I am going to play on

2

him, and of course you will assist me. I assured
him that I was to have nothing to do with this contest, that it was altogether beyond our powers, and
that this was the sentiment of the whole class. I
am of the opinion that under this impression he
will not hand in his name. He is the only one that
I fear, and I have resorted to this little trick to
switch him off while our train passes. What think
you of that?"

"Good for you!" was the response.

"Now," continued the leader, "let us finish our
arrangements without delay, and let them be known
to no living person outside of our circle. Professor
Lewis will not reveal names."

Having furnished an outline of his intended
movements, and his companions having satisfied
themselves with their leader's delicacies, the party
broke up, and before the setting of the sun the
names of Floyd, Baker, and Thompson were handed
to Professor Lewis as competitors for the prize.

CHAPTER II.

THE ARCH-DECEIVER BROUGHT TO GRIEF.

NOTWITHSTANDING Arthur's defense of Judge Mason and the principal, the words of Mark had left some impression on his mind. If the rest of the boys were to stand aloof, of course there would be no competition. He wondered that such a good and ready speaker should look with disfavor upon a measure which presented him such an excellent opportunity to win new honors. Well, he would think the matter over, and would be in no haste to hand in his name.

One evening, as the mother with her two children sat in their comfortable parlor, the sister thus opened the conversation:

"Arthur, the girls all say that the first oration prize will fall either to you or Mark Floyd, and nearly all hope that you will be the lucky fellow."

· "I thank them for their good wishes," said the brother; "but Mark ridicules the whole thing, and says that he and the rest of the class will have nothing to do with it. He was very anxious to win me over to the same opinion."

"Now, that is very strange!" said Alice. "It is not at all like him and the rest of the class! Arthur, I don't believe that he told you the truth."

"If he did tell the truth," answered the brother, "I don't see any use in handing in my name."

"My boy in this matter should not be governed by the action of his classmates," said the mother. "He should inquire what is right in the premises, and what are the wishes of Professor Lewis."

"That is so, mother," said Arthur. "I told Mark as much. To-morrow ends the week. I will give Professor Lewis my name and will begin to think of a theme."

"You ought to have done it before, Arthur," said the mother, in a pleasant tone. "You will always treat Mark Floyd with proper civility, but he is not the one to be admitted into your confidence. You may possibly find out before long that his advice to you on this point was not prompted by honest feelings."

The door-bell rang, and presently the smiling countenance of Professor Lewis was seen in the room. He began at once with the object of his visit.

"My chief business is with you, Arthur; but I am glad to see you together, and please so remain. Arthur, I have wondered why you have not given your name as a competitor for the oration prize. If there are any obstacles in your way that you feel free to mention I will be glad to remove them, if within my legitimate power."

"We were conversing on that very subject when the bell rang," said Arthur. "Some days ago Mark Floyd told me positively that he would have nothing to do with this contest, and that the other boys had come to the same conclusion. He said so much that I have hesitated in regard to the matter. But by the advice of my mother I shall most gladly hand in my name to-morrow."

There was on the professor's countenance a mingled expression of sorrow and pleasure as he replied :

" Arthur, the obstacles can be very easily removed. I will not mention individuals, but I will assure you that I have the names of a fair number of the members of your class that will enter the competition. The names must be all in to-morrow. Arthur, please call at my room to-morrow *evening* at nine o'clock, and hand in your name. If during the day, at any time before that hour, you are asked by any of the boys if you have handed in your name, please give them a very emphatic '*No !*' " And the professor, with a restored smile, bade the company " good-night."

" Arthur, don't you now see through Mark's plot ?" asked Alice, with much feeling. " He wickedly lied in order to get you out of the way."

" But Professor Lewis did not say that Mark's name is on the list," said Arthur. " He may not have lied in that after all."

" But he did lie in that !" said Alice, with much spirit. " Didn't I watch the professor's countenance ? In my opinion Mark's name heads the list, and very likely it was handed in on the very day when he assured you that he would have nothing to do with it."

" Then he is a very much worse boy than I

thought he was," said Arthur, reflectively. "Let us hope, Alice, that he is not quite so bad as that."

"It is very good in you, my boy, to talk in this manner," said Mrs. Trevor. "I am pleased with your kind spirit. We will hope as best we can; but, as things appear now, I greatly fear that Mark Floyd, for a very selfish purpose, has deliberately told you an untruth."

"And it would be just like him to lie again by saying that an oration written by another person was his own," said Alice.

"Not quite so fast, my darling," said the mother. "It will be soon enough to judge of that after the oration is delivered. Let us join with Arthur in hoping."

The next day young Trevor attended school as usual. Mark and his associates seemed cheerful, and yet they showed a degree of nervousness. Was Trevor's name given to Professor Lewis? or would it be within the limited time? were questions that gave Floyd much uneasiness. If up to that time he had not taken that step the probability was that he had abandoned the thought. They would try and gain this coveted information. Mark had given full directions how to proceed.

The school was out for the afternoon, and the scholars were on their way to their respective homes and boarding-houses. In the most friendly manner Baker asked his young friend,

"Trevor, do you think that I am responsible for the imperfect manner in which I recite my lessons when I do my very best?"

"I think that the most of your recitations are very good," said Arthur; "we all fail sometimes."

"I fail very often," said Baker, "and you never fail. If I had the ability that you and Mark manifest I would not hesitate a moment to enter this contest. I wonder that such a bright fellow as Mark Floyd should refuse to engage in it. Trevor, you will have an easy victory, for of course you have handed in your name."

"Of course *I have not*," said Arthur, with studied force. "Mark assured me that all the boys were going to stand aside."

"It would be embarrassing to be the only speaker," said Baker, "and, for one, I don't blame you."

By this time their roads parted. Each went his way well pleased with the conversation.

In half an hour Floyd had his company together in order to hear Baker's report. ·

"The scheme has worked splendidly," said Baker. "As far as Trevor is concerned the coast is clear."

"Give me his exact language!" cried Mark.

This was soon done to the perfect satisfaction of the leader. "Ha! ha!" he cried, "We are going to have things our own way! Keep shady, boys! Mum is the word. Let us stand together. You know that I am not backward in rewarding my friends. Make perfectly free with those oranges. There are plenty more where they came from, and my purse is far from being empty."

At nine o'clock that night Arthur Trevor's name completed the list of competitors.

It was a late hour and the door was locked. In

one hand Mark held a letter which he had just read, and in the other a certain manuscript which denoted a fair degree of age. He seemed to be in deep reflection, as if balancing possibilities. Upon the whole he appeared pleased, and yet not quite free from fear. He well knew that he was contemplating the performance of a dishonest act. He tried to believe that it partook of the nature of a joke, but that effort was vain. He was determined to make the venture. His deceptive, lying course for the past two or three weeks had greatly strengthened him in his dishonest career. He had read both the letter and the manuscript, and was revolving in his mind the contents of both, especially those of the letter. He looked at it again, and gave it a second perusal. It ran thus:

"And so you stand in need of a little help, eh? Well, Mark, I am in the same fix myself. I am not in need of an ' original oration; ' I have stacks of them laid away. If by exchanging commodities we can help each other let us proceed to business. Drink I must have. Drink I will have! It is killing me, yet I cling to it for dear life; I am about half drunk now. But, degraded as I am, I will say to you, beware of the bewitching devil! I am in the power of a demon, and my moral powers are crushed. I expect to live and die a drunkard.

"Now to business. I send you an original oration. It was never printed. My chum at college said it was prime, and copied parts of it into his diary. It was many, many years ago, and five hundred miles from Marvindale; so that there is not the least danger that it will ever give you any trouble. Mark, you are not engaged in an honorable business; but that is your own look-out. I am in need of money; so let us hurry up matters. If the oration suits you, copy it, burn the original, and send me ten dollars. I will pledge to you my eternal secrecy. JOHN BUDLONG."

"I think I will do it, Jack," said Mark to himself. "The parts that are too smart I will tone down to my own level. I will put in a sentence here and there; just enough to make it 'original.' Ha! ha! Yes, Jack, I'll do it, and, sot as you are, I know you will never go back on me. This time I must not only win the prize, but I must excel. So, Jack, for the present I bid you 'good-night.'"

Soon after all the names had been handed in, Professor Lewis privately informed each competitor that the contest would take place in four weeks at the Presbyterian church. From the nature of the situation, as the reader fully understands, the contestants were as retired in their preparations as circumstances would permit.

The day arrived, and the exercises were to begin at 8 P. M. The notice had been widely circulated, and much interest was manifested on the part of the people. The villagers in large number hastened to the commodious building, while hundreds came from the adjoining country.

The audience was called to order by Professor Lewis, who said: "Ladies and gentlemen, it is not a common practice to ask for original orations from the class of the second year. But in many instances a departure from settled customs has proved to be a healthy improvement. We have not deemed it expedient to have a printed programme. You will be the more interested in learning the names of the competitors as one by one they are called and appear on the stage."

The first speaker was Mr. Baker. He chose for his theme "Truthfulness." He was followed by Mr. Thompson, on "The Elements of Success." Fred Williams was then announced, who gave the audience "The Reward of Perseverance." He was followed by Thomas Jones, who chose "Cicero" for his theme. Mark Floyd then marched on the stage in a graceful manner and spoke on "Life's Responsibilities." He left the platform under the full conviction that he was the last speaker for the evening and that the first prize was ready to drop into his hand. Smiles were exchanged between the plotters, but when the name of Arthur Trevor was called Floyd's countenance turned pale. The theme was "Moral Integrity." The young orator left the rostrum amid loud cheering.

"While the adjudicators are getting ready their report," said Professor Lewis, "the audience will be entertained with vocal and instrumental music."

In about twenty minutes Dr. Parker stood on the stage and said, "Your judges have fully agreed on the following brief adjudication: Mr. Baker's oration possesses many valuable thoughts. The delivery was on too high a pitch, and less violent gestures would have been an improvement. Mr. Thompson's oration possessed many 'elements of success.' It was marred by several grammatical defects and was not thoroughly committed to memory. Mr. Williams's oration is creditable as a composition, and the delivery, upon the whole, was commendable. Mr. Jones might have selected a subject more suitable to his age, but his effort was worthy of praise. Mr. Trevor, for a person so young, showed wonderful proficiency both in matter and oratory. Your adjudicators are extremely sorry to be compelled to state before this audience that Mr. Floyd is not legitimately in the contest. The prizes are for original orations. They have in their possession the most positive proof that the one he delivered was originally written many years ago by a young man at college. We hope that Mr. Floyd will be able to show that he was mistaken in regard to the terms of the contest.

"The first prize is awarded to Arthur Trevor, and the second to be equally divided between Fred Williams and Thomas Jones."

This was followed by loud applause. The victors were called on the stage and publicly rewarded. While the band played the large audience dispersed, well pleased with the entertainment and with the verdict of the judges.

Dr. Parker, who read the adjudication, was John Budlong's chum at college, who had copied parts of the oration into his diary, as mentioned in the poor drunkard's letter to Mark Floyd.

As the reader may well judge, Mark and his

dupes were overwhelmed with confusion. They hastened together to the chief plotter's head-quarters. So sure was he of receiving the first prize that he had made preparations for a gay time of feasting on a large scale. The disappointment was crushing, and his defeat double. He not only failed of getting the prize, but was also disgraced before the whole assembly. He could not plead ignorance, for on this very point the class had been faithfully warned by Professor Lewis. Mark's countenance denoted anger and defiance, while his two companions showed a degree of shame and some sorrow.

"Well, boys," said Floyd, with a forced smile of indifference, "we have been badly worsted. Baker, Arthur must have lied to you when he said that his name had not been handed in."

"I presume it was handed in that evening," said Baker. "I don't believe that Arthur Trevor ever told a lie. The lying was all on our side, and the punishment, at least a part of it, has quickly followed."

"I should judge by your whining tone that you are going to play the coward," said Mark, with a sneer.

"Call it what you choose," said Baker, "but for days I have been ashamed of the part that I was acting, and I have no particular fault to find with the manner in which it has terminated."

"And I would advise such cowards to leave my premises, and make their humble confessions to the powers that be," said Mark, in an angry mood.

"The best advice you ever gave me," said Baker, "and I will take it under my serious consideration."

CHAPTER III.

CONFESSION, DEFIANCE, AND AN INVITATION.

ON Monday morning, after chapel service, Professor Lewis said: " I have a painful duty to perform, and it must be done in the presence of the whole school. A most cowardly plot of deception and falsehood was concocted to keep away a fellow-student from participating in the late oration contest. The chief mover in this iniquity was Mark Floyd. In addition to this he has been guilty of dishonesty in presenting as his own before the audience the production of another person. Mark Floyd, what have you to say for yourself in view of this disgraceful conduct?"

" I have no confessions to make, and I ask for no favors," was the spiteful reply.

Without making any remarks on Floyd's language the professor went on, " I am sorry to know that in this proceeding Mr. Floyd was assisted by at least two members of his class. Of this we have abundant proof. I trust that on the part of these two gentlemen a more becoming spirit will be manifested than that which we have just witnessed."

At this point Mr. Baker left his seat and handed Professor Lewis a folded paper. The professor first read it to himself, and then, in harmony with the request of the subscribers, he read it before the whole school :

"We, the undersigned, confess with shame and sorrow that, in yielding to the persuasion of a member of our class to use deceptive and false measures for the purpose of keeping Arthur Trevor from the oration competition, we were ungentlemanly, unkind, and even wicked. We most humbly ask the forgiveness of Professor Lewis, Judge Mason, Arthur Trevor, and the whole school. If punishment cannot be avoided, we pray that it may be of such a nature as to spare as much as possible the feelings of our parents and friends.

"JOHN BAKER,
"JAMES THOMPSON."

"I would say to these two young men that, although their conduct in this matter was all they confess it to be," continued the professor, "yet, in making this frank statement before the whole school they show that they are capable of noble and worthy deeds. Mr. Floyd, you would better call back your defying words, and join with these young men in their confession."

"Never!" cried Floyd. "I detest the sneaking cowards."

"Then I have only to say," said Professor Lewis, "that John Baker and James Thompson are suspended for forty-eight hours, and that Mark Floyd is hereby expelled. You will now quietly go to your respective classes, and diligently attend to your studies. Let what you have witnessed this morning be an incentive to all to follow in the paths of truth and magnanimity."

Judge Mason's brother, Hiram, was a rich merchant in the city of New York. At an early age he had left the country for the metropolis, and procured a situation as an assistant book-keeper in a large house. Such was his proficiency in this department, together with his moral integrity and the interest he manifested in the success of his employers, that he was soon promoted. In the course of a few years his services were considered so essential to the house that, for fear he might be induced to accept offers from other houses, they offered him a share in the profits, and he became a junior partner. In about five years after the formation of this partnership he married a young lady from the country, with whom he had become acquainted during his school-days, the daughter of a farmer in good circumstances. She was well-educated, fair in personal appearance, slightly vain in her aspirations, a little inclined to claim superiority over her equals, and yet possessing a very commendable degree of kindness, sympathy, and affection. Such was Mary Downer, who captivated the heart of the thriving young merchant of the metropolis. She was taken to a fine mansion, well furnished, with competent servants to do her bidding. The married pair lived happily. The wife, although cherishing an excellent opinion of herself, entertained a far higher opinion of her husband ; and it gave her unbounded pleasure to believe that Hiram Mason had but very few equals, if any, on this terrestrial ball. This was well, and it served to keep Mrs. Mason's aspirations within a circle that was not extravagant. At the time of our story they had been married about nineteen years, and had an only child, a daughter, verging on seventeen. By this time Hiram Mason was rich, even in the New York sense of the term. He stood at the head of a large commercial house, and was considered worth at least a million, while yet only forty-five years of age. At his fine mansion on Fifth Avenue he was the same kind, genial man that he was twenty years before. Parties attended, and given, where so often " vanity of vanity" made itself prominent, failed to make our merchant a gay worldling. While yielding to his wife's wishes in all things that did not involve a sacrifice of moral principles, his soul was often sick in view of the utter worthlessness of scores and hundreds who moved in what was termed " the best society." He was a full believer in orthodox Christianity, but had never identified himself with any branch of the visible Church. In his younger years he had sat under the Methodist ministry, but since his marriage he had gone with his wife to a church of another communion, of which she was a member at the time of our story. Helen, the daughter, was exceedingly amiable, and her affectionate nature was visible in her countenance. Her strong love for her parents showed itself on all occasions. She possessed in rich abundance the noble moral traits of her father. She had shared in the privileges of the Sabbath-school of the church she attended, and had often listened to interesting remarks touching Christian doctrines both from her teachers and superintendent. She was not a stranger to serious thoughts in regard to her spiritual condition, and often felt a longing desire to be a genuine Christian and a member of the Church. But the deportment and aspirations of those of her associates who did belong to the Church were of such a nature as to repel her from seeking that relation. In them she looked in vain for that consecration and self-denial of which she had read so much in the New Testament. And what would it avail her to unite with a church where such a large proportion of the members vied with non-professors in the strife for worldly pleasure?

She was young, but for years these inconsistencies proved to be stumbling-blocks in the path of Helen Mason. Hitherto she had said but little in regard to this point, but occasionally she would startle her mother with questions touching vital experimental piety that would make Mrs. Mason uncomfortable for hours.

The mother in her lively imagination gave her daughter and only child a most splendid future. First, she saw her a reigning belle—a star of the first brilliancy, a leader in fashionable circles, admired by a dozen of the metropolis's wealthiest young men; after this the honorable lady of a splendid mansion, leaning fondly on the arm of her husband, while men in livery hastened to act her pleasure. The mother pictured spacious halls, sparkling diamonds, costly costumes, enchanting music, and graceful cotillons. Let us hope that high Heaven has in store something infinitely more brilliant and honorable than that for the daughter of Hiram Mason.

Mark Floyd, while on his way homeward, put together with considerable ingenuity a string of lies which measurably satisfied his father. But in less than a week the brewer received a long letter from Professor Lewis giving a minute account of the whole matter, together with the defiant spirit his son had shown on the Monday following the prize contest. The father, although a rough, swearing, immoral man, had sense . enough to know that Professor Lewis's version was the correct one. His subsequent interview with Mark was a scene of intense passion. The parent was exceedingly angry and the son stubborn and defiant ; so much so that the rich brewer saw fit to give Mark a very thorough shaking. This he did with perfect ease, for he was a large man and physically powerful. This was not the first boisterous interview between father and son, nor the first time that Mark had tried to account for his conduct with a falsehood. The shaking was a new process. But instead of proving a " savor of life unto life," in the case of this depraved boy it had the contrary effect. While suffering this brief but sharp chastisement he fully made up his mind concerning his future course. The next morning he was not to be found on the premises. He had left for parts unknown, and for his traveling expenses he had burglariously taken from his father's office the moderate sum of four hundred dollars. The father, being perfectly satisfied that Mark was the thief, and being abundantly rich, made no ado about the theft nor did he trouble himself in regard to the whereabouts of his son.

One morning, while at breakfast, a servant brought Mr. Hiram Mason a number of letters. He hastily glanced at the different directions and selected one.

"This is from Marvindale," he said as he opened it.

"Yes, and from Uncle James," said Helen, when she saw the familiar handwriting.

The letter was as follows:

"MARVINDALE, *May* 15, 18—.

"DEAR HIRAM: As a family we are well and happy. We unite in the most earnest manner in sending you and yours an invitation to spend a few weeks this coming summer at Marvindale and make our house your most welcome home. We long to see you and enjoy your society. We have not the attractions of the popular watering resorts, but we have a beautiful village, a delightful lake, trusty boatmen, and the most healthy region in the State. I am sure my charming young niece would enjoy our country life splendidly. You know we have a commodious house, and if it would please you to bring some friends with you it would certainly please us.

"The closing exercises of our academy, when a large class shall graduate, will take place on the 25th

of June. This will give Marvindale a lively appearance, and I think you would be pleased with the
proceedings. Let us hear from you soon, and
please do gratify us in this our most urgent request.

     "Yours, for myself and family,

                "JAMES MASON."

"Well, my dear, what think you of that?" asked
Mr. Mason, addressing his wife.

"I had purposed to go to Newport or Saratoga,"
was the answer. "It must be rather dull in that
little village. There are but very few there who
move in the best society."

"And what do you mean by 'the best society?'"
asked her husband, looking at Mrs. Mason with
some earnestness.

"I mean such society as we mingle in in this
city, or at Saratoga—the society we meet at our
evening parties," said the wife.

"I understand," said Mr. Mason, with a meaning
smile. "I have watched what you call 'the best
society' for years, and, to tell you my honest opinion, I consider it, as a whole, superficial and trashy,
abounding in vanity, conceit, and mental weakness.
I would gladly exchange it for one where the people make free use of common sense."

"My dear, I am sorry to hear you speak so before
your daughter, who is just being introduced into
society," said Mrs. Mason.

"Mary, I speak chiefly on our daughter's account,"
said Mr. Mason. "I should be exceedingly sorry
to see her following in the vain and frivolous foot-

steps of very many young people who move in what is termed 'the best society,' whose great effort in life seems to be to outstrip each other in devotion to dress and gayety, while their moral and intellectual natures are sadly neglected. If in Marvindale Helen would not find a large number of young people·who are far better entitled to the term 'best society' than hundreds who claim it in New York I am very much mistaken."

"I would be sorry to take Helen anywhere against her will," said Mrs. Mason, looking at the daughter, who seemed to be deeply interested in the conversation. "Where would you rather visit this summer, dear; at Newport or Marvindale?"

"My dear mamma, you should not consult my wishes at all," said Helen. "I shall be glad to follow my parents. But since you have asked me I will say that I have not the least desire to go to Newport or Saratoga, and that nothing on earth would give me more pleasure than to visit our dear relatives in Marvindale. And, mamma, even if I had arranged to go somewhere else that letter from my dear Uncle James would have changed my mind at once."

"That settles it," said Mrs. Mason. "But, Helen, you are a strange child, I must say. You know John and Maud Farrington talked about going with us to Newport. I am afraid they will be disappointed. Perhaps they will be pleased to accompany us. Your uncle says that we can bring friends, and it would make it more agreeable for you."

"Not for me, dear mamma," said the daughter.

" I would rather be free with my Cousin Hattie, to go and come where and when we pleased, and not be tied to any city friends, especially those of the Farrington stamp."

" Helen, you should not permit yourself to speak like that of one of the first families in the city," said the mother, with some feeling, while the father indulged in well-pleased laughter.

" Mary," said he, " I cannot, for my life, see what you find in the Farringtons to admire. They are rich, it is true, and they make quite a show. Farrington is a good fellow in his way. His wife is proud and haughty. Maud is much like her. John is a silly, conceited dandy, and a very worthless member of society."

" Why, my dear Hiram ! What has come over you this morning?" said his wife. " I never heard you talk like this before."

" Well, Mary, to tell you the truth," was the reply, " I am heartily sick of hearing inferior and worthless persons pronounced 'the best society,' simply because they live in palaces and have servants in livery. I don't wish to have Helen fall into such a delusion, and I am happy to know that she is not inclined that way. If John and Maud Farrington desire to go with us, by all means let them come, and if you will not get more than enough of their society before we return I shall be disappointed."

Mrs. Mason, for all this, was not displeased with her husband. Even when he opposed her in some of her propositions she was still firm in the opinion that he stood nearer perfection than any other man.

CHAPTER IV.

A BIRTHDAY-PARTY AND AN ACCIDENT.

THE sun shone brightly in a cloudless sky. The day had arrived in which the inhabitants of Marvindale and the regions about wère deeply interested. There were exhibitions in painting and drawing, exercises in vocal and instrumental music, recitations, declamations, original essays and orations from a large graduating class composed of young ladies and gentlemen. Among the spectators in a favorable part of the building were found our friends from New York, Mr. and Mrs. Hiram Mason, their daughter, and a young gentleman mentioned in the last chapter who had concluded that his presence would greatly add to the comfort and importance of the company.

To Helen the exercises in all their features were interesting. She listened with pleasure and astonishment to superior playing by young ladies brought up from their infancy in the country, and to original essays which proved that their authors were young maidens possessing cultured minds. She gazed on superior oil-paintings and fine pencil-drawings. She listened to eloquent declamations and talented orations; all this from young people the majority of whom had never seen a large city. She compared these performances with the abilities of many of her New York acquaintances, who formed what her mother termed "the best society," and the comparison in her mind was any thing but flattering to her gay companions of the metropolis. The class clothed itself with honor. Arthur Trevor took the lead and stood the highest, but they all did grandly, and never had the closing exercises given better satisfaction.

When the company had reached the spacious parlors of Judge Mason Helen was the first to express her feelings touching the day's doings, and this she did in her usual warm and impressive style.

"Why, Cousin Hattie," she cried, "I am perfectly astonished and delighted! Every thing was splendid!"

"I am really glad, Cousin Helen, that you have been so well pleased," was the modest reply. "I had some fears that the exercises would fail to meet your expectations."

"O Hattie! they were far beyond what I expected," was the reply.

"I must agree with Miss Helen, that for a country exhibition it was quite creditable," said John Farrington, in a lofty, patronizing way.

"And I must inform Mr. Farrington that his language does not at all agree with mine," said Helen. 'For a country exhibition,' indeed! John, those exercises would have been a credit to any academy in the city of New York. Do you know of one young lady within the circle of your acquaintance that ever appeared to better advantage at the close of a four-years' course than did a number of those ladies to-day? Do you know of one young man of twenty years in your set that can eclipse in talent, deportment, and scholarship those young men of to-day, especially Arthur Trevor?"

"Well, really," answered Mr. Farrington, with some embarrassment, "come to think it over, I don't know that I can."

"Then why use the language 'for a country exhibition?'" asked Helen. "I think you had better call back those words."

"I call them back, Miss Helen," said the vanquished John. "The words were not well chosen."

This brief colloquy, and especially the way it ended, pleased well the company. Even Mrs. Hiram Mason enjoyed the easy manner in which her daughter had quitted herself. But in deference to the feelings of the millionaire's son she saw fit to say:

"Helen, dear, I am afraid that in your enthusiasm over the exercises your language to Mr. Farrington was not as gentle as it ought to have been."

"My dear mamma will remember that Mr. Farrington and myself are not strangers to each other," said Helen. "There is no danger that a little plain talk will give offense; is there, John?"

"Not the least bit!" said John. "Mrs. Mason, your daughter's words are all right, and she never stood higher in my estimation than she does this minute."

This bit of effusion was received in silence, and

it was plain that on the minds of all present it left an unfavorable impression.

In a few days after this Judge Mason, in his usual happy way, said at the breakfast table: "In a little over a week my young niece here will reach the seventeenth anniversary of her birthday. If in harmony with the feelings of her parents, as well as her own, I would consider it a very great pleasure, as well as an honor, to give her a birthday-party. Nothing would please our young people better than to have an opportunity to show their respect for one who a few days ago spoke so nobly in their praise."

"O Uncle James," cried Helen, with her face glowing, " how kind you are! I am not worthy of such particular notice. But if papa and mamma are willing I am sure I shall be delighted."

"To be sure we are willing," said her mother, "and your uncle is very kind. Of course the company will be select, and not large."

" We can leave all that to the superior judgment of this family," said her husband. "Any company that they shall see fit to invite will be select enough for us and an honor to our daughter."

"Should the weather be agreeable," said the judge, "we shall go to one of the groves on the lake shore. The young people will enjoy swings and boating. We shall not be able to confine the company to any exact age, but my sister may rest assured that all of them will be highly respectable; not in point of wealth, but in that of morals."

This was said so kindly that Mrs. Hiram Mason

in conscience could find no fault; and yet she felt
that in those kind accents there was a slight reproof,
and, furthermore, there was in her mind a degree of
conviction that it was deserved.

The day arrived and the weather was charming.
The preparation was perfect, and nothing was wanting to make the birthday-picnic a perfect success.
About thirty young people had been invited from
the village and its surroundings. There were also
a few married persons, particular friends of Judge
Mason's family. Helen rendered herself highly
agreeable to all. She was lively and cheerful, with
a happy smile for each. Never before had she
looked so lovely in the sight of her parents.

From the judge's residence they rode to the grove
in a number of carriages. Helen's mother intended
to have her daughter ride with herself and husband
and in company with Mr. Farrington. But in a
playful mood, as the young metropolitan stood ready
to hand her into the carriage, with a pleasant laugh
she stepped into another one, and, to the great
amusement of her father, sat by the side of Arthur
Trevor.

" Helen, darling, this is your carriage," said the
mother, while Farrington's countenance denoted a
degree of displeasure.

" O no, mother dear," said the girl; " on this day
you must permit me to mingle freely with my
country friends."

"All ready !" cried Judge Mason, and the forward carriages moved, while Mr. Farrington, with a
disappointed visage, took his seat by the side of

Mrs. Mason, and in a short time the company arrived at its destination.

The facilities for enjoyment were all that could be desired. The grove was enchanting, and the lake mirrored the heavens above with the tall trees that grew on its banks. There were boats in abundance, and many of the young men from their early childhood had been perfectly at home in the management of a "skiff." Helen had never before experienced such a perfection of social pleasure, and the joy of her heart beamed in her countenance. She distributed her words and smiles among all, and her village and country friends were charmed with her natural and spontaneous kindness. To this general enjoyment there was one exception. John Farrington was not happy. He was respectfully treated by all, but he was not a center. The young people were too much bent on having lively enjoyment and showing their respect to their young friend, the queen of the party, to lavish attention upon a person who seemed to consider himself their superior.

For some time Arthur Trevor had noticed that Farrington looked displeased, and it gave him some uneasiness. In the goodness of his heart he greatly desired to make his friends from the city cheerful and happy, and, volunteering his remarks chiefly to Miss Helen, he said:

"I would be really pleased, Miss Mason, to have Mr. Farrington join us."

"Then by all means ask him, Mr. Trevor," said Helen, with a pleasant smile.

"Perhaps an invitation from yourself personally would be more acceptable," said Arthur.

"On this occasion there is no necessity for such formality," said Helen. "An invitation from you in behalf of the company will be sufficient."

So Arthur hastened to the spot where the young man stood, when the following conversation took place :

"Mr. Farrington, you are respectfully invited to join us in our innocent merry-making."

"Do you represent any one besides yourself?" asked the New Yorker, a little stiffly.

"You are invited in the name of the whole company. That was my instruction from Miss Mason."

"It would have pleased me better if Miss Mason had come herself."

"I ventured to give her that opinion before I started, but she did not deem it necessary."

"And I don't deem it necessary to accept this kind of invitation."

"I am afraid," said Arthur, "that our country ways fail to give you pleasure. Miss Helen, however, seems to be well pleased."

"So I see," said the young man ; "Miss Helen can adapt herself to any kind of society."

"Of course you mean any good and respectable society," said Arthur, feeling somewhat hurt ; "and so can any young person who is endowed with a fair degree of amiability and common sense. Miss Helen is glad to join in any society selected by Judge Mason." With that Trevor left, and with a slight peculiar smile on his lips he rejoined the company.

"And John does not come, eh?" said Helen.

"Mr. Farrington does not accept the invitation," was the answer.

"Let no one be troubled on that account," said the young beauty.

Just then her father and mother were slowly passing by. Helen rushed up to them, warmly embraced them, and cried out,

"Is not· this most delightful? I never was so happy in all my life!"

"But why is not Mr. Farrington with you, my dear?" asked the mother.

"I cannot tell his reason, mamma," said Helen; "he has been politely invited to join with us and has flatly refused."

"I will go and see John myself," said the mother; "I think I can persuade him to join you."

"If the young gentleman cannot consent to be one of this company without being persuaded, let him keep away," said the father in a tone which the mother well understood. "Now, darling, go and join your young friends, and be as happy as you possibly can." And off the maiden ran, with a heart full of genuine pleasure.

The judge, being one of the politest men in the world, treated Farrington with every mark of respect, and although he thought it strange that he stood aloof from the young people, he said not a word which would indicate that he had even noticed it.

"We have a pleasant retreat here, Mr. Farrington," said the judge.

"Most lovely!" was the answer, and desiring to throw some covering over his sulkiness he added, "For an hour I have been admiring the bewitching scenery."

Soon, the young friends in a merry procession were seen approaching the spot where the elderly people sat. Helen's face beamed with joy. Her maiden associates had beautifully decorated her brow with choice roses and flowers. They came on, waving bright little banners, and singing:

> "In friendship sweet and joy complete,
> From city, hill and dale, we meet;
> We deck her brow with roses gay,
> On this her joyous natal day.
>
> "From yonder city great and grand,
> She comes and joins our rural band;
> With banners gay we join the lay
> On Helen Mason's natal day.
>
> "May angels bright in robes of light,
> Watch o'er our friend from morn till night;
> And thus we sing, and honors pay
> To Helen on her natal day."

This feature was a surprise, even to Judge Mason, and it pleased him wonderfully. The parents were affected to joyous tears. When the singing ended Helen ran to her uncle and warmly embraced him.

"O my dear Uncle James, how can I ever thank you enough for this day's enjoyment? And how can I ever sufficiently thank these my young friends for what they have done?"

"I am a thousand times rewarded, my dear niece, by the happy expression of your countenance," said the judge.

"And I will venture to answer for the young people, including myself," said Arthur Trevor, "that to us the day has been one of unmixed pleasure, and that we esteem it an honor to be permitted to join in this delightful anniversary."

"And I will say in behalf of Mrs. Mason and myself," said the New York merchant, "that we thank you all for the manner in which you have treated our daughter. From what I saw at your closing exercises the other day, and from what I have witnessed on the present occasion, I am well convinced that refinement and intelligence are plants that thrive most beautifully in villages and country towns. Providence has cast my lot in the metropolis, and I have prospered in business; but the remembrance of my country life and the society of my early days grow dearer to me every day I live. I am heartily glad to enjoy your society even for a short time. As a family we shall go home greatly profited by this visit to Marvindale. Should you come to New York, call and see us; and I will assure you that you will find the same smile on our faces at our residence in the city as you do to-day on the shores of this charming lake."

This brief address was loudly cheered. Farrington saw that he had missed his opportunity. He knew that any complimentary remarks from him after his treatment of the young company would not answer, and for once he wisely held his peace.

Attending this party there was a Mrs. Armstrong, a relative of Mrs. Judge Mason. She was a young widow whose husband had been dead about four years. She had with her an only child, a little girl six years of age. Lily was charming, and lively in her temperament. Throughout the day she had been an object of interest, and her brilliant childish remarks drew the attention of all.

It was about three o'clock in the afternoon, and some eight or ten of the young people, with a number of others, were standing near a bridge crossing a deep stream which a few rods below emptied into the lake. Mrs. Armstrong and Lily were also there. The child in merry glee ran hither and thither and was in the very height of enjoyment; now in the bushes, then on the green grass, again on the bridge. She was perfectly fearless, and her mother during the day had often warned her against going too near the lake embankment. The little one, on a full run, had crossed and recrossed the bridge several times, and no one thought that she would place herself in any dangerous position. When no eye happened to see her she partially climbed the railing of the bridge, stooped over, lost her balance, and fell into the deep waters below. In falling the child screamed, and her cry was answered by a loud wild wail from the whole company. They ran in frantic terror and cried for help. Not far away Arthur Trevor, with Helen and some others, stood. The cry brought him to the spot in a few seconds. The child was struggling in the water and drifting into the lake. To throw off his shoes, coat, and vest, was but the

4

work of a moment.   He ran down the embankment, plunged into the water, and swam for the current. Lily by this time had sunk, but Arthur well knew that she would come up—where, he was not so sure. On the shore among the ladies there was a continued wail of weeping, while the swimmer kept a sharp look for the appearance of the child.   Fortunately her little struggling form reached the surface close by.   A few bold strokes, and Lily was saved. Then on the shore the weeping was converted into a shout of thanksgiving.   Arthur, with his charge, did not have to swim ashore, for another young man promptly reached him with a boat, and they were soon landed.   The child, owing to the short time she had been in the water, was soon restored and tenderly cared for.

The gratitude of the mother cannot well be expressed.   She fell on her knees, clasped her hands, looked up, and cried, " I thank thee, O my heavenly Father, for restoring to me my only precious darling!"   She rose, and with a countenance that cannot be described cried, " Where is he?   O, where *is* he?"   She saw Arthur, ran up to him, and silently kissed his cheek.   There were many others present that would have gladly done the same, but by a process of self-denial they did not obey the impulse. His praise was on every tongue, and the city Masons were loud in their admiration of his noble act.

" This is in keeping with his whole movement," said Judge Mason to his brother's wife.   " Every few days we hear something to his credit.   He is an honor to his mother and an ornament in society."

"I believe you, brother," said Mrs. Mason, with a tear in her eye. "How he plunged into the water from that high embankment, and how nobly he accomplished his purpose! I shall not forget the scene as long as I live."

John Farrington, who had wandered away to nurse his sulkiness, now returned, and was astonished to see on the countenance of Mrs. Hiram Mason signs of deep feeling.

"O, Mr. Farrington," she cried, "we have had such a time in your absence! Little Lily Armstrong fell into the river from the bridge, and was carried by the current toward the lake. And you should have seen Mr. Trevor's grand plunge into the river to save the drowning darling—which he did! O it was noble!"

"To those who had never witnessed diving or plunging I dare say the sight was very interesting," said Mr. John Farrington; "but to me, after having seen some of the finest exhibitions in diving, Mr. Trevor's exploit would have been a very tame affair."

Mrs. Mason looked at him in perfect astonishment, and for the first time she utterly despised him. She made no reply. Her daughter, however, with suppressed indignation answered:

"So, then, we are to understand that in your estimation the sight of a brave young man who at a moment's warning plunges into the stream from a high embankment and saves the life of a little girl that has already sunk, and restores her to her almost frantic mother amid the joyful shouts of the spectators, is a very tame affair compared with the sight of a few worthless fellows that dive for the amusement of the crowd, from whom they get a few pennies.   Surely there is no accounting for taste!"

"But I thought your mother referred to the simple plunging," said the rebuked dandy, getting himself still deeper in trouble.

"Ah! now I understand," said Helen; "you thought that mamma was excited over the beauty of the plunge, and not over the saving of the child." And with a peculiar smile, which the young man did not enjoy, she joined her young companions.

About four in the afternoon it was deemed advisable to retire from the grove.   With the exception of John Farrington all had been greatly delighted.   The guests, with their friends, returned to the village in the same order as they came and scattered to their various places of abode.

CHAPTER V.

A METHODIST MEETING, AND WHAT THEY THOUGHT OF IT.

IT was Saturday afternoon, at the tea-table, and the conversation turned upon the religious services in the village on the morrow. The guests from the city had spent one Sabbath in Marvindale, and on that day there were no public services in the Methodist church, the minister having been called away. Rev. James Bunting had now returned, and would officiate on the Sabbath and administer the sacrament of the Lord's Supper.

"We have a most excellent minister; at least so we think," said Mrs. James Mason. "He is thoroughly devoted to his pastoral work and very able in the pulpit. The church is in a far better spiritual condition than it has been for many years."

"We never go to a Methodist meeting," said Mrs. Hiram Mason. "We shall go to-morrow, however. It will be quite a novelty."

"It strikes me, my dear, that 'novelty' is not exactly the proper word to use in regard to religious worship," said her husband.

"Sister meant no more than that the mode of worship would be somewhat different from that of her own Church," said Mrs. James Mason. "I think, however, she will forget all about the novelty when she hears Mr. Bunting."

"It can't be possible that this village minister can surpass in eloquence our own Dr. Darling," said the New York lady. "We are charmed with his preaching every Sabbath."

"I cannot say as much for our minister," was the reply. "Instead of charming us with eloquence his terrible earnestness often makes us tremble. Like the prophet of old, he shows 'the house of Israel their transgression' and pronounces a woe upon those 'who are at ease in Zion.'"

"For my part," said Mrs. Hiram Mason, "I don't fancy such preaching. Do you, husband?"

"I cannot say that I do, Mary," said her husband, with a smile. "We are not apt to fancy any preaching that rebukes us for our sins and short-comings. But it is not always the preaching we fancy that will do us good. You say we are charmed with Dr. Darling's preaching. But what good does it accomplish? Does it lead any one to true repentance and to cry for mercy?"

"I am sure that a large number have united with the church under his ministry," answered his wife.

"I admit that," said her still smiling husband. "But does their church membership interfere in the least with their former behavior? Just think them over. Do they not attend dances, theaters, comic exhibitions, play cards, and drink wine just exactly as they did before, while the prayer-meeting is turned over to a mere handful of old persons? It strikes me that it is high time for that church and congregation to hear preaching that they would not fancy."

"I know where a pretty big share of Mr. Darling's seven thousand dollars a year comes from," said Mr. Farrington, who had listened with some interest to the conversation. " Our family would never submit to any attack on dancing, theaters, card-playing, and respectable wine-drinking. There is no danger that Dr. Darling will be such a fool as to indulge in any such Methodist nonsense."

" I would respectfully remind Mr. Farrington that we are the guests of a Methodist family, and that we are sitting at a Methodist table," said Helen.

" Ah, surely," said John ; " I might have chosen different words."

Mr. Farrington's unmannerly blunder put a stop to the conversation in that line, and, by the ingenuity of Judge Mason, it was easily diverted to another channel, and every thing was pleasant.

In good season on Sabbath morning the judge's family, with their guests, were seated in the large and beautiful church, which was well filled. The services were opened by a most attractive reading of Isaiah liii. Then was given out the familiar hymn :

"All hail, the power of Jesus' name,"

and soon the thrilling melody of old " Coronation" filled the house. This was followed by a most earnest and impressive prayer, in which the man of God seemed to plead as in the immediate presence of the Almighty. Another hymn was given out :

" Forever here my rest shall be,"

and the pathetic " Avon," in melting strains, was

sung by hundreds of sweet voices. The text was announced: " Therefore, if any man be in Christ, he is a new creature: old things have passed away: behold, all things are become new." 2 Cor. 5, 17. A very brief synopsis is given:

It is evident from the text that all men are not in Christ. There are thousands of regular members in evangelical churches throughout the land who are not in Christ, and never have been. If we are in Christ in the sense of the text we have been "justified by faith," experienced a genuine change of heart, "transformed by the renewing of our minds," "begotten again unto a lively hope," "have peace with God through our Lord Jesus Christ." We are "new creatures." We possess the mind and nature of the Saviour, and our spiritual hearts beat in happy unison with the great heart of the Redeemer. "Old things have passed away." Every thing that is not in harmony with the mind of Christ is abandoned, and the whole bent of the soul is heavenward. This is the New Testament view of those who are in Christ. And I rejoice to know that such Christians are found by the tens of thousands. They come out from the world, deny themselves, take up their cross, and follow their Lord and Master. But I am sorry to confess that there are thousands in the churches who make a profession of love to Christ who prove by their behavior that they are "lovers of pleasure more than lovers of God."

" Brethren and sisters, ' the world will love its own,' and we are not at all astonished when we see the non-professing throng rushing after vanity,

> "'And vainly strive with earthly toys
> To fill an empty mind.'

"But the situation becomes more alarming when among these are found thousands who profess to be the disciples of the humble Nazarene and members of his visible Church. Many of these are leaders in worldly gayety, fashionable dances, and regular patrons of theaters. They are in the Church, but we fail to find in them a single element of vital godliness.

"Let no one think that I am drawing upon my imagination in order to make a picture. I am dwelling upon sorrowful and sad truths! Is it any wonder that non-professors stand aloof from the cause ·of Christ when members of the Christian Church are found rushing into the most frivolous wordly gatherings?

"But here let me say, with St. Paul, 'Beloved, we are· persuaded better things of you.' Although I thus speak to the glory of God let it be known that the members of my charge have come up to a high degree of spirituality, and they look upon these carnal pleasures as worthless trash. With the poet they can sing,

> "'Vain, delusive world, adieu.'

"At the communion to-day we expect the baptism of the Holy Ghost. Spirit of burning, come! Let us now sing,

> "'When I survey the wondrous cross
> On which the Prince of glory died.'"

The familiar tones of " Rockingham" were now heard, and the audience "filled his courts with sounding praise."

The minister said that all members in good standing in other evangelical Churches were cordially invited to the table of the Lord.

The sacrament season was deeply affecting. God was in his holy temple! A hallowed spiritual atmosphere filled the sanctuary. Heaven seemed very near, "and glory crowned the mercy-seat." It was a season long to be remembered, an exhibition on a small scale of the raptures of the upper sanctuary.

The friends from the city remained until the communion was over, and the Mason family were deeply interested. Mrs. James Mason asked her sister to go with her to the table. She shook her head, but her countenance denoted nothing in the shape of indifference or displeasure. On the contrary, there were tears in her eyes and her lips quivered.

Soon after returning from the church the company, with the exception of Farrington, was seated in the parlor, when Helen, in the fullness of her young heart, broke out:

"O, my dear Auntie Mason, your minister is wonderful! I never had such feelings in all my life! I shall remember that meeting as long as I live!"

"I trust, my dear, that you will sweetly remember it after you have passed away from the scenes of earth," said her aunt.

"Every word he said in regard to pleasure-seeking professors of religion was true. The members of our own church in the city are living proof of the correctness of what he said. Now, mamma, dear, is not that so?"

"It is so, my darling," said the mother in a low voice that was not quite steady. "Thanks to your father, I have not indulged in those things myself, but I have justified them in others. I am free to confess that the last two hours have produced a wonderful change in my mind. I only wish that all the members of our church had heard what the minister said and had witnessed the whole of the impressive service."

"Mamma, I have longed to be a Christian for a long time, and I have tried to pray in secret. But I knew that I could have no spiritual enjoyment in a church where nearly all the young are almost wholly given up to worldly pleasure."

The father was deeply and favorably affected by the words of his wife and daughter. Turning to his brother he said:

"James, there seems to have been a special providence in that kind letter of invitation you sent us. I never in my life so much desired to be a true Christian as I did this morning under your minister's preaching."

"Hiram, you are 'not far from the kingdom of heaven,'" said the judge, with his face glowing with happiness. "God is preparing you and your family for a grand mission, and in his own good time he will tell you what it is."

Here Mr. Farrington joined the company, and,

not knowing the situation, volunteered one of his blundering and offensive remarks. In all probability he had bestowed upon his first sentence some labor, and expected it would produce an effect.

" Well," said he in a pompous way, " this morning we have had a clear demonstration of the wonderful effect of animal magnetism."

" And were you one of the animals magnetized, Mr. Farrington?" asked Helen.

" I should think not," said John, with a touch of resentment. " It requires but a fair degree of culture and intelligence to be proof against that kind of preaching."

" I see," said Helen. " You have been protected from the minister's animal magnetism by your culture and intelligence. Papa, mamma, and myself, have been wonderfully affected by his preaching. According to that, it must be owing to our lack of culture and intelligence."

" Miss Helen, I think you are indulging in a joke," said John.

" I am in sober earnest," said Helen.

" I am very much astonished," said Farrington. " Had I known, my language would have been somewhat different. I give you all credit for culture and intelligence."

" And still we were not protected from the influence of the sermon," said Hiram Mason, with a peculiar smile. " Mr. Farrington, please explain."

Just then lunch was announced, and to Mr. Farrington's great relief he was excused from the unpleasant task of harmonizing contradictions. Soon he was thoroughly engaged in something for which he was far better qualified than for the discussion of philosophical points.

On Sabbath evening again the guests attended service at the same church. First they went into the prayer-meeting held in the large session-room, which was well filled. The meeting was conducted by the minister. The singing was grand and inspiring and the prayers earnest and reverential. Several ladies led in vocal prayer. This Helen had never witnessed before. Then came a season of speaking, in which a large number took a part. Our three friends were deeply interested in the testimonies they heard, and astonished at the intelligent manner in which the speakers expressed themselves. In this meeting Arthur Trevor took an active but a modest part, and in his remarks he affectionately urged his young friends to seek without delay the salvation of their souls.

In the public service the church was thronged, and the Gospel was " in the demonstration of the Spirit and with power." The closing part was deeply pathetic, and the meeting ended amid a halo of glory.

Our friends were again in the same parlor, and they fondly hoped that John Farrington, in view of his humiliating defeat in the afternoon, would see fit at this time either to remain silent or say something that would be moderately sensible. But in this they were disappointed. Being pretty well convinced that hitherto he had not been very fortunate in his manner of expression, he was pleased with the conviction that he was now prepared to say something that would please the company, especially the family of Judge Mason, and in this confidence he proceeded:

"I have noticed one thing: Marvindale has a fair number of pretty girls. I sat in a very good position to see their faces, and made it my special business this morning to compare several of them with some of my young lady acquaintances in the city, and I must say that in beauty of countenance they stood the test well."

For a few moments there was perfect silence.

"It was exceedingly fortunate for Mr. Farrington that Judge Mason's pew was so favorable to his peculiar mode of worship," said Mrs. Hiram Mason, in a tone of voice and with a facial expression which John had never heard and seen before, and he began to fear that his speech had not proved to be a success.

"John," said Helen, "to-morrow, under your own signature, send what you told us to the *Herald* and *Tribune*. Of course you can enlarge on the wonderful physical perfections of these Marvindale beauties that took your whole attention during the hour of worship. And you might say that this peculiar devotion of yours protected you from a strong current of animal magnetism issuing from the pulpit."

"And this is the pay I get, eh, for praising up these country girls?" said John.

"Mr. Farrington," said Mrs. Mason, "the account you have given us of the working of your mind this morning under that wonderful sermon was shocking, and you deserve a rebuke."

"We'll now attend to family devotion," said Judge Mason, while his daughter placed before him the sacred volume. He read the first portion of the fifth chapter in the gospel by Matthew, embracing the beatitudes. This was followed by a most earnest prayer, closing with that of our Lord, in which the company vocally united.

CHAPTER VI.

ANOTHER BLUNDER AND AN EXIT.

AS far as John Farrington was susceptible of any thing approaching affection, Helen Mason, more than any other person, had touched that very small department of his heart. She was fair, intelligent, sparkling in conversation, and the only daughter of a wealthy man. What more could he ask? Mrs. Mason, touched, and that not very lightly, with a fashionable infirmity which is anti-republican as well as anti-Christian, had smiled upon this young son of a millionaire, and had seen in him very satisfactory materials for a son-in-law. But from time to time she had witnessed very clear evidences that her daughter was not favorably inclined in that direction. He often called at her home, and Helen always treated him with familiar kindness. But after his departure she would laugh at his egregious blunders and silly remarks, to the amusement of her father, but not of her mother.

Some plain and yet very kind family conversations which took place between the receiving of Judge Mason's invitation-letter and their leaving for Marvindale had somewhat moderated Mrs. Mason's opinion touching this young man of fortune. But she still clung with considerable tenacity to those pictures of Helen's future which her fancy had drawn in such brilliant colors. Her candid judgment, when permitted to come to the front, told her plainly that John Farrington was not a person of moral worth, and that he was deficient in those points that would attract persons of talent and culture. But then he belonged to one of the " first families" and moved in the higher circles.

In several of the conversations alluded to, her husband in his own peculiar way had analyzed before her what she insisted on calling " the best society," and the process had revealed to her unwilling eyes a state of things that greatly disturbed her. It seemed to be a candid investigation. But could it be possible that that which for generations had been called "the best society" was three fourths counterfeit, and so much of the counterfeit in the church to which she belonged? She had great confidence in her husband's judgment, but, for once, was he not mistaken? Mrs. Mason was perplexed even before she left the city.

Hiram Mason's expressed opinion of John Farrington's mental powers caused his wife to pay closer attention to the sayings and behavior of the young man, and to her great mortification she found that nearly every thing he said justified the correctness of her husband's words. He had a fair command of language, but generally it clothed superficial and absurd ideas; and thus it continued until, as the reader knows, she became thoroughly disgusted with him.

On Monday morning at the breakfast-table John appeared a little gloomy and not overwell pleased.

They naturally concluded that this was owing to
the reprimand of the night before.   From his sullen
looks, however, they drew the consoling thought
that now at least he would confine himself to listening.   But this was not so to be.   Knowing that
he must soon return he deemed it prudent to offer
a few remarks.

"I was just thinking of what that young Trevor
said in the prayer-meeting last evening.   His words
were these: 'Religion is profitable unto all
things.'"

"John," said Helen, "Mr. Trevor did not use
the word 'religion,' but *godliness.'*"

"It means the same thing exactly," said John.
"And what rank nonsense that is! I wonder if godliness is profitable to thieving, robbery, forgery, and
a dozen other things I could name?   Godliness
would knock every one of them in the head."

"And would not that be profitable, Mr. Farrington?" asked Helen.

The question was not exactly a logical one, and
the young lady knew it, but it was enough to baffle
John on the spot.

"Why—let me see—profitable? Yes, I suppose
so," said he. "I wonder if that is what the fellow
meant?"

"No, it was not," said Helen.   "By the way,
whom do you mean by the fellow; Arthur Trevor,
or the author of the sentence?"

"I mean Trevor, of course. I was not aware
that he was quoting from an author," said John.
"And who was the author?"

"It was orginally used by an aged clergyman in a letter to a young minister," said Helen.

"But that doesn't prove that the sentence is correct," was his reply. "Aged ministers often write very foolish things."

"We are in the habit of believing that this old gentleman's writings are perfectly correct," said Miss Mason.

"Perhaps, for the information of the company, you will give us the old dominie's name, and that of the young chap to whom he wrote," said John.

"For your own personal information I'll do it," said Helen, with a smile. "The elderly gentleman was St. Paul. The young minister was Timothy. You will find the 'rank nonsense' in his first letter, fourth chapter and eighth verse." And taking a small Testament from her pocket she read : "But godliness is profitable unto all things, having promise of the life that now is, and of that which is to come."

Let not the reader suppose that John Farrington was overwhelmed with confusion. He was not of that make. He felt somewhat humiliated, and it grieved him to have his ignorance of the Scriptures so exposed. But in such trials he was always wonderfully sustained by his conceit, and so he simply said :

"It would have been much better for Trevor to have mentioned the name of his author."

During that morning the young man put his things in order ready for a departure. Before leaving he desired to have a few words with Mrs. Hiram

Mason and daughter, and the interview was soon granted.

"I am of the opinion that I have devoted as much of my time to this stupid place as I can afford. I am fully determined to leave on the afternoon train, and no effort or persuasion on the part of any one can change my mind," said John.

"Of course you will act in this matter as you think best," said Mrs. Mason. "I know enough of this family to assure you that you are welcome to remain here as long as you can make it agreeable to yourself. I think, however, you will find no one that will be inclined to persuade you to remain longer at a place you pronounce ' stupid.' "

"My rank and position, as belonging to one of the richest families in the city, and moving in the best society, entitle me to a little more notice from these country fellows, and, to tell you the truth, I have not received that treatment from yourself and daughter which I had a right to expect. I cannot put up with it, and I am going to join my friends at Newport, where the people understand good manners."

"Mr. Farrington," said Mrs. Mason, "I could easily answer your insulting language in terms of severity, but, as you are going to leave, I will say no more. Come, Helen, my dear, we have had enough of this." And the mother and daughter left the room.

In the afternoon a carriage came after John and his trunks, and in a very stiff and pompous manner he bade the family of Judge Mason good-bye.

On the following Sabbath at the Methodist church there were very clear evidences of divine power. Such were the manifestations of God's Spirit in his convincing influences during the evening sermon that the minister, instead of dismissing the congregation as usual, went down to the altar and said:

" I am well convinced that there are many in this assembly who are ' weary and heavy laden' and desire spiritual rest. Under this conviction I cannot close this meeting without giving such persons an invitation to come forward and kneel at this altar while we sing."

A large number, mostly young persons, went forward, and the space was nearly filled with weeping penitents. The exercises continued for an hour. So great was the feeling that a meeting was announced for Monday evening. The revival spread, and continued nightly for several weeks, and some two hundred professed conversion. Among these were found Hiram Mason and his daughter, while the mother, who was already a church member, was ' transformed by the renewing of her mind.' "

While the meeting was yet in progress Mr. and Mrs. Mason were under the necessity of leaving for the city, while Helen was permitted to remain a little longer.

At an afternoon visit at Mrs. Trevor's there were together, besides the family, Judge Mason, wife, daughter, and niece. Rev. Mr. Bunting and the revival naturally came up as subjects of conversation.

" In a few weeks he must leave us for another

field," said Judge Mason, " and, of course, in one sense we all feel sorry."

" Is not that an unfortunate feature in your church government, Uncle James?" asked his niece.

" Sometimes it has that appearance," was the answer, " but, in reality, I think it one of the most favorable things in our church polity. To this, in all probability, we are indebted for the presence of Brother Bunting among us. And where he goes next, the people will have no reason to complain of the itinerancy."

" I readily see those points," said Helen, " and I thank you for calling my attention to them."

" People often say, ' It is too bad for ministers to leave when all would be glad to have them stay,' " said the judge. " But are not such partings a thousand times more pleasant to the ministers than if the people were glad to get rid of them ?"

" They are, certainly," said his niece ; " and to the people also."

Just then an expressman called at the door with a small package for Arthur Trevor. Alice took it and handed it to her brother in the presence of the company, and said :

" Arthur, be very careful in the unpacking, for it may contain some dangerous explosives."

" It is rather small for that," said the brother, " and I don't think of any body at this moment that would wish to hurt me."

" It may be possible that Mark Floyd has sent

you his compliments," said the sister, laughing. " But come, let us see what you have."

The brother, with some embarrassment, opened the package, and, after a number of unfoldings, he came to a splendid heavy gold watch and chain. On the casing was engraved beautifully the following :

" *Presented by Mrs. A. L. Armstrong, as a token of gratitude, to Mr. Arthur Trevor, who saved her only child from drowning.*"

Arthur was deeply affected and the company greatly rejoiced.

" In this case it has been more blessed to give than to receive," said the judge.

" It is a magnificent present !" said Mrs. Mason.

" And it comes from a magnificent lady," said Mrs. Trevor.

" And to a magnificent gentleman, why don't you say, Hattie ?" said Helen.

" But my city cousin was too quick for me," said Hattie.

" Let us call it magnificent all around," said Alice.

The afternoon was spent most cheerfully. The Trevors were highly pleased with Helen Mason, while the young lady was delighted with the Trevors.

It was the first evening after the arrival of Mr. and Mrs. Mason in New York, and soon after supper. The servants had been summoned to meet the master and mistress in one of the parlors.

There they sat in mute astonishment, not knowing why they were thus called together, some of them seriously fearing that their services would be no longer required. They were not kept in long suspense, for Mr. Mason spoke:

" I have called you together for household worship, and to inform you that from henceforth this house is to be a house of prayer. At this hour of evening, daily, at the ringing of the bell, you are respectfully requested to meet at this room for family devotion. I trust that this change will be pleasing and profitable to you all. In time of prayer it will please Mrs. Mason, Helen, and myself to have you kneel."

He then opened the sacred book and read in an impressive manner the 91st psalm : " He that dwelleth in the secret place of the Most High shall abide under the shadow of the Almighty." The reading being ended they all reverently knelt, and Hiram Mason offered unto the Lord his first family prayer. He was not without some embarrassment. It was something of a cross, but it was faithfully taken up, and the Lord wonderfully blessed him. The prayer was earnest and simple. The language of the tongue was the expression of a full and honest heart. When the worship was over, the servants quietly left, to attend to their various duties, greatly astonished and well pleased. That family altar erected that evening at the residence of Hiram Mason was never taken down.

CHAPTER VII.

THE "BEST SOCIETY" ANALYZED.

THE next evening, soon after family prayer, the bell rang, and Rev. Dr. and Mrs. Darling called, and were ushered into the parlor, where they were soon joined by Mr. and Mrs. Mason. The meeting, of course, was a happy one, after an absence of several weeks.

"And so you have returned in excellent health and spirits," said Dr. Darling, directing his remarks to Mrs. Mason. "And how did you enjoy your country visit? I was afraid that it would prove rather dull."

"And so was I, before we started," said Mrs. Mason, "and I so expressed myself. But I have been happily disappointed. To me, as well as to Mr. Mason and Helen, it was by far the most delightful and profitable summer visit we ever experienced."

"That is very high praise indeed," said Dr. Darling, " especially when it comes from a person who has visited Newport and Saratoga. What could there be in a village like Marvindale to give you such exquisite pleasure?"

" Several things," said Mrs. Mason. " The people there are so good, kind, affectionate, and intelligent, that they won my heart in spite of my former foolish and blind views in regard to country people. Then came Helen's birthday-party, which her uncle gave her. It was a time of perfect social enjoyment. But the grand feature of our enjoyment was of a spiritual nature.''

" That must be a new feature in a summer resort, and we must hear all about it,'' said Mrs. Darling, casting a sly, merry glance at her husband, which Mrs. Mason noticed.

She then rehearsed to the minister and his wife all about their experience in connection with Mr. Bunting and his most wonderful pulpit powers, the nature of his sermons, the picture he drew of fashionable worldlings in the Church, the sacrament scene, the prayer-meeting in the evening, the spirituality and devotion of the young people, the sermon on the following Sabbath evening, the altar service, and the grand revival that followed. "Mrs. Darling,'' she said, with her face beaming, "it was wonderful beyond description. During those meetings I had a clear view of myself as a cold, formal, fashionable woman of the world in the Church, wholly destitute of that spirituality that insures 'fellowship with God through our Lord Jesus Christ.' Through the influence of those meetings, which my proud spirit once despised, I have found genuine consolation, and so have my husband and daughter.''

" We have now reached a point where I must turn you over to Dr. Darling,'' said the minister's wife in a tone that strove to be amiable. " I will say, however, that we heard something of this from our young friend, Mr. Farrington. We thought that perhaps it was one of his pleasant jokes, but your own story corroborates all that the young man said."

" As far as I can judge," said Dr. Darling, " this Mr. Bunting is one of those sensational preachers who are capable of producing religious excitements that are of no benefit either to the world or the Church."

" With all due respect to your judgment, Dr. Darling," said Mr. Mason, promptly, " I must say that your estimate of the gentleman is wholly erroneous and unjust. He is a quiet, modest man, a profound scholar, and deeply spiritual. He moves the people by his entire consecration to his work, and his earnest, eloquent pleadings with those who sit under his ministry. He is as free from the sensational element as was Peter at the house of Cornelius."

" I would do the man no injustice," said Dr. Darling. " I dare say he understands the class of minds he has to deal with. Such preaching would utterly fail before a highly-cultivated audience."

" I think you are mistaken again ; worse than you were before," said Mr. Mason, with a peculiar smile. " From Sabbath to Sabbath he stands before a highly-cultivated audience, very much more so, in my opinion, than your own city congregation."

" Mr. Mason," said Dr. Darling, perfectly astonished, " I think you are laboring under a sad mistake. Mr. John Farrington assures me that they are lacking in refinement and culture."

This was altogether too much for Mr. Mason's gravity, and in spite of an effort he broke out into loud laughter.

"Pardon this rudeness, doctor," he said, "if it must come under that name; but that was a little more than I could stand."

"And yet I fail to see where, in what I said, the laugh comes in," said the minister, who was not easily offended.

"I will tell you," said Mr. Mason. "The authority you produced for believing that the Marvindale people lacked in refinement and culture seemed to me as highly comical. A young man that is notoriously deficient in those traits, and who makes himself detestable by his ignorance and lack of good manners, is hardly the right person to sit in judgment on the refinement and culture of a community."

"I was not aware that Mr. Farrington was deficient on those points," said the pastor. "I have often met him at evening parties, and from the society in which he mingles I took it for granted that he was on a par with his fellows."

"We know, my dear, that Mr. Farrington is not what you may call brilliant," said Mrs. Darling. "But then, as long as he moves in the best society he must be respected as such."

"I have had a good deal to say for years about 'the best society,'" said Mrs. Mason. "I now look upon the term as it is used, as a sham and a cheat. I confess that I was a part of that cheat myself. What is there in what is called in this city 'the best society that entitles it to that superlative distinction? Is it a high grade of morality, amiability, intelligence, and a hearty enlistment in all measures of moral reform? Not at all. What is called 'the best society' abounds in frivolous characters given up to dress, dances, and theaters. Now, in all candor, Mrs. Darling, why should such a society be called 'the best?'"

"But you should remember, Mrs. Mason, that in this society there is a large number of church members," said Mrs. Darling.

"I know there is," was the answer; "but in a multitude of cases they outdo non-professors in their devotion to worldly gratifications, and, to all appearance, they are 'lovers of pleasure more than lovers of God."

"Could the village preacher hear your words, Mrs. Mason, he might well be proud of his achievement," said the pastor.

"Don't give the village preacher too much credit," said Mrs. Mason, "for through the instrumentality of my husband my eyes were partly opened to see these things before I left the city."

"Well," said Dr. Darling, "we are right glad to see you home. I am not sorry to see this great change in you and Mr. Mason. Your strong language has furnished me materials for reflection. It may be true that in our best society, as we call it, is found much counterfeit. I will look into this matter a little closer. I thank you for your plain, fearless words. I am comparatively young and inexperienced, and what I have heard may do me good."

They rose to leave, and the parting on both sides was perfectly friendly.

Helen had been at home two days. Her mother had gone out, and the daughter sat alone in the parlor, thinking over in a happy frame of mind the wonderful things she had seen and heard in Marvindale, while her young heart throbbed with grateful emotions. The bell rang, and in a few moments Clara Downing and Grace Doyle rushed into the room and warmly embraced their young friend.

"Why, Helen!" said Clara, "that country visit must have agreed with you, for you look splendid."

"Thank you, Clara," said Helen; "my time passed away delightfully. I never was so happy before."

"And did you find a cultured society in such a place?" asked Grace.

"Indeed I did!" said Helen, smiling. "The young people were so intelligent that at times I felt embarrassed."

"Helen Mason, I am perfectly astonished!" cried Clara.

"And so am I," said Miss Doyle.

"But why should you be astonished?" asked Helen. "With good educational advantages, sitting under the ministry of talented ministers, with ready access to large libraries, I don't see why they should not be as intelligent, and more so, than those who live amid the excitement of a large city."

"Helen, we will not debate with you, for you will beat us every time," said Clara, "and we like you all the better for it. But now to business. There are to be unusual attractions at the Broadway Theater to-morrow night. We are going with our brothers and we greatly desire the pleasure of your company. We shall call with the carriage at half past seven. If you are not otherwise engaged we hope that you will go with us. It will be splendid!"

"I am not otherwise engaged," said Helen, in a firm voice. "But, girls, let me tell you, once for all, that I shall never again go to a theater, nor to any party where they dance and play cards."

"Helen Mason! What has come over you?" said Grace Doyle.

"While away I have experienced, as I believe, a genuine change of heart. I have fully consecrated myself to the Lord for time and eternity. This is also the experience of papa and mamma. O, girls, I love you dearly! You are members of the Church, and is this constant running after worldly pleasure consistent with the religion of the meek and lowly Saviour, who said that in order to be his disciples we must deny ourselves and take up the cross?"

"But if it is wrong," said Clara, "why doesn't Dr. Darling say something about it, either in the pulpit or out of it?"

"Perhaps he has never seriously considered the subject," said Helen. "He may yet. If on your knees you consult your Saviour, *He* will never advise you to attend theaters and dances."

The girls thought it was time to go, but before leaving they fondly kissed the fair lips from which had dropped those earnest, solemn words.

One morning before the breakfast-hour, while Mr. Mason was examining the pages of one of his morning papers, his eyes rested on a paragraph which greatly moved him.

"Call in your mother, Helen," said he, with his face beaming with gladness. "I find something here that both of you will be glad to hear."

In a few moments Mrs. Mason was in the room, and both mother and daughter waited for a further revelation. The father read the following:

"At the session of the W—— Conference, which closed its labors yesterday, Rev. George Bunting, D.D., was transferred to New York East Conference and appointed to the St. Thomas Methodist Episcopal Church, in this city. It is understood that, aside from his profound scholarship, the gentleman is one of the most effective pulpit orators in the Church. His success at Marvindale was wonderful."

Helen was the first to respond, which she did by clapping her hands. "Once I did not look favorably upon this moving among Methodist ministers; but see how beautifully it has worked in this case!"

"Beautifully indeed!" said the mother. "As an instrument in God's hand he has done for us a wonderful work that we shall never forget. I feel as if we ought to put ourselves under his pastoral care."

"O, mamma, dear, I am so glad to hear you say that!" cried Helen. "I am almost sure that papa feels as I do."

"I had no intention of asking your mother to change her church relation," said the father. "I fully believed that God, by his Spirit, would lead us all in the right way. As I feel now I am strongly inclined to avail myself of the tender care of that good man who, under God, has led us into the fold of Christ."

In due time the minister arrived and preached his first sermon to the people of his new charge. The house was crowded, and the ministry was "in the demonstration of the Spirit and with power." The audience was deeply affected, and hearty responses were heard from brethren whose hearts were full.

Before the benediction was pronounced one of the church officials stood in front of the congregation and said that Dr. Bunting would be glad to take by the hand any and all who would come up to the altar after the meeting was closed. A large number went forward and were introduced to the new pastor. They were all strangers. At last came three—a husband, wife, and daughter.

"Bless the Lord! Here we meet again," cried the minister, and the hand-shaking was exceedingly cordial. There was no time then for prolonged conversation, but they gave him the street and number of their house, and he promised to call on a certain day of that week—which he did—and on the next Sabbath the family was received into the church; the mother by letter, the father and daughter on probation.

6

CHAPTER VIII.

A MEETING AT FARRINGTON'S AND "THE COMING OF ARTHUR."

BETWEEN Helen and her Cousin Hattie there was now formed a regular correspondence of the most affectionate nature. The following will show the reader the state of Miss Mason's mind and throw light upon the situation:

NEW YORK, *Sept.* 20, 18·—.

"DEAR COUSIN HATTIE: I thank you from the depth of my heart for all of your good letters, and especially for your last. I have read it over and over, and it has yielded me a great deal of pleasure and profit. I am very glad to know that your new minister met such a warm reception and that he is doing such a grand work. I had some fears that the overwhelming popularity of Brother Bunting would prove to be unfavorable to his successor. Those fears were groundless. The Methodists adapt themselves most grandly to their wonderful itinerancy. I have formed a large circle of new acquaintances, young ladies of moral worth and deep piety. Their conversations prove to me exceedingly valuable, so different from the fashionable talk that I have heard for many years.

"Since it became known to our former set that we have forever abandoned theaters and dancing-parties many of them treat us coldly, and some spitefully. But I have reasons for believing that we have convinced several that 'the pomp and vanity of this wicked world' can never be harmonized with the religion of Christ.

"We are heartily engaged in church work. In addition to the regular meetings, which we greatly enjoy, we have a number of organizations, one of which is the Systematic Benevolent Society. In this mamma takes a very active part, and with the hearty consent of papa contributes large sums of money. I am a member of the Society myself, and together we often go to the abodes of the poor and destitute, examine the circumstances, distinguish between vice and virtue, and then we consult together as a Society in regard to the most needy and deserving. Through this benevolence and a kind word of advice we not only cheer the hearts of hundreds but we gently lead them to the Saviour and the Church.

"Every day I fondly think of Marvindale and the few happy weeks I spent there. What a society of young people! They are splendid! Alice Trevor— I dearly love her. Her ringing sweet laughter is yet in my ears. And her tall, straight, handsome, intelligent—brother. I almost added *captivating;* but you see I didn't. The list is too long to mention by name. They are all down on my book of remembrance. Kind love to my dear uncle and aunt and many others. Write often, my dear Hattie, to your   COUSIN HELEN."

Mr. Farrington's father, or John's grandfather, was

a rich man, and when he died left a vast amount of city property to his only son. Like his parent, this son was a keen business man, temperate in his habits, and somewhat quiet in his manners. His wife was of a different temperament, fond of society and well known as a leader in fashionable circles. By her orders her family had a private box at several theaters and opera-houses, and the Farrington carriage was very elegant. In addition to this she was a member of an aristocratic church, and was as attentive to her monthly communion as she was to her weekly theaters and dances. This costly round of amusement did not at all disturb her husband, who knew that, owing to the abundance of his income, there was not the least danger. Sometimes he would accompany his family to those gay gatherings, but oftener he stayed at home.

The Farringtons contributed largely to the support of the church, and it was chiefly through Mrs. Farrington's influence that Rev. Dr. Darling had received a call to become the pastor of " Mount Zion."

It was now over three months since that conversation took place, when the minister and his wife sat in Mr. and Mrs. Mason's parlor soon after their return from Marvindale. The words of truth and soberness to which the pastor of Mount Zion listened at that time were not forgotten. He left the house under a degree of conviction that the wonderful change in that worldly, fashionable woman was not brought about by a fanatical enthusiast. In addition to this there arose in his mind the serious question, " Has my ministry among this people been of the evangelical apostolic stamp?'' This question he revolved in his mind, but he would wait awhile and examine it more thoroughly before he would decide upon an answer. He would watch the result of this sudden transformation and see if the Mason family would persevere in their new departure. This he did, and in the father, mother, and daughter he saw a most beautiful specimen of Christian life. In each of them the fruit of the Spirit was found in rich abundance.

On one Sabbath evening, when there was no service in their own church, Rev. Dr. Darling and his wife availed themselves of the opportunity of hearing Dr. Bunting. They went in late, and took their seat near the door, where but few noticed them. The Methodist minister on that Sabbath evening was in one of his most effective moods; eloquent, learned, convincing, persuasive, and pathetic. When the meeting closed Dr. Darling and his companion hastened away, and said but little until they reached their home.

" Well, my dear,'' said the minister, "we have heard the Rev. Dr. Bunting.''

" We have,'' said the wife, " and without asking your opinion of the man and the sermon I am quite ready to give mine. I think it was a grand specimen of gospel preaching.''

" I perfectly agree with you,'' said the husband. " I never was more interested in a sermon in all my life. I am now fully convinced, my dear, that my ministry has not been of the right stamp. I have not purposely neglected my duty. A new light has broken upon me, and by God's help I will be faithful to my convictions."

"And God *will* help you, my dear," said Mrs. Darling as she kissed his heated brow.

They knelt together before the Lord and made a new consecration. They rose from their devotion under a sense of God's favor and approbation.

It was evening, and there sat together in Mr. Farrington's elegant parlor the family, with a number of others, ladies and gentlemen, who had met to consult in regard to some particular church arrangements. These having been disposed of, the conversation, as usual, branched out into different subjects.

" Mrs. Farrington," said Mrs. Randall, "what has happened to Dr. Darling? I am sure that of late he has greatly changed in his manner of preaching, and in my opinion the change is decidedly an unfavorable one. I am sure this could not have escaped your notice."

"O no, indeed," said Mrs. Farrington ; "we have noticed it and talked about it among ourselves. It gives me great uneasiness, for you know that through my influence chiefly Dr. Darling secured his prominent position among the city pastors. This change is visible not only in his pulpit efforts, but also in every thing else. His remarks at the close of the last communion service in regard to those church members who patronize theaters and who are never seen in the prayer-meeting were exceedingly out of taste. I was perfectly astonished and very much provoked.''

"He might have known that his remarks would have been offensive to a great many,'' said Mrs. Randall. "Those who enjoy prayer-meetings of course are at liberty to attend them. As for me, I think they are decidedly flat. His sneering allusion to the theater would be more becoming in a Methodist preacher than in the pastor of Mount Zion.''

"So I say!'' said John Farrington in a loud voice. "I had more than enough of that stuff in Marvindale, and we can't tolerate it in our church. It will not take long for mother to put a veto on Dr. Darling's lingo and stop his nonsense.''

"If your mother has such ready power over lingo and nonsense I would advise her without any delay to try her hand on you,'' said his father, with an expression of countenance that was not amiable.

"John has his outspoken, blunt way,'' said the mother, in a manner apologetic. "Dr. Darling has no truer friend than John Cicero Farrington.''

"Does any one know of any reason for this change in Dr. Darling?'' asked Mrs. Randall.

"I think I do,'' said Miss Grace Doyle, a young lady before mentioned. "Soon after Helen Mason returned from the country, Clara Downing and myself went to see her, and before we left we invited her to accompany us to the Broadway Theater on the next evening. She then told us that she had attended theaters and dances for the last time. Her words and her manner so affected us that we have not attended a theater since. We went and consulted our minister, and he frankly told us that from the conversation he had with Mr. and Mrs. Mason, and from watching their daily lives, he became convinced that his ministry had not been what it ought to have been.   He feared that many of the members of his church were 'lovers of pleasure more than lovers of God.'   He seemed to feel very deeply, and said that, God helping him, he would try and do better.   He prayed with us and advised us not to attend theaters and dances.   That, in my opinion, accounts for the change in Dr. Darling's preaching."

"Upon my word!" said Mrs. Farrington, in rather an angry tone.   "The change is bad enough, but to think that it was brought about by listening to those insane Methodists is humiliating beyond description.   Ho, ho!"

"You may call the Masons 'insane Methodists' if you choose," said Miss Doyle, "but their insanity has rather a strange way of showing itself, I must say."

"Grace," said the elder Mr. Farrington, "I would be pleased, for one, to know the features of this Mason insanity."

"Well," said Grace, with a smile, "they are exceedingly kind, amiable, affectionate, and intelligent. Each evening at a certain hour after supper, all the servants assemble with the family in one of the parlors for prayers.   They attend strictly to Sabbath service as well as to their class-meeting and prayer-meeting during the week.   Mrs. Mason and Helen are daily engaged in works of benevolence.   They go among the poor, the sick, and the destitute, and give freely of their money for nearly all charitable

institutions.   That is the way this insanity shows
itself, Mr. Farrington," said Grace.

"Thank you," said the man of the house. "It
would be a grand thing if such insanity were con-
tagious.   But in a little gathering like this it is not
pleasant to get into disputations, so let us touch
upon some other subject."

"Just as you please, Mr. Farrington," said his
wife, and, feeling very confident that in one gentleman present she would find an ally, she continued,
"but I would like to hear a few words from Mr.
Barnard."

"I am afraid that Robert will be too plain-
spoken," said his wife. "Sometimes he is a little
harsh in his remarks.   I think you would better
excuse him."

"Yes, please excuse me," said Mr. Barnard. "I
am but a poor judge in such matters, and Kate is
right."

"You are a member of our church," said Mrs.
Farrington, "and you ought to have something to
say."

"I belong to the church," said the candid Barnard, "but I don't pretend to be a Christian ; and
if I did pretend, who under heavens would be such
a consummate fool as to believe me ? Kate and
I go to meeting on Sunday morning, and in the
afternoon, if the weather is fine, we drive to Cen-
tral Park.   On week nights we go to the theaters
and dances, and never think of going to prayer-
meeting, where a few Christians meet.   That is the
kind of life *I* live; and is not this true in regard

to more than half of our members? And until very lately there was nothing in Dr. Darling's preaching that interfered in the least with this kind of life; and, to tell you the truth honestly, I secretly despised him and his jingling, ornamental essays, when his own church members by the scores, and I among them, were on a full run toward hell. Now I begin to like him. I hope he will give us what we deserve, and I will stand by him. If any church on earth needs 'hell and damnation' preaching we are just that very church."

"Well," said Mrs. Farrington, greatly disappointed, " things are taking a strange turn, I must say. Grace, please give us some music, and that, I presume, will be acceptable to all."

Miss Doyle went to the instrument and played one of her brilliant pieces and ended with a song.

.   .   .   .   .   .

One morning, before Mr. Mason had left his house for his place of business, a letter from his brother was handed to him which read thus:

"DEAR HIRAM: Without delay, and with the greatest pleasure, I answer your letter. Arthur Trevor is just the young man you need. I have tried him thoroughly, both as book-keeper and salesman, and he has given perfect satisfaction. He has in him all the elements of a successful merchant. In addition to his business capacity he is amiable and kind—so much so that from his childhood he has been a universal favorite—and, better than all, he is deeply pious. Of course I shall not mention the subject to him. I leave that to you. He will undoubtedly accept your offer with thanks, for, with all his humility and gentleness, he has much ambition. When Arthur Trevor leaves Marvindale tears will freely flow. But it will be far better for the young man. Our love to sister and niece. Your brother, JAMES."

"He will be such a help in our church," said Helen, in a voice that was not quite firm. "Mamma, don't you think he will be splendid in our Sabbath-school?"

"Arthur Trevor will be splendid in any place, my dear," said the mother.

"I will write to him at once," said the father. The following letter was penned, and reached Marvindale the next morning.

"MY DEAR YOUNG FRIEND: I write to you on a matter of business. Our trade of late has greatly increased, and I need an assistant book-keeper. Judge Mason assures me that you are fully competent for that position as well as for other departments in my store. I will give you a fair salary and put you on the way for promotion. If you can accept the position please let me know when to look for you. Yours truly, HIRAM MASON."

The answer promptly came, which was as follows:

"MR. MASON, DEAR SIR: I thank you for your kind offer. After having consulted my mother and Judge Mason I gladly accept the position, with the full purpose, to the best of my ability, to give you satisfaction. In two weeks from to-day, Providence permitting, I will take the morning train for New York. Respectfully yours, ARTHUR TREVOR."

At the time appointed the young man was met at the depot by Mr. Mason, and was taken to an excellent boarding-house, in close proximity to the store, and furnished with very comfortable quarters.

On the next morning he was shown by Mr. Mason through every department of the vast building and given to understand that, for his own benefit, he would not be wholly confined to book-keeping. It was evident that the interest the proprietor felt in this young man was deeper and of a different nature from that taken in the generality of his clerks.

Nothing had been said to Mr. Bunting by the Masons in regard to Arthur's coming. They thought they would give the pastor a surprise. Although the young man sat in the pew with them the minister did not see him. At the close of the sermon Arthur's church letter was handed to the minister. He looked it over, and his countenance changed. He then remarked: " I am delightfully surprised. I hold in my hand the church letter of a young brother from my former charge, with whom I have been well and happily acquainted for two years. If the young man were not present I might say much more." He then read the letter, and commended Arthur to the affectionate regards of the membership.

CHAPTER IX.

IN SEARCH OF A MODEL, AND HOW IT WORKED.

REV. DR. DARLING became still more pointed and convincing in his sermons and more spiritual in his pastoral visitations. Dissatisfaction increased on the part of the majority, led on by Mrs. Farrington, whlle a good number seemed to be well pleased with the new departure. The pastor, rather than stay in a divided church, saw fit to hand in his resignation, in which he admitted the sad failure of his ministry. He had no unkind word for any one. He soon received a number of calls, and finally became the pastor of a strong church in a western city. Mount Zion remained in a bad state, Mrs. Farrington running the machinery with a high hand. The few devoted ones sought a more congenial home, and the church, like her former Laodicean sister, increased in goods and wanted nothing.

One day there came into Mr. Mason's store a well-dressed gentleman and inquired for the proprietor. He was shown to the private office.

"Mr. Mason," said the stranger, "my name is Ostrander. Here is my card. My father for many years has been in trade at New Orleans. Our business has so increased that we have concluded to build a new store on an extensive scale. At the request of my father I came north in search of a perfect model. I have been informed by several merchants that your building, in many respects, is the most convenient in the city. I would take it as a great favor to be shown through your house."

"It will give me the greatest pleasure to show you through the building myself," said Mr. Mason, rising. "We shall begin at the bottom." And both left the private office. The proprietor showed the stranger through every part. Their stay below was somewhat protracted. Every door was carefully examined and marked down in a blank-book which the stranger held in his hand. They then went into the parts above. When the survey was ended they re-entered the street floor. The southern gentleman expressed himself as perfectly delighted with the building, and in very strong terms thanked Mr. Mason for his great kindness.

At that moment Arthur, from a distant part of the store, had a full clear view of the stranger's face, and was startled to find that he was none other than his former classmate at Marvindale, Mark Floyd. His first impulse was to go and speak to him, but he concluded to keep out of his sight, and wait to hear from Mr. Mason the nature of the interview. From what he had learned of Floyd after his expulsion from school he was well convinced that at this time he was on some errand of mischief. The stranger, with a polite bow, left the building, and Mr. Mason returned to his private office with strengthened opinions concerning the perfections of his large house.

In about an hour after this, Arthur, wishing to ask Mr. Mason some questions touching a little discrepancy between certain figures, went into his private office. These were soon adjusted.

"Arthur, did you notice that young man with whom I went through the building about an hour ago?" asked Mr. Mason.

"I did indeed," was the reply; "I know him well, and I have been wondering what he wanted."

"*You* know him well!" said Mr. Mason, in astonishment. "I don't see how that can be. He told me his name was Ostrander, and his father a merchant in New Orleans; that they intended to build a new store, and wanted to secure a good model."

"I am not mistaken in the man," said Arthur. "His name is Mark Floyd. His father is a rich brewer. Mark was my classmate for a year and a half in Marvindale. He was expelled for deception and lying. He went home, robbed his father of four hundred dollars, and ran away. In all probability he belongs to-day to a gang of thieves."

"Arthur, sit down," said Mr. Mason. "We must talk this matter over a little more. If you are correct it has a very serious appearance."

"Mark Floyd has several peculiarities of features," said Arthur, "and by me they could not be mistaken. He is a constitutional liar and a depraved wretch. By a deception that may claim ingenuity he has got a full knowledge of the interior of this building and what it contains."

"And what is your explanation of this strange movement, Arthur?" asked Mr. Mason.

"It admits of but one explanation," was the answer. "That fellow, with his comrades, has an eye on this building, with burglarious intentions. If it would be pertinent in me to give advice I would say that the store should have a double outside watch."

"I am so thankful that you happened to see the villain and recognize him," said Mr. Mason, by this time well convinced that Arthur was correct. "We shall be on our guard, and I will see that the watch shall be strengthened."

In a room reached through dark, winding, mysterious passages, were assembled at a late hour of the night about a dozen men in rough high revelry. Owing to the depth of their hiding-place and its remoteness from other apartments their boisterous proceedings did not disturb any quiet sleepers. This was one of their rare jovial nights in which they were permitted by their chief to indulge freely.

"Well, Nero," said the chief, who was perfectly sober, addressing himself to Mark Floyd, "have you found a right model for your new store at New Orleans?"

"Prospects grand!" said Nero. "Abundant treasures! Success sure!"

"Three cheers for Nero!" said the chief. But the company refused to cheer.

"No disrespect must be shown to your superior!" cried the chief.

"We don't receive the skulking coward as our superior!" cried "Rob Roy."

"That we don't, by a long shot!" cried another.

"Silence, you drunken fools!" cried the chief again. "Have you no regard for your sacred obligations?"

"Much more than Nero has," answered "Robin Hood." "We meet dangers, but he skulks. We bear his insolence no longer."

The chief saw at once that threatening would not answer, and said: "To-night, my boys, you are somewhat heated; to-morrow you will be sorry for what you have said. In our very next operation Nero will take the most dangerous post."

To this there was no reply, but sneering countenances plainly told that Mark Floyd was detested by the majority of the gang. His selfishness and conceit were as visible in the New York burglar as in the Marvindale student.

One Tuesday afternoon Mr. Mason received by mail this strange communication:

"Mistar Maysun this is munda look out for thirsta nite the man from neu ar leens wil bee a rownd plees thro this in tha fiar,   wan hoo nose."

Mr. Mason at once sent a boy to inform Arthur that he was wanted at the private office, and in a few minutes the proprietor and his clerk were closeted together.

"Trevor, how is this to be explained?" asked Mr. Mason.

"It is often said ' there is honor among thieves,' " said Arthur, "but they often quarrel and betray each other. Mark Floyd could never remain long in any society without creating enemies. In my opinion this is one of them, and he desires Mark to fall into a trap."

"But does not this warning endanger himself?" asked Mr. Mason.

"He well understands that he is not to be one of the number," said Arthur. "The gang in all may number twenty, when only four or five are employed at the same time."

"Arthur," said Mr. Mason, "Your theory is reasonable. We should reveal this matter to the chief of police. Let us go at once."

In a short time they were in the office of that city official, and they revealed to him the whole, from beginning to end.

"And from all this what is your theory?" asked the chief.

Mr. Mason referred him to Arthur, who briefly and clearly gave the officer the same view as he had given Mr. Mason.

"Young man," said the chief, smiling, "when you wish to leave Mr. Mason's service come to me, and I will put you on the detective force. Your theory is perfectly correct, and I am very confident that we are about to grab a gang of burglars that have so far escaped. Mr. Mason, I will have a strong force of my best men at your place on that night, and I believe I shall have to see that sport myself. I shall be the first one to call. I will have on no uniform. See that I am directed at once to your private office. The others will follow at short intervals, in citizen's dress, and let them also be shown to your office. Last of all shall come a small chest marked 'For Mr. Mason.' This shall contain a number of things that we shall need. Say nothing about it to any one; I will see that the preparations will be complete."

It was Thursday, just after dinner. "Mary," said Mr. Mason, "I will eat supper down town. I have a certain business transaction to see to of such a nature that it will keep Arthur and myself busy until a very late hour."

"O well, that is all right," said Mrs. Mason; "you have told me, and I shall not be uneasy."

The night was rainy, dark, and tempestuous. The winds howled and there were but few pedestrians seen in the streets. Mr. Mason had told one of his clerks that he expected a number of gentlemen to call upon him that evening and that they were to be conducted into his private office.

Mr. Snyder, the chief, arrived first, and was followed by four more at short intervals, and at last came the chest before mentioned.

"Trevor," said Mr. Mason, "the night is so very rough, give the order from me to close the store at once. Let the lights be left as they are."

The order was given, and soon all the clerks had dispersed and the doors were locked.

The front half of the store's basement was elegantly fitted up and contained among other things many valuable articles in gold and silver. The room back of this contained unopened packages. In the rear were two doors opening into an alley. Into this basement the police force, with Mr. Mason and Arthur, entered. They soon reached the rear.

"Mr. Mason," said Snyder, "did your friend from New Orleans pay much attention to this room?"

"More than to any other part," was the reply. "He examined the rear door very closely, and inquired about the width of the wall."

"Exactly," said the chief. "This is the only place where they can force an entrance, and it will take them but a short time to enter the room."

"But how?" asked Mr. Mason, with some astonishment.

"Well," said the chief, "they can easily dislodge those stones and make an opening for the smallest of their number to get through, who will then remove those iron bars. They can do that with far less noise than to break that heavy door."

"But can they do all this without being overtaken by the watch?" asked Mr. Mason.

"To-night they can," answered the smiling chief, "for I have ordered the watch not to molest them unless they see them coming out of this building unarrested. But where is to be our hiding-place? The performance will be in this room, and of very short duration. They are to be suddenly knocked senseless and handcuffed before they know what is the matter. Mr. Mason, I see a door there; does it lead into a room?"

"It does," was the answer, and the door was opened.

"This is just the place," said Snyder. "Tom and Fred, you go after the chest, and we shall put ourselves in working order."

The chest was brought and carried into the hiding-room. Each officer put on his uniform, armed himself with a heavy club and a revolver, and provided himself with a pair of handcuffs.

" Now, Mr. Mason and Mr. Trevor will go up and extinguish the lights and then come down and stay with us in our little room, where we shall wait for our guests. It is a grand night for burglars, and I don't think they will neglect it," said Mr. Snyder.

This order was at once obeyed, and in a few minutes Mr. Mason and Arthur returned.

" One thing more," said the chief: " they must not be permitted to enter that front basement. They will break that lock in a second. Place some heavy substance in front of that door; something that they cannot easily remove. This will give us a little better advantage to dispose of them."

This was soon done. " Now let us get into that room and make ourselves as comfortable as we can until we are relieved."

In a moment all was silent and dark. Seven persons sat together in the little waiting-room. Not a whisper was heard. Nothing seemed to astonish Mr. Mason more than the confident manner in which the chief spoke and acted. The theory of Trevor seemed plausible, but, after all, did it amount to any thing stronger than a probability? These were questions that somewhat troubled Mr. Mason in that dark, silent hiding-place. If the burglars should not appear their situation would be somewhat ludicrous. The storm raged in all its fury, and the darkness in the alley was deep. The hours passed away, and a clock in a neighboring steeple struck the hour of midnight. The chief sat next to Mr. Mason. In about ten minutes after the clock struck Mr. Mason felt his hand gently tapped by that of the officer. He listened with all his powers, but could not hear a sound. He felt the same tapping again, and now, indistinctly, he could hear a certain movement on the outside. His heart beat quickly. It soon became evident that the wall was attacked. There was no pounding, but by some method the stones were being removed with but very little noise. Before long, substances fell on the inside. Mr. Snyder and his men now all at once rose to their feet. The watchers could now hear busy footsteps. More stones fell into the room, and from a brief stillness it was clear that the opening was completed. The crawling through was but the work of a few moments, and one of the gang was in the room. He felt for the door, removed the iron bars, and the door was opened. How many came in was not yet known to the officers, for as yet burglars and all were in darkness. The door was quickly shut and barred.

"Cover the opening, Nero, before we uncover the lanterns," said a voice on a very low key.

"That is done, worthy chief," said Nero.

"Now we are all safely in," said the master burglar. "Light!" And in a moment light there was. Through slight openings Snyder and his men saw five persons standing on the floor.

"Now, my men, you are to reap the biggest harvest of the year," said the chief burglar. "Nero, who knows all about the building, will conduct you to those valuables that will take the least room. Beyond that door you will find articles in gold and silver. Let each depart well loaded. Now, to work!"

"I see there are heavy boxes resting against the door," said Nero, "but we can easily remove them."

"Let them be removed at once," said the commander; and, while the robbers were in the act of removing the heavy obstructions, quick as lightning the policemen fell upon them, and by well-directed blows from heavy clubs the five burglars were laid senseless on the floor.

"On with their ornaments, my brave lads!" said the chief, and instantly their hands were bound together.

"Ha, ha, ha!" cried Snyder. "This is the neatest job that I have witnessed in years. While they are coming to let us have a smoke." And he handed his men some cigars.

As the prisoners recovered consciousness and looked around, the curses were terrible, and not fit to be mentioned here even with the assistance of dashes.

"Gentlemen, I think you have slept long enough," said Mr. Snyder. "It is high time for you to start for your lodgings. I shall be very happy to entertain you as my guests this stormy night."

"A thousand curses on your head!" cried Nero.

"Ah! I think I hear the voice of Mark Floyd, Esq., the once brilliant orator of Marvindale Academy," said Mr. Snyder. "Hail, Nero! I fear the new store at New Orleans will prove a failure. By the way, would you not be pleased with a sight of one of your schoolmates—Arthur Trevor, for instance?   Here he stands.''

"Mark," said Arthur, "I·am sorry to find you in this situation."

This would have affected some pretty hard characters into tears.   But not so Mark Floyd.   He broke out in the most abusive language imaginable.

" Enough of this," said Mr. Snyder.   " My men, help those fellows to their feet and march them to the station-house."   And this was done.

Mr. Snyder remained.   " Now," said he, " I have a bit of information to give you.   You wondered why I felt so positive in regard to this matter. About two hours before you and Mr. Trevor came to my office the other day I received this letter, which, owing to its horrid spelling, I will read to you myself :

"'MR. CHIEF OF POLICE: I belong to a gang of burglars, and I know I am a hard, miserable wretch ; but when a man shows me kindness I don't forget it.   Six years ago I stole some goods from the store of Hiram Mason and was arrested.   I told him I was very sorry.   He talked to me like a father, pleaded for me before the judge, and my sentence was very light.   Now, a part of this gang—and I am telling you the truth, so help me God—is going to rob this Mr. Mason's store on next Thursday night, led by Nero, the meanest devil that ever breathed. That man's store is not going to be robbed if I can help it; and if those that will go at it get nabbed so much the better.   Now you know all about it.   I send you this because I have not forgotten the kindness which Hiram Mason showed this poor wretch six years ago. I am going to leave the gang to-night.   THAT IS ALL.' "

"Mr. Mason, I presume you remember this fellow," said Snyder.

"Very well, indeed," was the reply; "and his statement is perfectly correct."

"Your communication came from the same chap," said the chief, "and he has repaid your kindness with compound interest. Now I'll go. This matter will cost you but little time or trouble. It is not often that I accompany the boys, but this time I could not withstand the temptation."

The prisoners pleaded guilty, and were sentenced to State prison for terms varying from seven to fifteen years.

CHAPTER X.

RAILROAD CALAMITY, A SCREAM, AND THEN JOY.

ARTHUR'S great proficiency in store and business matters was on the increase. He had the full confidence of his employer, and his kind, amiable ways won the regard and respect of his fellow-clerks. His fine, manly appearance and gentlemanly bearing were highly complimented by all who had the pleasure of his acquaintance. In the church, also, his influence was constantly increasing. To his mother and sister he was deeply devoted, and the correspondence between them was uniform and affectionate.

How Rev. Dr. Darling was progressing in his western church may be known from the following part of a letter written to the Mason family:

"DEAR BROTHER AND SISTER MASON: It is now over a year since I became the pastor of 'this church, and the Lord has been better to me than all my fears. My feeble efforts have been blessed in the salvation of many souls. I have learned much from my former failure, and I am 'determined to know nothing among men save Jesus Christ and him crucified.' Our social meetings are spiritual and largely attended.

"I look back with gratitude to that interview we

had in your parlor on an evening soon after your return from the country. The weighty and solemn truths which then fell upon my ears astonished me, and became the foundation of a better life and a more spiritual experience.

"Mrs. Darling joins me in sending affectionate regards to yourselves and Miss Helen.

"Yours, in the Gospel,

"JOHN DARLING."

Arthur Trevor had now been in the employ of Hiram Mason for three years, and had reached the age of twenty-four. He had received special privileges and advantages in the large emporium from his very first advent. He was very deep in his employer's confidence. Mr. Mason often had business to attend to in country towns and villages, and in this he had found that Arthur was perfectly reliable.

On an errand of this nature he had been sent to a town on the western border of Massachusetts, and it was not certain how long he would have to remain. One morning, just before breakfast, Helen was the first one to open the morning papers. She was by herself in one of the parlors. She was attracted by this heading: "A SERIOUS ACCIDENT ON THE HARLEM ROAD. A LARGE NUMBER BADLY, AND SOME FATALLY, INJURED!" She passed the details of the accident in search of the names of the injured, and among the first she saw "Arthur Trevor, of New York, ribs and arm broken, with severe bruises on face and head. It is feared that he received serious internal injuries." The maiden uttered a loud scream and began to sob aloud. Both parents rushed into the room in a moment.

"Helen, my child, what is the matter? Tell me at once!" said the father.

"O, papa, forgive me for screaming! I couldn't help it!" cried the girl. "I did not know that I was so nervous. Railroad accident, and Arthur is terribly, if not fatally, injured!"

"Your screaming was perfectly natural, my child," said the father. "Show me the article!"

By this time Mrs. Mason was louder in her weeping than was the daughter, while the father, with quivering lips and a pale countenance, examined the article.

"It says, 'The wounded that were able to travel reached the city last night,'" said Mr. Mason. "Heaven grant that he may be among the number!" He ran out of the room, rang a bell, and his coachman stood before him.

"Now, Edward," said he, "have the double carriage ready as soon as you possibly can. Mr. Trevor is badly hurt. Make all haste, my man."

"My dear, while Ed is getting the carriage ready we will just take a bite to keep us from fainting. You must go with me!" said Mr. Mason.

"And, Hiram, we must bring him home with us if he is able to ride," said Mrs. Mason, through her tears.

"That is my intention," said her husband. "Let us take with us a few pillows. Helen, darling, bring them down."

In a few minutes the carriage was hastening at a

rapid rate toward Trevor's boarding-house, and Helen was in her chamber bowed before her heavenly Father in behalf of one who was very dear to her heart.

The boarding-house was reached. Mrs. Mason went to the parlor, while her husband hastened to the office.

" Mr. Rogers," he asked, " has Trevor arrived ?"

" Mr. Trevor is here and much injured," said Rogers ; " but his injuries are not of a dangerous nature. He has a broken arm and a badly bruised face and head."

" Then you think his condition is not dangerous ?" said Mr. Mason, with his face brightening.

" Nothing dangerous, I'll assure you," said Rogers.

" Thank Heaven !" said Mr. Mason, and hastened to inform his wife.

He then returned to the office and informed Mr. Rogers that under the circumstances he thought it was best to take Trevor with him to his own house. Mr. Rogers was of the same opinion, and said :

" I am sure that you can do better for him than we can. We sent for Dr. Bailey early this morning and—but here he comes."

The doctor, accompanied by Mr. Mason and Mr. Rogers, went up to Arthur's room. He was lying down partly dressed, with his head bandaged. He reached out his left hand, which was eagerly grasped by Mr. Mason.

" For a short time they have spoiled your beauty, Mr. Trevor," said the doctor, in a cheerful voice ; " but in two or three weeks we'll have you as good as new. Pretty hard knocks, I must say, but fortunately they'll leave no permanent marks. Have you any broken ribs?"

" My ribs are all right," said Arthur. "I have a broken arm, with a bruised head and face, and so far as I know that is the extent of my injury."

"Let us feel that broken arm," said the physician. "See how gently I can do it! That will do for the present. Mr. Mason and his good wife have their carriage below, and they claim you as their guest for a few weeks. Before noon I will call to put your arm in good shape and to attend to your face and head."

The young man was deeply affected, even to tears. "I am sorry to give you so much trouble, Mr. Mason," said he.

"Not another word, Arthur."

The young man was assisted. Shawls were put over him, he gently walked down and was met by Mrs. Mason with a smile that touched his heart. Pillows were arranged, and he was placed in a comfortable position. The husband and wife joined him, and the carriage moved very slowly while Arthur's aching head rested on the bosom of Hiram Mason.

At the Fifth Avenue mansion the young man received every attention that kindness and affection could bestow. Here it would be an easy matter to dwell at length upon a dozen little incidents that occurred during those few weeks. He suffered much bodily pain and some fever. On the other hand he experienced unspeakable bliss in the full assurance that his genuine love for Helen Mason was no stronger than that of the young lady for him, and that all this was in perfect harmony with the feelings of Miss Mason's parents.

Arthur in the early morning following the accident had caused a dispatch to be sent to his mother assuring her that his injuries were not serious, and she heard from him almost daily while he was an invalid.

He was cordially greeted by all in the store when he resumed his duties, and at the church there was much rejoicing on seeing his face and on hearing his voice again.

In about one year from the time of the accident, and when that scream from Helen showed her nervousness, or something else expressed in one syllable, that fine residence was crowded with smiling guests. It was evident from the line of elegant carriages seen in that part of the fashionable thoroughfare that the occasion was not one of small importance. Judge Mason and his family were there. Mrs. Trevor and her beautiful Alice were present. Mrs. Armstrong and her sweet Lily were among the guests. Clara Downing and Grace Doyle moved quickly hither and thither. There was a large representation from St. Thomas's Church. Under the circumstances a clergyman was necessary, and Rev. Dr. Bunting was chosen, who was present with his amiable wife. The ceremony was brief and impressive. Arthur Trevor and Helen Mason were pronounced "husband and wife, in the name of the Father, and of the Son, and of the Holy Ghost."

Helen was not separated from her parents. In the same commodious house they lived as one family, in the enjoyment of health and happiness. Arthur became a partner in the business, a man of wealth and great influence. Helen, with her mother, continued in her labor of love among the poor, while hundreds arose and called her blessed.

OTHER
STORIES OF COUNTRY AND CITY.

SHARP WORDS ON OLD FLINTROCK CIRCUIT.

CHAPTER I.

THE CONFERENCE.

A HARD charge was old Flintrock. That little word "hard" has several significations, especially when applied to circuits. Sometimes it conveys the idea of the amount of labor to be accomplished, sometimes the long and difficult distance between the appointments, and sometimes it refers to the temper and disposition of the people. The word when applied to Flintrock means all of these together, and if the reader can think of any other kind of "hard" in all probability that old circuit was then entitled ·to it. At nearly all of the appointments things were in a loose condition. The congregations were small, and lacking in proper attention. Young people often trifled during prayer and preaching and had gone unrebuked. The brethren, many of them, had no

family altar. The prayer-meeting had a sickly ex-
istence, and the class-meeting was attended by only
a few. Financial affairs were sadly neglected, and
only two or three brethren could be found in the
official board that cared any thing about the matter.
The minister's salary was always put down at a low
figure, and even that small sum was never paid in
full. There was but one Methodist church on the
whole charge, and that was at the village from which
the circuit took its name. But there were several
out-appointments, where preaching was had once in
two weeks at the respective school-houses. Some
of these were not far from the village, but the brethren would carelessly stay at home until the " once in
two weeks" would come around. Some of them
said that the folks at the " Rock" were rather "stuck
up," and they were charged with pride and exclusiveness. Official members would invariably get
tired of their minister before the end of the first
year and demand a " change." Yes, Flintrock was
a hard circuit, and the ministers knew it, and to be
" read out" for that well-known spot was never considered a feather in any body's cap.

The year had come to a close and the itinerants
were on their way to Conference, which was held
that year at N——. In those days they were not
conveyed in elegant railroad coaches rushing along
at the rate of thirty or forty miles an hour, for this
was over forty years ago. The majority of them
drove their faithful ponies and were often two or
three days on the road, stopping at the houses of
good Methodists, where, as a rule, they found a

hearty welcome. Well, they would reach their destination, and as fellow-laborers would exchange most friendly salutations. I think the demonstration of good feeling in those days was more enthusiastic than at our modern Conferences. It is possible that their extensive circuit-riding and their battles with winter storms and oppressive summer heat were more conducive to an overflow of soul than are our modern little stations and our one appointment itinerancy. In richness of apparel they were far behind our modern preachers. Their "allowance" was very small, and in many instances it was not paid. They flourished no gold watches or costly sleeve-buttons. Their suits were plain both from principle and necessity.

Among these hardy sons of the ministry at this Conference was found John B. Sharp. His preaching talents were excellent, and with the ministers he was a favorite. He had the rare faculty of combining great plainness of speech and an excellent temper. In completely demolishing an opponent, or in administering reproof in "words that burned," his countenance would give unmistakable proof of a kind spirit and good intention. While others, in softer words, would give mortal offense, involve themselves in trouble and fail in their object, Brother Sharp would gain his point and retain the good will of those whom he rebuked. The appointments he filled were not of the first class, and sometimes they were not of the second. There was something which no one ever knew that kept him down. His inferiors one after the other marched into good stations. This, of course, he noticed, but he did not complain. He was cheerful and happy, and never asked for any particular favor of either bishop or presiding elder. For two years he had served the Fairport appointment with such a degree of success that the Watchford Station was very anxious to secure his services.

Rev. Samson Keener at this time was the presiding elder of Sahara District. He was a powerful preacher, especially on points bearing on distinctive Arminian theology. He was just such a man as high Calvinists would be sorry to meet in public debate. Once, before they knew his strength, they made that mistake. They were put to flight with terrible slaughter. Let not Brother Keener be blamed for his non-intercourse with his preachers touching their destination. At that day among the presiding elders that was considered a rule clothed with more than ordinary sanctity and very seldom departed from; and if occasionally through his nomination and influence an appointment was made that seemed to be wholly destitute of *human* wisdom it gave the people an opportunity to gaze in wonder on the mysterious workings of that Providence whose ways are past finding out.

A few days before the session of this Conference two brethren representing the Quarterly Meeting Conference of the Watchford Station called on the presiding elder, and the following conversation took place:

"Brother Keener, we have called to see you in regard to our next minister," said Brother Candor. "We thought there would be no harm in asking for a certain brother if there was nothing in the way."

"That is a very delicate point!" answered the elder, looking profoundly solemn. "Your interests will be sacredly regarded in the cabinet. But when preachers ask for a particular charge, and charges ask for a particular preacher, it has a tendency to block the wheels of our glorious itinerancy."

"Our regard for the itinerancy is fully equal to yours, and we know something of Methodist Church polity," answered Brother Candor. "We put forth no claim. How can a simple and respectful request of this nature have a tendency to clog the wheels of the itinerancy?"

"Brother Candor, with all due respect to your age and ripe judgment," said Brother Keener, "I must say that you are not expected to know these things as well as I do. Such requests give us a vast amount of trouble."

"Then, as far as I am concerned," said Brother Candor, looking the presiding elder in the face, "you are released from all further trouble. I am prepared to go home and report this interview to my brethren."

"And so am I," said his companion, Brother Earnest, rising, as if ready to start.

This independence was something that Samson Keener was not in the habit of encountering, and, knowing the influence of these men, he saw at once that it would not answer for them to leave in their present mood, and he hastened to give the interview a more friendly turn.

"O, no, brethren!" he said, with some astonishment. "I did not mean to cast any reflection on *you*. I have always found you to be good men and true. Who is the preacher that you have in view?"

"John B. Sharp," was the answer.

"Indeed! Your aspirations are quite moderate," said Brother Keener. "Watchford is one of our best stations, and you are aware that Brother Sharp has never filled that grade of appointments."

"Yes, we are well aware of that," said Brother Earnest, "and to us it has been a matter of wonder for years why a man of such splendid preaching talents, with other perfections to match, has been kept away from our good stations, while some of them, at least, have been filled by men of very inferior abilities."

"I am not aware that that has been the case," said the presiding elder, with evident displeasure. "You pay but a poor compliment to the combined wisdom of the Bishop and presiding elders."

"We don't deny the wisdom," said Brother Candor; "we only fail to see it; that is all."

"I will give your request the consideration it deserves," said the elder, with some stiffness of manner; and soon the brethren departed for their homes.

"Watchford! Whom do you nominate for this station, Brother Keener?" asked the Bishop.

"Brother Minus," was the response.

"I have no wish to interfere with the legitimate business of another presiding elder," said Brother Fairhead, "but it seems to me that that strong station needs a person of more commanding pulpit talent than that young brother possesses."

" Bishop," said Brother Keener, " Brother Minus is a very promising young minister ; a fine scholar, and a graduate of Middletown. He has lately married the daughter of one of our wealthiest laymen. Sister Minus is exceedingly kind, amiable, and *benevolent*, as I know by experience."

Brother Minus was written down for Watchford, although several of the presiding elders pronounced it a " bad fit."

It soon came around again to the Sahara District.

" Whom do you nominate for Flintrock ? " asked the Bishop.

" May it please the Chair," said Brother Keener, " before I make the nomination I wish to say a few words in regard to this circuit. In many respects it is hard to serve. The majority of the members of the Quarterly Conference are peculiarly constituted, and I have to make a change almost every year. They need a strong man, and, fortunately, I have a brother on my District that will answer their purpose exactly. I nominate for Flintrock, John B. Sharp."

" Bishop," said Brother Sweet, " I cannot look upon that nomination with favor. Brother Sharp is one of our best preachers, and I have thought for years that we have not done him justice. I have a good station on my District where they would receive him with open arms. He is a grand good man, and to send him to Flintrock borders on the abusive."

Much was said *pro* and *con* on this question, when at last the Bishop remarked: " I am very confident that Brother Sharp's worth and talents are high. I am deeply interested in the man. Flintrock has been humored until it has become insolent. Instead of yielding to their unreasonable demands and foolish whims Brother Keener ought to have administered to them a severe reproof. It is evident that the circuit is cursed with worthless church officers who ought to be displaced or reformed. I think Brother Sharp would do the work. If I send him there I want him to have his own way, and I think he will come forth all right. But I will not appoint this excellent man to Flintrock without his full and cheerful consent. If he objects I will give him a station worthy of his talents. Brother Keener, please ask Brother Sharp to call at my room this evening at seven o'clock."

The presiding elder could not instantly make up his mind whether he was pleased or otherwise, and so he left it an open question. On that evening Brother Sharp had a long interview with the Bishop and came away with a smiling countenance.

At the close of the Conference the appointments were read in a clear, distinct voice, and it was noticed by several that a faint smile touched the Bishop's lips as he read, " Flintrock, John B. Sharp."

CHAPTER II.

THE FIRST WEEK ON OLD FLINTROCK.

IT is sad to think that nearly all of the perplexing difficulties on this circuit were owing chiefly to the lamentable inefficiency of a large number of its official members. In addition to a lack of energy they manifested a spirit of opposition to every thing in the shape of improvement or progress. Several ministers had undertaken in soft words to awaken them from their stupidity, but they were invariably met with either frowns or indifference. Their annual changing of ministers was, upon the whole, as pleasing to the retiring itinerant as to the Quarterly Conference. Indeed, to many of the preachers who had served them this had constituted the most pleasing reflection of the whole year. In most cases they had been men of quiet habits, peaceable disposition, and moderate abilities. They comprehended the situation and saw that it needed a desperate remedy ; but they lacked the moral courage to enter the fight. Under the conviction that they were not adequate for the emergency they left things as they found them, and perhaps worse. In the seclusion of their own study at the parsonage, when no official member or any one else was nigh, they would often tell these brethren in very plain language what they thought of them. Those were brave words, and had they fallen on the ears of those negligent officials, instead of those inanimate volumes and papered walls, perhaps they would have accomplished some good. But these peaceable brethren thought it was not advisable to create strifes, and hoped that some one would yet find his way to Flintrock that would give these worthless officials the shaking they deserved.

These lay brethren, ludicrous as it may seem, were nevertheless anxious for a revival. "Our paying members are dying off," they would say, "and quarterage is getting scarce, and unless we get a rousing 'reformation' it will be hard to get the preacher's pay." Yes, they longed for a reformation, not for the glory of God and the salvation of souls; that was not in their official line; neither was it for the sake of the preacher, but rather for their own profit in dollars and cents. Where is the circuit minister of long standing that has not heard words like those from *some* official brethren? These men in the midst of their moral stupidity would clamor for a revival and demand of the presiding elder to send them a man that would "get up a reformation."

Here it may be well to let the reader have a little knowledge of some of the members of the Flintrock Quarterly Conference.

Brother Goodier was a steward and class-leader, a man of some wealth, and a devoted Christian. He was liberal in his contributions, active in every department of the work, and a regular reader of the church paper.

Brother Tighter was a wealthy steward, but paid no attention to the duties of his office. He was a penurious worldling. The support he gave the Gospel was shamefully meager. He took no church paper, and his house had no family altar.

Brother Pompey was also a steward, and a very loud talker. He was of a swaggering disposition, quite illiterate, and abounding in slang expressions. He was just as apt to be in the right as in the wrong. There was in him a vein of kindness, and he was not stingy. He took no church paper.

Brother Sly was also a steward, and always rendered a cheerful assistance in keeping down the preacher's salary to the lowest figure. He was known among the young people as "Old Human Natur'," on account of his never-failing habit of using that term in all of his conversations. Of course he took no church periodical.

Brother Gruntly was a class-leader, but fortunately he never officiated in that line. He always conferred that honor upon the preacher. He was much given to grumbling and was at home in fault-finding. No *Advocate* in his house.

Brother Trembly was a good man in his way, but greatly lacking in moral courage. In the official meeting he would quietly submit to wrong measures rather than come in contact with the majority. His wife insisted on having the *Advocate*.

Brother Wiser was an excellent class-leader and steward, and always stood with Brother Goodier for reform, and was invariably voted down. He had taken the *Advocate* from its origin.

There were others in the official board but they were indifferent, or even worse than that.

Brother Goodier had just returned from Conference, which he generally attended if not too far away. No sooner was he seated than his daughter, a beautiful young lady of eighteen, said :

"And now, dear papa, tell us who is to be our minister for this year. I am almost afraid to hear. But, whoever he may be, he will be better than we deserve."

"Ella," said her father with a look she failed to comprehend, "when I tell you his name you will be perfectly astonished."

"Well, we may as well learn our fate at once," said she, "let us hear his name."

"My child," said the father, "you will be glad to hear that we are to have Brother Sharp."

"What ! John B. Sharp !" cried the girl in utter astonishment.

"That is the very name," said her father.

Ella in ecstasy ran up stairs to impart the news to her mother. They both came down smiling. "What a strange thing to send that splendid man to this place !" said Mrs. Goodier. "I am afraid that he feels sore about it."

"No, he cheerfully consented to come," said the father. "It is all right."

Here Walter, the son, a young man of twenty, came in with the closing part of old "Denmark" on his musical lips, to which he did splendid justice,

> "Firm as a rock His truth shall stand,
>   When rolling years shall cease to move."

"O, Walter !" cried his sister; "guess whom we are going to have for our new minister."

"Some one we don't deserve, as I learn from your laughing eyes," said Walter. "I pity him from the bottom of my heart."

"What would you say, Walter, if I were to tell you that John B. Sharp was the man?" asked the sister, with a sly look.

"I would say that Miss Ella Goodier was for once indulging in the most improbable fiction," said the brother.

"And yet, in sober earnestness, he is the very person," said Ella.

The brother for a while looked upon his sister in silent astonishment, and then, turning to his father, said:

"Father, what does this mean? I am really astonished. Well, John B. has a mind of his own and the courage of a lion. He would not be afraid to meet a whole regiment of devils. If I am not mistaken there will be some *sharp* words on Old Flintrock between this and next Conference."

The new minister arrived in due time, and for a few days, with his wife and two daughters, was entertained at the friendly residence of Brother Goodier, with whom he was well acquainted. From this faithful steward he gained all the information that he could desire touching the temporal and spiritual condition of the charge.

"These are discouraging truths to reveal to our new minister," said Brother Goodier, with tears in his eyes.

"I was fully aware that things were in a bad shape when I consented to come," said Brother Sharp.

" I am constantly praying for wisdom to move in harmony with the will of God. I shall endeavor to be kind to all, but at the same time I must lift up the standard of Christian holiness, and stand by the requirements of our Church Discipline. I have a very comfortable assurance that my labors will be blessed in reclaiming the backslidden and in the conversion of souls.'·

On Sabbath morning at Flintrock the congregation was very large. The minister delivered his message with " energy and power."   He had perfect liberty, and the sermon produced a strong impression. At the close of the last hymn he asked the congregation to be seated, as he had a few more words to say in which he was sure they would be interested.

" I thank you for the deep and respectful attention you have paid this morning to the preached word. Your earnest, solemn countenances prove to me that you come to the house of God to hear the Gospel, and not to satisfy your curiosity by gazing on a stranger. After having thus spoken in your praise I am sorry to say that to this general attention and solemnity there has been a slight exception. Throughout the service I have been greatly annoyed, and so have others, by the rude and trifling behavior of four young persons in the gallery. Such conduct in the house of the Lord cannot be tolerated, and I would kindly entreat those young persons from henceforth to abstain from behavior that is not only a violation of all the principles of good manners but also displeasing to God.

I hope these words will be kindly received ; but let it be clearly understood, and you are at liberty to proclaim it far and near, that no rude behavior in the sanctuary during divine service shall go unrebuked."

The benediction was pronounced and the people went to their homes. The closing remarks of the minister gave great satisfaction to all except the very few whom we shall mention hereafter. He was praised for his noble decision, and in the class-meeting, in which he was not present, there was a general good feeling as the result of their first Sabbath service.

In the afternoon the minister had an appointment at the "Yellow School-house," about four miles from the village. The house was full. The aspect of the congregation was less intelligent and less thoughtful than at the village. They had a choir made up of young people, who evidently "magnified their office." The minister spoke with great freedom and power. The general attention was good, but the singers behaved badly. There was the irrepressible whisper and winking, and they went so far as to exchange views on slips of paper, and Brother Sharp, only in fewer words than at the church, spoke of the trifling spirit manifested on the part of a few, and hoped he would never witness the like again.

After class-meeting he went home with Brother and Sister Gruntly, who lived close by. They were sociable and friendly, but there appeared to be an effort about it, and it was evident that their minds were not at perfect ease. Tea was soon ready and the minister was invited to sit at the table in another room. As he entered the dining-room he noticed the exit of a young lady into the kitchen on whose countenance rested something very much like a frown. He noticed also that this young woman was one of those who had figured prominently in the school-house choir.

The meal was progressing, while the conversation lagged.

"Where is Sallie?" asked the father, looking around.

"Sallie wishes to be excused," said the mother, a little stiffly.

"Methodism is not what it was when I was a boy, Brother Sharp," said Brother Gruntly, in a tone far from being cheerful.

"For which I am very thankful," said Brother Sharp. "We certainly ought to have made some fine advancement in forty years, and I am glad to know that we are progressing finely."

"I guess we have been progressing backward," said the man of the house, and he smiled in view of what he considered a very happy hit.

"No. Our course is onward and upward in every respect," said the minister. "We are progressing splendidly in piety, education, and liberality. Have you read Dr. Banks's article on that point in the last *Advocate?*"

"I don't take the *Advocate*," was the answer.

"I am sorry," was the reply. "I think if you were well posted in regard to the working of our

Church you would never say again that we were progressing backward."

" There is too much pride in the Church," was his next.

" If there is any, of course there is too much," was the answer. " But was not that the complaint when you were a boy? According to the number there was as much pride in the Church then as there is now, although it did not show itself in the same way."

" Then we didn't build costly churches with soft cushioned seats and worldly fixings," said Brother Gruntly, with the conviction that he had made a point.

" That was owing to poverty, and not humility," said the preacher. " I believe that God is well pleased with well-furnished churches if the people are able to build such. As to seats, I don't see why it is worse to sit on cushions in church than at home," pointing smilingly to a finely-cushioned rocking-chair near by.

The meal was over, and the company returned to the parlor to give room to Sallie, who soon resumed authority.

" Well, Brother Sharp, you gave us a powerful sermon and no mistake, but I fear that what you said afterward will break up the choir," said Brother Gruntly, feeling relieved after a performance he somewhat dreaded.

" It would be a blessing to the Church if all such choirs were broken up at once," said Brother Sharp, without the least hesitation. " They are a moral nuisance. A thousand times better to have no singing than that offered by those who have not sufficient regard for divine worship to conduct themselves with decency. I am always glad to encourage well-disposed and well-behaved young people in their efforts to sustain a choir, but when they fancy that being in a choir gives them a license to trifle, giggle, and pass written slips of paper around during divine service they should be undeceived at once. Such choirs, where I have any thing to say, unless they alter their ways, will certainly be broken up. Singing is a part of our public worship, and should never be conducted by a class of irreligious triflers. If they reform, and behave themselves, well. If otherwise, I shall consider myself doing God's service in breaking up the choir."

These words may seem to the reader as having been spoken on a high key, with an animated countenance and corresponding gestures. This was not the case. They flowed smoothly over the smiling lips of the minister in gentle accents, and Brother and Sister Gruntly were astonished to listen to such strong language in such a mild spirit.

Here the conversation ended, and soon the faithful itinerant was on his way toward the evening appointment at " Coon's Hollow," five miles away.

The school-house was well filled. They had a well-trained choir, who paid the most respectful attention, and from first to last there was nothing that approached levity or rudeness. The minister was happy in his work, and at the close of the meeting two young men rose for prayers.

After the service the preacher went home with Brother Wiser, where he remained that night. The family consisted of the parents, two sons, and one daughter. The sons were hardy young farmers, free from all bad habits, but as yet had not embraced religion. John was twenty-five and George twenty-one. Julia was eighteen, fair in form and features, with a well-developed mind and a devoted Christian heart. The family was universally respected. Brother Sharp was perfectly at home under their hospitable roof, and found to the joy of his soul that Old Flintrock Circuit could boast of some bright jewels.

The next morning, soon after breakfast, the new pastor, with a heart full of the consolation of the Gospel, was on his way toward the village, where loving hearts waited for his return.

The closing remarks on Sabbath morning, although highly pleasing to the congregation at large, did not give satisfaction to all. The four young persons alluded to were Frank Pompey, William Sly, Grace and Charity Tighter. The three brethren, from what they had already heard, were well aware that their children were the objects of the minister's remarks. But instead of standing by their faithful pastor they secretly cherished a degree of hardness. In point of property they stood on something of an elevation, and their children figured in what they considered good society, and never before had they been referred to as lacking in good manners. It is true he had not pointed his finger toward them, but all knew

whom he meant.   The fathers, however, were at a
loss how to exhibit their resentment.   They knew
that the minister had made a very favorable impression on the audience, but this bold movement of his
which touched their family pride must not pass
without further notice.   They did not stay in the
class-meeting, they hardly ever did, and, living in
the same neighborhood, they slowly walked together
toward home.

"Well," said Brother Tighter, in carefully meas-
ured words, "we have a man that can *preach*, there
is no mistake about *that*."

"I like his sermon tip-top," said Brother Pompey,
in a loud voice.   "Brother Humbler can't hold a
candle to him.   Didn't he rattle it off, though!   I
thought I was going to like him first rate.   But I
don't know.   I don't think it looked well for a
stranger like him to come down on our young folks
like a thousand o' brick.   If he had left well enough
alone and pronounced the benediction it would have
been some dollars in his pocket, I'll bet you on that.
He gave us a good pail of milk and then kicked it
all over."

"The brother don't understand human natur',
that's sartin," said Brother Sly.   "Supposin' they
was a little mischievous.   Sakes alive! what of it?
It ain't in the natur' of youngsters to sit stock still
as we do.   A preacher ought to understand human
natur'.   If he gets the young people mad he will
get a mighty slim donation."

"If the brother knew that his remarks was going
to hurt the feelings of members of the official board,"

said Brother Tighter, well pleased with the remarks of his companions, "I think he wouldn't speak as he did. I guess he will be glad to explain matters a little more to our liking."

"When it comes handy I will give him a piece of my mind and tell him what's what," said Brother Pompey.

"He is to call at my house to-morrow afternoon," said Brother Tighter, "and if you and Brother Sly should happen to come around about that time we may tell the brother something that will do him good."

"All right," said Pompey. "Let us *happen* to be around about that time. Ha, ha! Happen, eh? Sly, will you be on hand?"

"I'll try to," was the answer. "I don't know as I'll have any thing to offer, but I do hope that our minister will study human natur'."

They had now reached a point of the road where they had to separate, and each went to his home.

———◆———

CHAPTER III.

BROTHER POMPEY GETS THE WORSE OF IT.

"WATCHMAN, what of the night?" asked Brother Goodier, with his ever-welcome smile, when Brother Sharp returned on Monday morning.

"The day is breaking, bless the Lord!" was the cheerful, ready answer. "I am happy in my work.

At the Hollow two anxious souls rose for prayers, and the signs are glorious!"

"At that appointment we have some of our best members," said Brother Goodier. "They pull together in every good measure. How did things appear at the Yellow School-house?"

"With the exception of their choir, who behaved badly, every thing looked favorable," was the reply. "As in the morning, I delivered a short message on that point. I think there will be no occasion for repeating it."

"May Heaven bless you for your prompt and fearless course!" said the class-leader.

"It will all come out right in the end," said the minister. "I trust that my plainness of speech will always flow from a kind heart. From a few I may meet with coldness and even opposition, but it will be of short duration, and the end will be glorious. I look for a revival."

"Amen!" loudly responded Brother Goodier, who seemed to drink in the spirit of his pastor. "Old Flintrock Circuit has not seen a revival in many years, but I believe it is coming. Bless the Lord!"

In the afternoon, in harmony with his promise, the minister walked as far as Brother Tighter's mansion. The girls saw him approaching and felt somewhat inclined to shun him, but, having understood from their father that his remarks at the close of the sermon were to be criticised by Brother Pompey and Brother Sly, they concluded to remain.

Notwithstanding their parents' sympathy and

their own wounded pride, there was in their minds all the time the uncomfortable secret conviction that the minister was right and that they were wrong. Sometimes this inward impression would assume shape, and laugh at the inconsistency of Methodist parents in upholding their children in wrong-doing. Still, they tried to hope that the new minister would be somewhat punished during the interview. They had some fears that he would recognize them as the disturbers of the meeting, but they concluded that he would not. Their conclusion was correct.

Sister Tighter had some noble qualities. In her younger days she had enjoyed much of the power of religion and was a real worker in the church. Of late years she had in a great measure lost her spirituality, and with her husband had become somewhat worldly. Still she had great respect for the cause of God. Her daughters were her heart's great treasure, and in justice to the young women let it be said that, notwithstanding their levity in the sanctuary, they possessed many valuable traits of character.

Brother Sharp was met at the door by Sister Tighter, who received him with faultless politeness and with a very fair imitation of cordiality. The keen eye of the experienced minister saw in a moment that every thing was not exactly right. He was introduced to the daughters, who, in spite of their efforts to appear composed, showed much nervousness. But by the perfect and charming ease of Brother Sharp and the fascinating nature of his conversation, they soon regained their natural-ness. Brother Tighter, in view of what was to transpire, did not fully succeed in throwing off restraint.

The conversation was going on with fair success, depending mostly on the ready abundance of the new pastor, when Brothers Pompey and Sly happened to come. They had also happened to put on their "Sunday suits," in anticipation of happening to meet the new minister. After a formal introduction Brother Sharp saw at once that their coming was not accidental.

"Glad to see you," said Brother Pompey. "Hope for better acquaintance. Somehow or 'nother I didn't get a fair chance to speak to you yesterday."

"Perhaps you expected to meet me in the class-meeting," said the minister, in true honesty. "My afternoon appointment did not grant me that great pleasure."

This was an unintentional shot that was felt by others than Brother Pompey, and, no reply being convenient, there was a short pause.

"You had a rousing congregation and no mis-take," said Pompey, in a loud voice, "and you gave us an all-fired smart sermon. There is no going back on that. We think that old Samson Keener is a pretty big gun, but I guess the old fellow's got to cave in."

To this speech the minister seemed to be perfectly indifferent. He neither smiled nor frowned, but looked very much as if nothing had been said; but in his mind he was weighing and measuring the man who had let loose such a volume of sound. His estimate was exceedingly correct.

"A large portion of the audience was made up of young people," said Brother Tighter, preparing the way. "I don't know when I have seen so many of that class together before."

"And upon the whole," said the minister, "a more earnest and attentive company of young people I scarcely ever witnessed."

"Gracious! elder," cried Brother Pompey, on an elevated key, "that don't jibe exactly with that setting out you gave them before you pronounced the blessing."

"It harmonizes exactly with what I said yesterday," said Brother Sharp, in a pleasant tone of voice. "The 'setting out,' as you •call it, referred to only four persons in that large assembly."

Here the two sisters blushed.

"Young people are easily offended," said Brother Sly, "and it is a great thing in a minister to understand human natur'."

"Young people are *not* easily offended," said Brother Sharp, in his earnest style. "They are not nearly as sensitive as those who are advanced in years. They often get out of the way, but as a general thing they are not obstinate and mulish. As to human nature, I have studied it all my life, and I think that I understand it pretty well. As a proof that I have some knowledge in that line I will simply say that your object in meeting me here to-day is to call me to an account for what I said yesterday."

This was said in a manner so gentle and kind that it had a double effect. They were completely taken back, and even Pompey felt his courage giving way. He soon rallied, however, and said, " Well, I guess the elder has hit it this time. Tighter thought that this 'ere matter ought to be talked over a little ; and without going around Robin Hood's barn I am going to tell you at once that that speech of your'n at the close of the meeting don't set very easy on some minds."

" I am very glad to hear that, Brother Pompey," said the minister, with his usual smiling ease. " Speeches and sermons that sit easy don't do much good."

" But I mean that our young folks can't be lect-ured in that way without getting riley," said Pompey, " and if you get the youngsters down on you then you are a goner, and we thought we would better tell you."

" I have been eighteen years in the ministry, and my experience with young people has been quite extensive," said Brother Sharp. " I have never per-mitted rude behavior in the house of God to pass by unmentioned, and I never shall. I have had no occasion to mention the subject to the same con-gregation more than once. It will be so on this charge if older heads do not interfere. Don't you borrow trouble about me. The Lord may have given me as well as yourselves a fair degree of com-mon sense. The young people referred to will be all right in a short time unless they are injured by bad advice and bad examples from those who are

older. They may not have had the religious training that *your* children have had. They may have
been brought up in families where there are no family
altars. I most earnestly desire their salvation."

"We were only thinking," said Brother Tighter,
"that if the young people should go against you
your quarterage would come middlin' kind of hard."

"Brother Tighter," said the minister, with a broad
smile, bordering on a laugh, "the young people
will not go against me. They never did and they
never will. As to quarterage, that shall never prevent me from doing my whole duty. I am not
troubled about it in the least. My support will
come plentifully. If it does not come through you
stewards it will come in another way."

"That sounds kind o' independent," said Brother
Pompey.

"Not at all," was the reply; "I depend on God
and I have faith in the people."

"We find it pretty hard scratching to pay the
ministers," said Pompey, "and it ain't allus they
get paid up."

"And we ministers know it," said the preacher.
"Flintrock is understood to be the meanest circuit
in the Conference. You *never* pay your ministers,
and there is an impression among our preachers
that the majority of the official brethren don't care
whether they are paid up or not."

"Do *you* have that impression, Brother Sharp?"
asked Brother Tighter.

"Yes, I do," was the answer. "How can I have
any other impression? It is indifference on the

part of stewards that causes this perpetual deficiency.
I know that a few do the best they can ; the rest
are drones. Think you that on this large circuit,
with all its wealth, the small pittance of four hundred dollars could not be raised by men who had a
heart in the work and the welfare of the minister
in view? And another thing that shows indifference or penuriousness, or both, is the shamefully-
small sum paid by wealthy members of the official
board."

"I swan ! that is plain talk for a new-comer, "
said Pompey; " I don't know what to make of it.
How you can give it to us right and left in that way
and still keep as cool as a cucumber is more than
I can understand."

"With such an opinion of us," said Tighter, "it
must have been very painful for you to come among
us."

"I was consulted by the Bishop in regard to it at
an early part of the Conference," said the minister.
"He would not have sent me here without my full
consent. If I had said no, he would have given me
one of the best stations in the Conference. I said
yes, and came to Flintrock."

" Now, if that don't beat all creation ! " cried Pompey. "What do you think of that, Tighter?"

"And you have no doubt in regard to your quarterage ? " asked Brother Tighter, without paying
any attention to Pompey.

"Not a bit," said Brother Sharp; "I have faith in
God and I have faith in the people."

"The people will do fust rate if they are carefully

handled," said Brother Sly ; " it is not every minister that understands human natur'."

"Well," said Pompey, " somehow or 'nother we hain't stuck exactly to the point. Brother Sharp don't soften down the least mite on what he said yesterday. It's too all-killing bad to have the young people turn against him at the very start."

" Brother Pompey," said the minister, " I will ask you one question. Do you positively know of even one young person that is offended with what I said yesterday, aside from those four I referred to ? "

" Well, when it comes to knowin' for sartin," said Pompey, with some embarrassment, " I can't say that I do."

" I will ask another question. Do you really *believe* that any other young persons are grieved with my words ? "

" Hokie ! " said Pompey, in the vain endeavor to extricate himself, " the elder would make a smashing lawyer. I guess he would make out a case right or wrong."

" But you don't answer the question," said the smiling minister.

" Well, let me see ; what was it ? O, yes. Wal, since you squeeze a fellow right down to it, I guess I may as well own up that I don't really believe that any of the young folks was hurt except those youngsters that thought they would have a little fun," said Brother Pompey, wiping his face. " But I reckon it is time for me to be moving ; it is pretty near milking-time."

" It is the same with me," said Brother Sly, looking for his hat.

" Before these good brethren leave," said Brother Sharp, " let us have a word of prayer. We have pleasantly conversed together in regard to the interests of the Church of Christ. In these matters we are to seek wisdom of the Lord. It gives me pleasure to meet with you, and I trust that our coming together thus will be blessed of the Lord. Brother Tighter, are these young ladies in the church ? "

" No, they have not yet made a start," was the reply.

" I am sorry," said the minister, with a look that was all kindness and Christian love. " How much good they might accomplish if they would only give their young hearts to the Saviour ! Young ladies, I hope to see you genuinely converted to God. We will now call upon our heavenly Father."

The sisters had been attentive listeners to all that had been said, and from his first sentence the minister had continued to gain in their estimation, and more than once their cheeks burned with shame as they thought of their behavior in the house of God. The words of Brother Pompey had never sounded to them so decidedly flat, and they were pleased to see his embarrassment. They firmly resolved that they had trifled in the sanctuary for the last time. The preacher's few words addressed to them before engaging in devotion had reached their hearts, and although they had not bowed in prayer for many years they knelt down as if drawn by some magic power.

The prayer was deeply impressive. With holy ardor the man of God implored the divine Spirit to rest upon all present and upon the Church of Christ. He remembered the unconverted, and especially the young people. There were no vocal responses. From that company they could not be expected. But when the prayer was ended there was a moisture in those sisters' eyes which Brother Pompey noticed with perfect astonishment.

The two officials left, and the reader will be glad to know from their own lips their estimation of the interview.

"I tell you, Brother Sly," said Pompey, "I guess we have come out through the little end of the horn. I tell you he is just as keen as a razor. I feel just as if I had been drawn through a knot-hole. I never was so whittled down in all my life, and it looked all the time as if the fellow didn't half try. When he talked about the small contributions from official members didn't he hit the nail smack on the head? I am not very big on the pay, but I fork over as much again as Brother Tighter. He gave us a drubbing, but somehow or 'nother I like him better than I did two hours ago. How is it with you, Sly?"

"Well," said Sly, "it was a little tough to listen to some things he said, but I have made up my mind that after all Brother Sharp understands human natur'."

"Wasn't that prayer of his'n a stunner, though!" said Pompey. "And didn't it beat all to see them girls drop on their knees just as if they had been struck by lightining ! I'll bet my old hat that something is going to happen, and I guess we'd better git out of the way."

The two men now came to the end of the road and parted.

The minister tarried but a short time after the brethren had left, promising to call again with his family before long.

" Well, Luke," said Sister Tighter, " the meeting didn't go off just as you expected."

" Not quite," was the reply, " but perhaps it is just as well."

" Yes," said his wife, with some feeling, " and a thousand times better. My eyes have been opened to see things in a very different light from what I have ever seen them before. When Brother Sharp came here this afternoon I did not feel right toward him, simply because of what he said yesterday. Now I feel different. I love him as a faithful servant of Jesus Christ, and I am going to stand by him. Girls, what do you think about it by this time ? "

" Mother," said Grace, " I think Mr. Sharp is perfectly splendid ! I have not the least hardness toward him, and, to tell you the honest truth, I am heartily ashamed of my conduct yesterday, and I ask my parents' forgiveness while I promise never to do so again."

" And that is the way I feel," cried the younger sister, bursting into tears.

" You have not had the religious training which the children of Methodists ought to have," said the mother, with tears in her eyes. " I hope from henceforth to set a better example before my children. Luke, who is there in the official board that pays so little quarterage?"

"I don't know exactly what the brethren do pay," was the evasive answer.

"Well," she said, "I was glad that that did not hit *us*. We have many short-comings, but we are not guilty of withholding from our minister a generous support."

CHAPTER IV.

THE "RECEPTION," AND SOMETHING ABOUT LUKE TIGHTER.

ON the next Sabbath at the church the congregation was larger than on the Sabbath previous. Grace and Charity Tighter sat with their parents down stairs and paid the most earnest attention. This produced a very happy effect in the minds of many who feared that things would turn out otherwise. Frank Pompey and William Sly were seated in the gallery, and their behavior was blameless. The text was, "Woe to them that are at ease in Zion." It was a sermon long to be remembered on account of its deep searching power. Several attended the class-meeting who had neglected it for years, and made humble confession of their backslidings.

In the afternoon the appointment was at the "Quaker Settlement." There was a fine congregation, and the singing was conducted by a choir of well-trained singers. During the opening prayer

10

the minister was much disturbed by the rude behavior of a young man and a young woman sitting very near the desk. Before announcing another hymn he said:

"I stand before you as a stranger for the first time. I hope that our relation as preacher and people will be pleasant and profitable, but at the very start I must give you to understand that I shall never tolerate any trifling behavior in this place during divine service. I have been greatly shocked by a shameful levity on the part of two young persons during our opening prayer. I hope that I shall never witness this again during any part of religious worship."

There was a general expression of satisfaction manifested by the audience at this fearless stand taken by the preacher. On this occasion the text was, "Why stand ye here all the day idle?"

Before the congregation was dismissed a very respectable-looking gentleman asked permission to say a few words. The permission was given.

"I wish in the presence of this congregation to thank the reverend gentleman for his plain words touching unbecoming behavior in a place of worship, especially during the solemnity of prayer. This behavior, I am happy to say, is confined to a very few persons, and if it had been met by other ministers as it has by this gentleman it would have disappeared long ago. I am not a professing Christian, although I ought to be, but I am a lover of good order and good manners. I again thank the reverend gentleman for his timely remarks."

The audience were on the point of cheering, when Brother Sharp pronounced the benediction.

The gentleman was a wealthy farmer of the vicinity by the name of Edward Gates. He possessed brilliant talents and had been a member of the Legislature a number of times. He very politely asked the minister to call on him at his convenience.

The pastor took tea at Brother Trembly's, and was treated with much cordiality.

" I was terribly scared to hear you talk so after prayer," said Brother Trembly. " They richly deserved it, I know, for they are always cuttin' up, but when preachers scold it makes me feel nervous and unpleasant. I don't blame you one bit, but any thing of that kind spoils my meeting. But now that 'Squire Gates has backed you I feel better. I wish I was not so nervous."

"You had better wish you weren't so foolish," said Sister Trembly, with a good-natured laugh. " You ought to have cried amen to what the minister said, instead of feeling nervous. I felt as if I wanted to pat him on the back."

The evening appointment at the village was a grand success.

On the next Sabbath the " Yellow School-house " was crowded. Before the service commenced Brother Gruntly whispered to the minister that there was no choir, with a " Didn't I tell you so?" expression on his countenance. The members of the choir were all present, but had concluded to show the new minister that their fun during meeting was not to be interfered with without a show of resentment. There they sat, under the silly impression that their " pouting " was going to create a panic. Brother Sharp was one of the best singers in the Conference, and in that line he was fully prepared for any emergency.

" I am informed," said he, " that there is to be no singing by the choir this afternoon. For this accident, which often occurs, Methodists are generally pretty well prepared. If you have no objection I will be your chorister for this service at least. You are all invited to join in the song of praise. We'll sing five verses of the first hymn, to the tune of ' Northfield.' Let us arise and praise God."

The audience, with the exception of the choir, stood up. The people sang as they had never before, and the old school-house rang with the sound of pure melody.

The prayer was earnest and impressive, and in a particular manner the young people were presented before the Lord.

Next was sung, " When I can read my title clear," to the tune " Ortonville," and, it was grand. Then a powerful sermon was preached from the text, " For why will ye die?"

The evening meeting at the Hollow was a time of refreshing from the presence of the Lord. The seekers had found peace and were happy in their first love. The prospects were brightening, and the itinerant's heart was glad.

One afternoon and evening, when the minister and his family were fairly settled in their new home, a circuit gathering of a friendly social nature, which was well called a "reception," was found at the parsonage. Its object was to give the minister a welcome and to carry also in the line of eatables much more than would be necessary for that one occasion, the balance, of course, to remain at the preacher's house for the benefit of the inmates. At Flintrock these gatherings were quite popular, especially among the young people, not so much on account of the eatables as of the "good time" they enjoyed together. Unfortunately, former pastors, under the bad advice of some of the brethren, had reluctantly consented to let the youth indulge in those boisterous and vulgar plays made up of silly ditties, running, screaming, and kissing. Many of these ministers had been sick at heart in witnessing these rude performances in their own house, but, being new comers, advised by official brethren, they had lacked in the moral courage to carry out their own convictions of duty.

There was a large company of young people in a commodious front room up stairs. The evening was advancing.

"Come, isn't it about time for us to commence playing?" said Fred Nimbler, jumping up and standing in the middle of the floor.

"I am almost sure that playing will not be pleasing to our minister," said Walter Goodier.

"O, fiddlesticks!" cried Fred. "We always have playing at receptions. Why should he object more than other ministers?"

"Other ministers have objected," said Walter,

"but yielded to the wishes of others. Our last preacher, with tears in his eyes, said to father that he never was so disgusted with any thing in his life."

" Well," said Fred, defiantly, " we'll have our play any way; come on, girls!"

" No girl that respects herself will do any thing in a minister's house that would hurt his feelings," said Ella Goodier.

"And so I say," responded Grace Tighter. "We are here to respect our minister, and not for a frolic."

This from Grace caused much astonishment, for heretofore she had been a leader in these performances.

Just now the loud voice of Brother Pompey was heard on the stairs, and presently he was in the midst of the company.

" Mr. Pompey," said Fred, "we were just about starting a play, when Walter interfered and said he thought Mr. Sharp would not like it."

" I swow," said Brother Pompey, " I don't know what the minister does think of these huggin' bees. I am glad, though, that Walter did stick in a word. This yellin' and squealin' and kissin' and huggin' and tearin' dresses and tippin' over chairs I don't think a mighty sight of myself."

This was followed by a laugh and some applause, which did not at all displease Brother Pompey, who was conscious that he had made the best effort of his life.

" To me a reception is not worth a cent without a play," said Fred, showing a degree of displeasure.

"Well," said Pompey, "I am not much of a judge on the worth of victuals, but at the table a while ago I thought I saw a red-headed, big-mouthed chap of your size putting himself outside of a pile of biscuit, butter and cheese, pies and cold chicken, corn-beef and cabbage, pork and beans, and cold ham and pickles, that I would call worth a good deal more'n a cent."

Here was another laugh at the expense of Fred, and Pompey considered himself a hero.

"Some one might ask the elder," said Julia Nimbler.

"Would we not stand better in his estimation," said Walter, "if for his sake we voluntarily give up a practice which at any place is of very doubtful propriety, and especially so at the house of a minister? We are here to welcome our preacher, as Grace so properly remarked, and not to satisfy our desire for fun. I believe that I speak the sentiment of the great majority of this company, and I move that we dispense with playing, not only for to-night, but on all occasions when we meet in the interest of the church or pastor."

"I second that motion," said Grace Tighter.

"Brother Pompey will put it to vote," said Walter.

"Now let every mother's son and daughter of you sit down!" cried Brother Pompey, with his loud voice. "If you can't get seats just squat right down on the floor. I don't know as I can do this kind of business right up to the handle, but I will pitch in the best way I know. Now let all of you that think as I do, that Walter Goodier has hit the nail right smack on the head, and will agree to do as he wants you to, stand up quicker than you can say skat!"

They were on their feet in an instant, without a single exception. Fred Nimbler saw how matters stood, and gladly put himself with the majority.

"Well, now, if that don't beat the Dutch!" cried Pompey, well pleased with the response, and feeling that his own eloquence had strengthened the vote. "If my wife was here she would be tickled half to death, for she is awfully down on huggin' bees."

The evening was spent pleasantly, and at a seasonable hour the whole company was invited to come together down stairs, where Brother Sharp addressed them as follows :

"I thank you all for your presence and kind regards. Within a few hours I have formed the acquaintance of a large number. Our coming thus together must be profitable as well as pleasant. I hope soon to visit you at your houses and do what I can for your spiritual benefit. I thank these young people for their worthy deportment at the house of their minister. I have known of parsonages that have been disgraced by rude plays and amusements of very doubtful propriety. I am glad that the young people of Flintrock can enjoy themselves for an hour or two without resorting to these frivolities. Young people, you have my hearty thanks. Let us now unite in prayer."

The prayer was an earnest supplication in behalf of the people of his charge, and the reception reached a happy conclusion.

"Lucy," said Brother Tighter to his wife one morning, "it is time for us to be looking up something for our minister. Quarterly meeting comes next Saturday. I guess we can let him have some of that corn-beef, can't we?"

"Perhaps he doesn't want corn-beef," said his wife, rather dryly, "and if he does he would want a better article than we've got."

"I know it isn't first rate," said her husband; "but what is good enough for us is good enough for him."

"It is *not* good enough for us," said his wife, rather sharply, "and let us hear no more about that."

"Well, how are we off for lard?" asked Luke.

"But how do you know that Brother Sharp is in need of lard? He may have already more than he needs," said Lucy, in a manner that made her husband stare.

"But what *shall* we give him?" asked her husband, with a degree of impatience. "I must not go to the Quarterly Conference without quarterage."

"I don't intend that you shall," answered his wife; "but did you ever think that ministers, as well as other people, need money?"

"Money!" cried Brother Tighter. "I never pay money."

"But you will pay money after this, or I will pay it myself," said the wife, in a most emphatic manner.

"Why, Lucy, what has come over you?" asked the almost frightened husband.

"You will find out pretty soon what has come over me," was the stern reply. "That afternoon when Brother Sharp was here with Brother Sly and Brother Pompey he said that for years some of the official members on this charge had been shamefully stingy in their contributions. I had always thought that in addition to the little provision you carried to the preacher you paid also a liberal sum of money. I have just learned to my shame that I was mistaken. Now, Luke Tighter, you ought to be ashamed of yourself! Here you are, one of the most able farmers in the church, with abundance of cash at your command, and all the poor ministers have got from you for years has been a little lard, sausage, turnips, and onions; and for these you have charged more than you could get for them in the market. Now, Luke Tighter, perhaps you know what has come over me."

"I wonder where you got your news?" said Tighter.

"I got it reluctantly from those that know all about it," was the reply. "And now this wicked work must be stopped. Let poorer people, if they must, pay their quarterage in onions and turnips, but we pay money. And in view of your past stinginess I want you next Saturday to pay in cash ten dollars for this quarter, with the promise of three more tens during the year. What do you say to that?"

"I would like to say that you was crazy,"

said Luke, in amazement, " but I guess I hadn't better."

"Luke Tighter, I am perfectly sane, and I never was more in earnest in my life!" said the wife. " Now that the girls are away, I want the matter settled right here. I would be ashamed to have them know it. I have worked hard to earn this property, and my wishes are entitled to some respect. I want you to pay forty dollars this year for preaching, and that in money. What do you say?"

" Why, Lucy, if you are really in earnest, and you look very much as if you were, I'll do it, of course," said Luke.

"There!" said the wife, with a pleasant smile on her face, " let the past be forgotten." She went into another room, and in a few moments her clear voice was warbling " Coronation."

CHAPTER V.

THE CHARGE REDEEMED—A WONDERFUL LOVE-FEAST.

AT the quarterly meeting there was a large representation from every part of the circuit. The Saturday afternoon congregation was a marvel in point of numbers. The presiding elder looked around in astonishment, and could hardly attribute this wonderful change to his own popularity. Never had he seen the like at Old Flintrock. At the Quarterly Conference nearly all of the official members were present, and every thing wore a cheerful appearance. Brother Keener was in his best humor, and the preacher in charge wore a smiling countenance. Brother Goodier was the secretary. The minister's financial report was very encouraging. The secretary now took out of his pocket a roll of bills amounting to thirty dollars which he had collected in view of the quarterly meeting. Brother Wiser reported twenty-five dollars from Coon's Hollow. Brother Gruntly reported a smoked ham and a bushel of apples from the Yellow School-house, and Brother Trembly fifteen dollars from the Quaker Settlement, ten of which he was requested to say came from Squire Gates as a token of thanks to the minister for his timely service to those triflers during prayer. This created a smile.

"Is there any more quarterage to be handed in?" inquired the presiding elder. Brother Tighter left his seat, walked up to the altar, and, to the astonishment of the secretary, handed him a ten-dollar bill.

"How much do you wish to pay?" asked Brother Goodier, preparing to make change.

"I wish to pay ten dollars for this quarter and thirty more during the year." This was said so that all could hear. But in order to make it more emphatic the delighted secretary said aloud, "Brother Tighter this year will pay forty dollars in cash!" The astonishment was profound and almost embarrassing.

"It is no wonder that you look astonished," said Brother Tighter; "I am astonished myself. If you wish to thank any body you may thank my wife. She had just found out how much I paid for preaching, and the way I had to take it was a caution. I was glad to come to terms—forty dollars in cash. I am inclined to think that Lucy is right."

This created a degree of merriment, and some other close-fisted officials present thought the matter over and concluded to double their subscription. The quarterage was beyond all expectation, and the future looked bright. The love-feast on Sabbath morning was noted for humble confessions of past unfaithfulness and solemn vows for the future. At the public service the church was crowded. Brother Keener had a good time, while the quarterly collection far exceeded his claims.

On the following Sabbath at the Yellow School-house all the members of the choir were in their seats; they sang heartily, paid strict attention to the preaching, and a number of them seemed to be much affected. Brother Sharp took tea again at Brother Gruntly's, and this time Sallie, with a smiling countenance, sat at the table.

Just before the minister entered his carriage Brother Gruntly said, " I guess things are going to work all right after all. I was afraid it was going to break every thing all to pieces. The singers have had a meeting, and after much talk every one of them voted that you were right and that they were wrong; and they have signed a paper drawn by our Sallie, saying that they will never again whisper and giggle in meeting. Don't that beat all?"

" I am very glad to hear such good news," said Brother Sharp. " We have only to do our duty, and God will take care of his cause." He then left for the Hollow, where they had another pentecostal shower.

Seeing the minister could not attend the Sabbath-school, on account of his many appointments, he consented to teach a Bible class at the parsonage on each Wednesday evening. This was largely attended, and in addition to his explanatory remarks, addressed to their intellect, his earnest application of Bible truths was leaving a decided impression on their individual hearts. The weekly prayer meetings throughout the circuit were gradually increasing in spirituality and in attendance. This was specially true at the village. Many of the young people attended, and their countenances denoted genuine interest. The second quarterly meeting, which was conducted by the pastor, was a season of great interest. The text on the Sabbath was, "Prepare ye the way of the Lord; make his paths straight." The people were given to see that all that was necessary in order to have God among them in a sweeping revival was the "preparing the way," and it was evident that this was going on. This favorable state of things was not brought about by an accident. It was chiefly, under God, the result of an untiring effort on the part of their minister. He had begun with the official members. With the exception of two or three, their influence for years had been ruinous to the charge. For this it required profound skill, invincible courage, perfect honesty, and abundant love. In these requisites the man of God abounded. From the first he had set his heart on saving these brethren from their chronic stupidity, their criminal indifference, and their wicked worldliness. In a very short time he thoroughly understood them, administered his medicinal doses, and looked up to Heaven for success. He showed them their sins, and their transgressions to the house of Israel. He also visited from house to house, and as far as opportunities presented themselves he conversed with the unconverted part on the all-important subject of religion. On all occasions he had held up the banner of holiness and honored the requirements of the Discipline. His exhortations at the prayer meetings and the Bible class produced deep conviction. Add to this his powerful and earnest ministry, in which, with a tongue of fire, he denounced sin in the world and in the Church, and this favorable state of things will not seem strange.

In the fall of that year the pastor became convinced that "the set time to favor Zion" had indeed come. Throughout the charge on the part of a great many there was an earnest longing for the salvation of souls. The moral firmament gave unmistakable promise of " abundance of rain." After a full consultation with the brethren he concluded to commence a protracted effort in the village church. For some two weeks this meeting had been announced, and it was known far and near. Monday and Tuesday evenings were to be devoted to church work: humiliation, confession, and prayers for the baptism of the Holy Ghost to fall upon believers to prepare them to labor for souls. The meeting opened with the evident presence of God. There was a complete prostration before the Lord. There

were free confessions of worldliness, pride, penuriousness, neglect of family and private prayers and
the social meetings of the church.   There were
hearty shakings of hands between church members
who for years had treated each other coldly. These
meetings, although announced for the special benefit of church members, were attended by many of
the unconverted.

On Wednesday evening Brother Sharp preached
to a crowded house. He stood before them looking somewhat pale, while deep solemnity rested on
all.   He felt the weighty responsibilty of the hour.
He took his text: "Then how wilt thou do in the
swelling of Jordan?"   The closing part of this sermon was thrilling, grand, and terribly solemn.   Already, and before the invitation was given, there
were groans of penitence heard in different parts of
the church.   The minister, leaving the pulpit, continued his words of fire as he came down to the
altar, and there without an intermission he invited
all who wanted a Friend to stand by them in the
"swelling of Jordan" to come and kneel at the
altar.   No sooner were the words spoken than from
all parts of the house there was a rush forward.
Some wept aloud and cried for mercy; others were
silent and solemn.   The altar was soon more than
filled, and seats were vacated to make room for
mourners.   Then followed a season of prayer, and
many souls were set at liberty. Thus continued
the meetings in interest and power for some six
weeks, while about two hundred had professed to
have found salvation. The converts were from all

parts of the circuit, and far beyond. Nearly every family had been reached. The charge was completely revolutionized. All the young people in the minister's Bible class were converted. Among these were the sons of Brother Pompey and Brother Sly and the daughters of Brother Tighter. At the Quaker Settlement a number had embraced religion, among others Hon. Edward Gates, whose conversion was very bright and clear. At the Yellow School-house all the members of the choir had surrendered, and Miss Sallie Gruntly was a thorough worker. At the Hollow Brother Wiser's two sons were among the saved, together with a score of others. Shouts of praise vibrated through the valleys and echoed on the hill-sides.

Brother Sharp's donation was the largest by far ever heard of in that part of the country. In cash and other valuables it amounted to two hundred and fifty dollars. In the evening among the young people there was nothing heard of that famous "needle's eye that doth supply," but their young voices blended sweetly in,

"How happy are they who their Saviour obey."

The quarterage also came in abundantly, and the itinerant received much more than his allowance. By a unanimous vote he was asked to return for the second year, which, of course, he did, and the work progressed gloriously. Improvements became the order of the day. The church at the village was thoroughly repaired and beautified. Brother Tighter, at this time without an order from Lucy,

11

headed the subscription with a liberal sum. In this he was followed by Brother Sly, whose "human natur'" had of late greatly improved, and even Brother Gruntly freely gave twenty-five dollars. A new church was built at the Quaker Settlement chiefly through the liberality of Esquire Gates, while Brother Trembly had wonderfully improved in moral courage. The Yellow School-house was enlarged and painted a more attractive hue, but for years afterward it was known by the same old term. At the Hollow a neat church was built, and paid for before it was dedicated.

The last love-feast of the second year was a time of shouting and tears. Their beloved pastor, who had done so much for them, was about to leave. The testimonies were very numerous; but we can allude to only one.

Brother Pompey, with great tears running down his cheeks, cried out: "I am a poor, crooked stick, the best way you can fix it; but, thank God and Brother Sharp, I think I am in better shape than I was two years ago. I was a church member, I know; but what good will that do when you have no more religion than a snipe? I thank God for what Brother Sharp did for me. I once undertook to haul him over the coals at Brother Tighter's. I shall never forget that. It didn't take him long to take all the starch out of me, and I went home determined that I would never again make a big fool of myself. Ever since that afternoon, brethren, I have been trying to toe the mark a little better. I know I often get out of the way, and they tell me

I use too much slang. I think I am getting over that. Any how I am going to try my level best. Every now and then I have a big tussle with the old fellow, but I generally down him before we get through. He hates awfully to give me up, and sometimes he is as polite as a basket of chips; but I tell him : 'You can't come it, Mr. Devil, and you would better scud.' Brother Sharp, that dressing you gave us at Brother Tighter's that afternoon made us squirm, but it was the best thing that ever happened to us. At our house we are a happy family. I read the Scriptur' and my wife and the boys do the praying. I pray in secret every day, but I dasn't venture this old runaway tongue of mine to do that kind of business before folks. God bless you, Brother Sharp! and, whoever our new preacher may be, you may bet your life that Brother Pompey will come up to the scratch, and stand by him through thick and thin."

In spite of the betting phrase these remarks were well received, because every man, woman, and child knew that they were uttered in perfect sincerity.

At the next Conference Brother Sharp was sent to Watchford, where the congregation had greatly diminished under the preaching of Brother Minus. Here again, as in all his previous appointments, he was eminently successful. For years after this he served the most prominent appointments. After that he was a very popular presiding elder, and was repeatedly a delegate to the General Conference.

Here it may not be amiss to note a brief conver-

sation between Brother Sharp and his former presiding elder, which took place years afterward.

"Ah, Brother Sharp," said Samson Keener, "is
it not very clear to your mind that I was under
divine direction when I nominated you for Old
Flintrock?"

"I have never been so impressed, Brother Keener," was the smiling reply. "I think it would have
been more in harmony with the will of God if, in
unison with the modest and respectful request of
the brethren from Watchford, you had nominated
me for that station."

"But does not the wonderful success that followed
your labors at Flintrock prove most conclusively
that the nomination was from the Lord?"

"No; it proves nothing of the kind. My being
appointed by the Bishop in harmony with my own
will, after a friendly consultation, may have been
pleasing to God, but that does not prove that he
looked with favor upon the nomination. And even
if the whole thing had been wrong my labors might
have been blessed in the salvation of souls. The
will of God touching ministerial appointments is not
to be learned by their success or failure. And so,
my dear Brother Keener, I do not think that my
nomination for Flintrock was at all inspired by the
Holy Ghost."

Samson Keener made no reply. Perhaps he did
not feel quite sure that the nomination of Brother
Sharp for that hard charge was prompted wholly by
motives that would bear a pleasant recollection.

Flintrock became a desired field. At present the

original ground embraces two prominent stations. The older members have gone to their reward, while their children and grandchildren carry on the work. Brother Sharp is now advanced in years and waiting for his discharge. Walter Goodier is a worthy minister in the effective ranks, and his sister Ella, as a loving wife, cheers the declining years of a noted Methodist minister.

THE MAN WITH THE RUFFLED SHIRT;

OR,

MY FIRST WEEK ON L— CHARGE.

CHAPTER I.

THE JOURNEY AND MY FIRST SABBATH.

I WONDER if this is the case with the generality of my brethren in the ministry. It is so with me, at least. I now look upon many things as comparatively trivial that in my early days I considered as exceedingly sinful. I am often astonished at myself when I compare my present feelings and views with those that I cherished forty years ago. I am inclined to think that in this I relate the experience of a great number. They may, or may not, be ready to make the public confession that I do. Let that be as it may, I must say that in this year of grace, from some reason or other, I am not troubled, pained, tortured, and agonized by reason of the style of brethren and sisters' costumes, especially the sisters' bonnets, as I used to be when I was much younger in the ministry than I am to-day. I have often been led to inquire, Is not this change of mind and feeling the result of a gradual backsliding from the simplicity of the Gospel and from that ardent zeal for the glory of God which I felt in my younger days? Was not my judgment at that time, when warm in my first love, a safer one on this point than the one I now exercise after so many years of mingling more or less in fashionable and worldly societies? These questions, gentle reader, have been well considered. I have been for hours on the witness stand, and I have undergone a thorough cross-examination, and I am justified at the bar of my own conscience, at least, in the views that I hold, and I trust that they are in harmony with the will divine.

This may be considered as rather a strange way of commencing a story. Well, I have never taken any lessons in that line. I know nothing of the rules of story-telling or story-writing. I am not sure that there are such rules. If there are, I am not bound by them more than I am by Claude's *Essay on the Composition of a Sermon.* I think I shall be able, before I get through, to tell my story, and if I see fit to put the moral at the top, or in the middle, or at the bottom, that is simply a matter of taste.

It was in the summer of 18—. The Conference was closed, and my field of labor was to be L—— charge in Northern New York. It was by no means a "responsible" charge, as the term is sometimes used by Methodist ministers, and to be read out for that place was not considered a very high compliment, although it was a "fair" appointment. But at that time I was young, vigorous, hopeful, and confident; and with cheerful hearts the little family started for the new circuit. The journey was long, about one hundred miles, under the burning heat of a July sun. Of course we wondered and wondered why it was necessary to send us so *very* far away. We did not say it was wrong. O, no! In those days I was exceedingly " loyal," and looked upon the appointments coming from the Bishop and his advisers as having the signature of Jehovah attached. My views on that point also have been slightly modified since. But we reached the end of our journey. It was Saturday afternoon. We had been directed to put up at the hospitable mansion of " Father Rogers," and they were expecting us.

This family at that time consisted of the parents and their only daughter, Alice, a young lady about twenty-two years of age. Father Rogers had long been a local preacher and a class-leader, and was universally loved. He was well versed in theology, and in conversation he was easy and agreeable. Sister Rogers was very much like him. Alice had shared in good advantages, and her manner was cordial and mirthful. She was richly dressed and had on her person a few articles of jewelry. I inwardly sighed, and wondered if she was a Methodist. We were received with the warmest Christian sympathy, and within a very short time we felt perfectly at home. The children had thrown off restraint, and already Alice had become a great favorite.

On that evening the itinerant and his family were glad to seek an early rest. The household bowed in humble adoration, and we offered unto the Lord our evening sacrifice.

The next morning was clear and bright. The family was up betimes, and without any noticeable haste or hurry the work was completed, and we were ready for the service a long time before the hour arrived. The church stood but a short distance from the house and was visible from the room in which the venerable man and myself sat.

"Well, Father Rogers," I asked, "what is the spiritual condition of the members at large on this charge?"

"A positive knowledge of the heart belongs only to God," was the reply; "but, judging from appearances, I trust that the members generally strive to do their duty and make their way to heaven."

"I am glad to hear that," I replied. "You say truly that God alone can read the heart. But to me it is perfectly evident that the Methodist Church is drifting fearfully from her ancient moorings toward sure destruction. It has got so that in our congregations you see no difference between the world and the Church. Professing Christians are as gay in their dress as the worldlings. In days of yore Methodists were known by the simplicity of their apparel; but it is so no longer. Vital godliness is departing from the Church, and we need not be mistaken, for ' By their fruits ye shall know them.' "

"I admit that by their fruits ye shall know them, Brother C.," answered Father Rogers. " But is it safe to take a mere article of dress or a piece of jewelry as a proof of a wicked heart in one whose daily walk and works give unmistakable evidence of love to God and of an earnest zeal for his glory? When I was younger I used to feel very much as you do. The sight of a little breastpin on a Methodist sister, or a little artificial rose on her bonnet, would shock me, and inwardly I would conclude that such a person could not enjoy religion. I am still decidedly opposed to any vain display. But a long life of experience in the Church has convinced me that a few articles of dress, whether plain or gay, are very unsafe criterions whereby to judge of a person's religious excellence or moral worth in a community."

" Father Rogers," said I, with a degree of warmth, " while I greatly respect you for your age and piety I am sorry to hear any thing from your venerable lips that can in any manner be construed into an apology for this worldly vanity in professing Christians. We are not to be ' conformed to the world,' but to be ' transformed by the renewing of your mind.'"

" And yet, Brother C.," replied Father Rogers, with a humorous smile, as he scanned me from head to foot, " *you* seem to be pretty well conformed to this world as far as its fashion is concerned. Your coat is cut in the latest style. Your pantaloons are far from being in the fashion of the apostolic age. Your neck-tie has a very modern appearance. Your hat, yonder, is a magnificent ' stove-pipe,' and your boots look to me as if they had been made on a very fashionable and worldly last. I am well pleased with your appearance. I am gratified to see our new minister so tastefully clad. And yet it seems to me that, from your own stand-point, you must admit that, so far as *dress* is concerned, you are somewhat 'conformed to this world.'"

All this was said so kindly and smilingly as to impart double weight to every word, and I began to feel that the veteran had with my own Scripture put me in a position that was far from being comfortable, and I was glad to know that it was near meeting-time. I replied, " As far as my garments are concerned I will assure you that I have never bestowed a thought upon their fashion or style. They were ordered, they fit me, and I wear them. That is all."

"And I think, Brother C.," said the veteran again, " that it would be exceedingly unkind as well as unjust in any one to accuse our new minister of worldly conformity because he wears a suit of clothes similar to those of his neighbors. The proof of our moral transformation is not to be found in the cut of a coat or the style of a bonnet. I have learned to value people according to their moral and religious worth, and not by their dress or profession."

I was certainly surprised to hear this language from an *old* Methodist. I had never heard the like before, and although I considered myself well prepared to sustain my views on this point, for some reason I found that I was confused, and a reply was not quite ready. To my great relief Father Rogers said :

" Let us be going. Brother C., we will resume this talk some other time."

The services proceeded as usual. The congregation was large and attentive. I felt a comfortable degree of liberty, and was cheered during the sermon by a number of responses in the shape of " amen" and " glory," and once or twice an emphatic " hallelujah " echoed through the house. After an earnest invitation for all the members to tarry for class-meeting the benediction was pronounced.

A very fair number tarried, and, knowing that before me stood the majority of the members of the charge, I paid particular attention both to their outward appearance and spoken experience. To my sorrow I thought I saw clear exhibitions of pride and worldly conformity. In the public service my attention had been drawn toward a singularly-dressed man, whom I instantly concluded to be a vain worldling who came to make a display of his singularity and to hear the new minister. Be it remembered that I arrived at this conclusion from the man's apparel, and from no other cause. His deportment was perfectly correct and his attention strict. But to me his dress was enough to settle the question of his moral condition. He wore a black velvet coat, a yellow vest, and white trousers, from the waist of which hung a short, massive gold watch-chain, ending with a couple of golden seals. But what struck me more particularly was a very fine white ruffle projecting from his shirt bosom. Judge of my astonishment when I found this ruffle-shirted gentleman in the class-meeting. I looked around and examined the countenances of those present in order to ascertain if others were astonished as well as myself. But no! Then it was evident that the man was at home, and one of the fraternity. I will mention but few names in connection with this class-meeting, but enough to answer our purpose. Brother Frothingham was evidently *poor*. His garments denoted him as such. He was glad that they had a minister at last who was not afraid to preach against pride and popularity. It was all dress and fashion, and the cause of Christ was languishing. He had often asked their former pastor to preach on pride, but he didn't do it. But now he believed the set time to favor Zion had come. Halleluiar! Sister Frothingham believed in that religion that had life and power in it. When God converted her she was converted all over, soul and body. She felt it from the crown of her head to the end of her toes. It pained her soul to see Methodist sisters following the vain fashion of a wicked world and thus giving the lie to their profession. At last I came to the man with the ruffled shirt. Father Rogers with a smile spoke his name—"Brother Sterling." I looked upon him with a degree of amazement and wondered what *he* would have to say. He spoke on rather a low key, but quite distinct. In a second I found that he was an Englishman. "It is all of grace! It is all of grace!" said Brother Sterling. "Twenty years ago, in Old England, the good Shepherd found me a poor wandering sheep on the barren mountains of sin and unbelief, and led me into the fold, and ever since then I have lain down in green pastures and by the side of still waters. Brethren, if there is any good in me it is all of grace, and to God be all the glory!" All this from the man with the ruffled shirt and the massive watch-chain! There was a ring of sincerity about what he said, and I found on looking round a number shedding tears. I had purposed to say something to this man touching worldly conformity, but when he sat down I concluded to let it pass. How thankful I have since felt that I did not at that time follow the impulse! The class-meeting closed. The new minister was introduced to many present, all of whom gave him a hearty welcome with a warm invitation to call at their houses. "I hope Brother C.," said Sister Frothingham, "that you will not do as some of our former ministers have done. They could make themselves mighty familiar in fine houses, where the women folks dress in silks and play on the pianner, but their visits to the poor were few and far be-. tween, and sometimes as scarce as hens' teeth." I told Sister Frothingham that her being poor would not prevent my visiting her. This answer caused a general smile, which at that time I did not understand. We scattered, and I returned to the hospitable mansion of Father Rogers.

"Well, Brother C.," said the venerable local preacher, after we were fairly seated, "you see that we have a few at least in L—— that will take great pleasure in giving you all due assistance in carrying forward the dress-reform movement."

"I would not run from one extreme to another," I replied. "I have no desire to see the sisters at-tired in Sister Frothingham's style. I was not at all pleased with her remarks. But I have often noticed that there is a tendency in the poor members of the church to charge pride on those who are in better circumstances. So we must have charity for Brother and Sister Frothingham."

"If you put down the Frothinghams among the poor you will make a very great mistake," said Father Rogers. "Mr. Frothingham is nearly the richest man on the charge. He has all the appearance of poverty, and I often think that he has all the experience of poverty. That coat that he wore to-day has been his Sunday garment for fifteen years, and it bids fair for years to come. Both he and his wife are forever harping on pride and dress, and, whatever may be the merit of the subject in itself, from them it always does harm. Their influence in the church is any thing but favorable. They generally make a great ado over every new preacher, and invariably wish a change at the end of the first year. You may look upon these remarks as being uncharitable, but they have led so many new ministers astray by their noisy demonstrations that I deem it my duty to set you on your guard, and if you find them better than my description I shall greatly rejoice."

"But what about the man with the ruffled shirt, Father Rogers?" I asked. "I certainly was favorably impressed with what he said; but how can any man that enjoys religion permit himself to indulge in such vanity of dress? I had not the least idea that he was even a professor of religion, much less a *Methodist.* I certainly was surprised when I saw him in the class-meeting. The idea of a ruffle-shirted Methodist!"

" Now we come back to our first point of discussion," said Father Rogers, with a smile on his lips; "and I wish for no better subject to test our theory than this man of the ruffled shirt and the heavy watch-chain. Ten years ago he came from England with his two sisters, one a young lady and the other a child of twelve years. The older sister married, and now lives in the West. The younger is unmarried and superintends the house for her bachelor brother, who owns a large and beautiful farm about two miles from this place. They came to this country with regular certificates of membership, and their Christian walk has been blameless. Brother Sterling dresses now very much as he did then. The first time I ever saw him he had on a velvet coat and a ruffled shirt. I never saw a person more indifferent to the changing forms of fashion. He is a man of property, and it is all at God's service. He abounds in every good word and work, temporally and spiritually. He is loved and respected by the whole community. His attendance at the sanctuary is constant. His contributions toward the support of the Gospel are liberal and cheerful. He well understands our theology and church government. He is a ripe scholar and understands several languages. He is as humble and unpretending as a child. His love and regard for the ministers are proverbial. All this you will see for yourself, and a vast deal more, between this and the next Conference. Thus this man has stood among us in all the beauty of holiness for a dozen years, and those that know his moral worth are not disposed to meddle with the style of his shirt or the weight of his watch-chain."

Father Rogers waxed warm in the praise of his English neighbor. I certainly was much surprised to find my man of "worldly conformity" set up so highly. I had all confidence in my worthy host, and concluded that the account was correct. Again I found my usual ready utterance wanting. I simply replied:

"It is very possible that I have wrongly judged persons on account of my views of dress. I will give the subject more consideration."

CHAPTER II.

SOME PASTORAL CALLS.

TWO days after this, in company with Father Rogers, I called to see a number of the members. After what I had heard on the Sabbath I concluded that Sister Frothingham must not be overlooked. On our way thither my faithful guide remarked: "Brother C., in all probability your feelings will be hurt more than once before you will leave that house. If you escape you will be the first Methodist minister that ever proved so fortunate. It will be under the garb of pretended sanctity. But be assured, my dear brother, that you are not to judge of this charge by the Frothinghams. Our people are good and kind, and they

12

never rush to the throne of judgment to pass a sentence on their fellow-men."

I assured him in return that I was fully prepared to meet all features of mind and disposition, and on we trotted until we found ourselves in front of the Frothingham mansion. We entered. It was evident from Sister Frothingham's habiliments that on this afternoon she was not expecting "company." If she was acquainted with St. Paul's injunction, "Let every thing be done decently and in order," in all probability she had given it an exclusively *spiritual* meaning, for the interior appearance of her kitchen was far from being a proof that the good advice had been heeded. We found her as we generally find the pictures of sweet rustic maidens in the magazines—shoeless and stockingless; while her hair was permitted to enjoy a holiday and run in any direction its fancy might dictate. She was engaged in spinning flax.

"Good afternoon, Brother C.," she said; "you have catched me in a fine fix. You see I yet stick to the old fashions. I tell Simon what was good enough for our fathers and mothers is good enough for their children. 'A penny saved is a penny 'arned.' I don't run after every new-fangled notion. It seems to me that the world is getting crazy after new things, and the Church is as bad as the world. Sit down, Father Rogers. Huldah, bring a chair from the spare-room, and run to the back lot and tell your father that the new minister is come. Sister C., I noticed, didn't stay in class Sunday. I presume she was tired. I tell Simon that women nowadays can't stand nothing. It wa'n't so when I was young. If they would only take hold and work as I did when I was a girl I guess they wouldn't be such a puny, sickly set. When Sister C. gets over being tired of course she will stay in class. There was a good deal of fault found with our other minister's wife on that account. If any body should set a good example it should be the minister's wife. Well, well, when I begin to talk I don't know when to stop."

But she did stop for a while, not, however, before she had made a very unfavorable impression on my mind. Her language in regard to my wife touched me keenly, and I replied with as much composure as I could command:

"Sister Frothingham, I am happy to inform you that Mrs. C. is an ardent lover of our means of grace, and is always present unless unavoidably detained. I tell you this to relieve you from any further embarrassment."

"And let me say in behalf of the wife of our former minister," said Father Rogers, "that there was but one family on the whole charge that ever found fault with her. She was a beautiful specimen of a true Christian lady, and in her absence I must defend her."

"Conscience sakes! Father Rogers, you needn't get huffy about it!" replied our sister. "I guess there are no bones broken. When I was—"

But just in time to prevent another outpouring Brother F. came in from the "back lot." It seems that he had witnessed our arrival and Huldah's journey had been rendered short.

"Glad to see you," said he as he took my hand. "Father Rogers, why didn't you put your horse in the barn?"

"O, we are not going to make much of a stay," was the reply. "The horse is all right. Brother C. thought he would like to make a few calls."

"How much of a family have you, Brother C?" asked Brother F.

"I have a wife and two children," I replied.

"O, that ain't *very* bad," replied the man. "Some of our ministers have so many children that they figur' up pretty middlin' high for a weak charge; don't they, Father Rogers?"

"That is a point that gives me no trouble," replied the veteran, with much earnestness. "When the minister's claim is high the brethren pay accordingly. They find no fault. If Brother C. had sixteen children instead of two some would stick to their old figure, and that a very low one."

Simon was evidently hit, but not much hurt. His "well-beloved," seeing the situation, concluded to come to the rescue, and so replied:

"It takes a heap more to support a preacher's family than it used to. Twenty years ago they were willing to live like common folks. But pride and popilarity has crept into ministers' houses as well as others. I often tell Simon that if they would live and dress as plain as we do we wouldn't hear so much complaining about money and quarterage and such like stuff. But, dear me! they are often as stuck up as the world's people. I hope Brother C. will not think that I am alludin' to his family; but that is true of some of our ministers, and Father Rogers knows it."

"Father Rogers does *not* know it!" was his emphatic reply.

"Nancy," interposed Brother F., "I guess we better drop that subject; you know Father Rogers and us could never see alike on these matters. But from some parts of Brother C.'s sermon on Sunday I think he must side with us."

This put me in an uncomfortable position. I utterly detested the spirit that prompted their remarks, and yet much of the language they used was very much like my own, and no one knew it better than did Father Rogers. I dare say that he rightly judged my feelings and rendered very timely aid.

"It is hardly fair to draw Brother C. into this talk," he said, with a restored smile. "He will have plenty of time after this to make known his views, and we hope to profit by them. We came here to make a friendly call, and not to argue questions."

This, to my great relief, had the effect of changing the tone of the conversation, and in a few minutes we were more at ease. In the course of remarks touching various church enterprises Brother and Sister F. instinctively shrank from all measures that required any thing in the shape of advancing money or even labor. Designedly or otherwise, my good Father Rogers touched on points that were peculiarly adapted to show the new minister the close and penurious disposition of the Frothinghams.

"Our church ought to be shingled over," said Father Rogers. "In heavy rains it leaks in many places."

"I guess a little patching would answer for the present," said the man of the house.

"We have patched long enough. The house needs a thorough shingling, and if we all do our part as God has prospered us it can be easily accomplished," was the reply.

"How was the state of religion on your last charge, Brother C.?" asked Brother F., evidently wishing to turn to something *cheaper* than shingles.

I replied, "There was a very good state of spiritual prosperity when I left, and the finances were attended to with punctuality."

"What we need on this charge is a rousing revival," said Brother F., "and I hope that Brother C. will be able to git up a reformation."

"I hope so too with all my heart," answered Father Rogers. "Let the reformation commence at once, and, to begin with, let the church be shingled. But for this we must raise money. Come, now, let us push this subscription"—handing it to Brother F. "I have put my name down for what I thought was right, but if it is not enough I will give more. In what way can we better start a reformation than in showing proper respect for the sanctuary?"

Brother F. reluctantly took the paper, read the heading, folded it up again, and handed it to Father Rogers. Then turning to me inquired:

"How long have you been in the ministry, Brother C.?"

I told him I was commencing my sixth year.

"Brother Frothingham," said Father Rogers, "Brother C.'s goods are at B. station, and they must be brought up this week. You have good strong horses and you will go after a load, won't you?"

"Let—me—see," was the slow reply, while he cast a glance toward Nancy.

"I guess," said Nancy, "that Simon has all he can do with the horses at home this week. This is a busy time with us. I dare say that Brother Sterling can send teams for the goods; he generally does such things."

"So he does," was the reply, "and will most gladly do it again. But is it best to permit that good man to carry burdens which fairly ought to rest on other shoulders?"

"If he does it with pleasure," said Sister F., "I guess it won't hurt him."

"It may not hurt *him*," was the reply; "but it will hurt those who will not touch these burdens with one of their fingers."

"Brother Frothingham," said Father Rogers again, "Brother C. would be glad to get a little help in the line of money. He tells me that his purse is pretty low. I guess we had better make him up a little sum; it will cheer him among strangers."

"Land o' mercy!" cried Sister F. "I guess you have come to a poor place for money. We have to spare every cent we can rake and scrape to make the last payment on the west farm."

"We have more turnips than we really need,"

chimed in the husband. "I can spare Brother C. a few."

"And I can let Sister C. have a little yarn," added the wife.

"And in the fall we shall butcher a crittur, and Brother C. can have a fore-quarter," said the man of the house.

"Well," said Father Rogers, "we have several calls to make, and we must be going."

"You will pray with us, Brother C.," said Brother F.

Nancy stopped her wheel, and I tried to pray with feelings which I never shall forget. The interview had left on my mind a most painful impression. During the prayer the responses of the man and his wife were loud and frequent, "Amen" and "Bless the Lord" being the favorites.

We left, and, once out of that house, I felt greatly relieved, and came very near resolving that I would never enter it again.

On that afternoon we made several short calls on families belonging to the church. They were brief seasons of genuine delight. The hearty Christian welcome I received and the favor with which every measure of Father Rogers was met convinced me that my lot had fallen in pleasant places.

About four o'clock we came to the beautiful residence of Brother Sterling. The premises were nicely laid out, and in a manner indicating at once that the design was not American.

"This is the English of it," said Father Rogers. "Brother Sterling's taste is very fine. His knowledge of farming and gardening is almost perfect."

We were met at the gate by the owner of the house. Yes, sure enough, there he was—the man with the ruffled shirt. He was glad to see us. The horse was put in charge of a servant and conveyed to the stable, while Father Rogers and myself, in charge of the worthy host, were conducted to the house.

He was attired much the same as he was on the Sabbath; but, from some reason, a wonderful change had come over me, and I was not much discommoded by his peculiarity. He at once in the most modest and quiet manner led the conversation in a strain that became to me delightful and even captivating.

Presently his sister came in, a fine-looking young lady, still retaining that freshness of complexion so strikingly visible in English countenances. I had been introduced to her on the Sabbath, and this, our second meeting, was free from restraint. I thought her dress denoted a degree of worldly vanity, but her manners were so very agreeable and her very nature so thoroughly happy that, for the time being, at least, I postponed any mental reflection upon her personal piety or Christian character. Her real goodness of heart beamed forth in her smiling lips and laughing, sparkling eyes; and her intelligence and culture stood out in her wide, prominent brow and faultless address. It was evident that she was every thing to her brother, who looked upon her with eyes of deep affection.

"We are truly glad that you have called on us," she said, smiling. "You have come so late and your visit will be too short. But I will not find fault; I dare say you have made other calls."

"That is true, Mary," said Father Rogers; "but I knew all the time where we were going to stop and take tea."

"You are a downright good Father Rogers," said Mary, with laughing eyes, "and see now if I don't give you an extra good cup; and now please excuse me while I leave and try to make good my promise." And Mary, clothed with smiles, left the room.

"That dear girl is a world of comfort to me," said her brother. "She was left an orphan at an early age, and when quite young she subjected me to some care and anxiety. But since then she has repaid me a thousand times. She is very happy herself, and she appears to impart her nature to those around her. It may not seem in the best of taste to thus speak of my own sister, but to me she is one grand source of joy and consolation. Her vivacity does not intrude upon her devotion. Mary is an ardent lover of our Lord Jesus Christ and deeply attached to the Church of God."

"This is the united testimony of the whole community," said Father Rogers. "Mary is universally loved and esteemed. She is an ornament in society and a pillar in the spiritual Zion."

"Well, Brother C.," said the man with the ruffled shirt, "we most cordially welcome you and your family into our midst. Your name and former labors are somewhat known to us. You have served good charges and you have been well supported. In point of wealth our charge does not stand as high as some you have served. But you have come among a warm-hearted people that will feel it a pleasure to co-operate with you spiritually and see that your temporal wants are all supplied. We invite you to our homes and our hearts. Father Rogers will tell you that, with perhaps one exception, the families of our church are always a unit in regard to their love for the pastor and his family."

I was certainly affected. Not so much by what he said as by the manner in which it was spoken. There was a peculiar affectionate earnestness in his voice and way that is not easily described. And, although the offensive ruffle was right before my eyes and the golden seals at the end of his watch-chain, I felt a certain moisture gathering in my eyes while my heart was "strangely warmed." I briefly replied:

"I heartily thank you, Brother Sterling, for your cordial greeting. From what I have already seen I am well convinced that I am among warm friends."

"I tried to get Brother Frothingham to go after a load of Brother C.'s goods to the B— depot," said Father Rogers, "but I did not succeed."

"You must have been sorely disappointed," was the smiling reply. Then turning to me he inquired: "How many loads will the goods make, Brother C. ?"

"The goods are well boxed," I replied, "and they will make two fair loads."

"Brother C., I will send for the goods to-morrow, and Father Rogers, you need not look any farther. This is a favor that is generally conferred on me, and perhaps on this account Brother Frothingham felt a little delicate. Brother C. will find the parsonage convenient and in good repair.   By the way, Father Rogers, how about that church shingling?"

"It should be attended to without any delay, Brother Sterling," was the reply. "In rainy weather the church is greatly injured.   I have drawn a subscription, and a sufficient amount should be raised to complete the whole job."

"It may take you some time to circulate that paper," said Brother Sterling. "The shingles had better be procured at once and the work commenced. I have more than half enough on my premises which I don't need, and if you say how soon you can use them I will see that they will be there. The rest we can secure by the time they are needed. Let us hurry this matter through."

"A blessing on your kind head and heart!" said Father Rogers, with some feeling. "I will agree that on Monday of next week, at eight o'clock, there will be a strong force of the brethren and friends on the ground to make short work of it."

"All right," said the man with the ruffled shirt. "The shingles will be on the premises on Saturday afternoon."

While this conversation, and much more I might mention, was going on, my mind could not help contrasting this family with the Frothinghams. There was another thing which often came up in my mind as I witnessed the true devotion of this man to the cause of his Master and the kind manner in which he spoke of all. I thought how very wide of the mark was my estimation of Brother Sterling as I gazed upon him for the first time on

the previous Sabbath morning in the house of the
Lord. The conviction broke upon my mind with
unmistakable force that it was wholly unsafe to
judge of a person's spirituality or moral worth on the
one hand by an article of dress, or on the other by
a high-sounding profession. It was during my first
week on L— charge that I promised God and my
own heart I should be more careful and charitable,
and that I should strive to the utmost of my ability
to give "honor to whom honor" is due.

In about an hour Mary returned to inform us that
tea was ready, and we sat down at a table richly
spread. The sister presided with ease and dignity.
Her remarks were perfectly suited to the occasion.
She was lively and brilliant, within proper bounds.
She wore what I considered a valuable breastpin,
and there was a very light gold chain around her
neck. These articles gave me some uneasiness for
a time, but such was the general flow of good feeling at the table that I soon forgot all about the
ornaments and gave myself up to the charm of the
occasion.

After tea I asked Mary to give us some music.
To this she readily consented, but before commenc-.
ing she said, with a humorous smile:

" I am not sure, Brother C., but that this will give
Sister Frothingham an occasion for another lecture.
This, I presume, is the very 'pianner' to which she
referred."

" Mary!" said the brother, "I know, dear, you
will say nothing unkind of Sister Frothingham."

" Not for the world, my dear Gordon!" replied

Mary. "I only feel somewhat concerned for the safety of our new minister."

"Give us the music, Sister Mary," said I, "and I will risk all harm."

"Very well," said she; "and I call Father Rogers to witness that I am not responsible for the consequences." Then, as a kind of prelude, she gave us an exhibition on the key-board which showed that those notes were under the control of a master.

After one very brilliant instrumental piece she sang, in a deep, full, rich soprano, the celebrated "I know that my Redeemer liveth," with which Jenny Lind had so recently thrilled the country. I had not heard it from the Swedish maiden, but I possessed sufficient knowledge of music to know that the piece at this time was very finely rendered. We had it in its plain English fullness, without any of that affectation and lisping which is often witnessed at homes and concerts.

·After half an hour of very pleasant conversation Father Rogers deemed it advisable to leave. Again the new pastor was requested to lead in prayer, and a hallowed influence seemed to fill the room. It is true there were no loud responses, but there were silent invocations that accompanied the vocal prayer;

> "And Heaven came down our souls to greet,
> While glory crowned the mercy-seat."

Before we left the house Brother Sterling handed me a twenty-dollar bank-note, remarking, "I dare say it will come handy. If at any time you should stand in need of pecuniary aid please let me know it, for through the blessing of my heavenly Father

I am in circumstances where I can be of assistance
to you without in the least embarrassing myself, and
it will afford me much pleasure."

I looked upon the money with a degree of wonder, for it was the largest sum I had ever received
at one time from a single person as "quarterage."
I tried to thank him as well as I could, and then I
thought of the man with the ruffle who sat before
me on Sabbath morning, and then I thought of the
minister in the pulpit who made up his mind that
that man was a vain worldling.

CHAPTER III.

IN WHICH ALICE GIVES A PIECE OF HER MIND.

ON our way homeward for some time the conversation was not very brisk; but on my part,
at least, reflection was very busy. Father Rogers, I
have no doubt, pretty well knew what was going on
in my mind. I could readily see by his smiling countenance that he had been abundantly pleased.

The silence at last became a little embarrassing
to me and I started the conversation :

"Father Rogers, I find that your praise of Brother
Sterling was not at all exaggerated. He more than
justifies all you said."

"And you will find him the same kind, faithful,
reliable, benevolent soul the year round," said Father Rogers. "And you can readily see by this
time, Brother C., how well we can afford to let him

be his own judge in regard to the style of his dress. His sister partakes largely of the same nature. You have seen to-day that she is a cultivated, finished young lady; and yet there is not a respectable poor person in this town whose society she would shun. She is the first of her sex in deeds of charity, and her kindness to the poor is well known. She is faithful to all the means of grace, and never, in any company, does she shrink from acknowledging her Saviour. It is true, she wears a fashionable bonnet and a gold watch. She can well afford it, and for this Sister Frothingham pronounces her proud. I never saw a young lady in all of my life that gave more substantial proofs of genuine humility than does Mary Sterling."

"Brother Rogers," said I, "I am free to confess that after the conversation I have had with you on this subject, and after what I have plainly witnessed at the respective houses of Brothers Frothingham and Sterling, my views on this point of pride have been greatly modified. My theory of judging from the mere dress led me to a most erroneous conclusion. I condemned a most worthy servant of the Lord, and gave unmerited credit for Christian humility to persons of a worldly, penurious, and uncharitable spirit. I deem it a duty and feel it a relief to make to you this confession. The experience of the last few days I trust will prove to me a most valuable lesson."

Father Rogers undoubtedly would have replied but already we found ourselves at the gate, where Alice and the two children stood ready to receive

us. Father Rogers took care of the pony, while
the rest of us went into the house, where Mrs. C.
sat with Sister Rogers.

"Well, Brother C.," said Alice, "I hope that you
have been well pleased with your first visits on
your new charge. Indeed, I know that with but
one exception you have been delighted with the
people."

"Why make that exception, Sister Alice?" I
asked. "Why could not all of our visits have been
pleasant?"

"I learned before you started that you were to
call on the Frothinghams," was the reply, "and that
fully answers your question. No person of fine feelings, minister or otherwise, can remain at that house
for ten minutes without being utterly disgusted."

"Alice, my dear," remarked the mother, "you
are using strong language."

"I simply speak the truth, mother," was her reply,
"and the language is much milder than the case
would justify."

"But, my dear," said the mother, "it may be possible that Brother C. found things otherwise; and
why should you thus express yourself in the absence
of any actual knowledge in the premises?"

"My dear mother," said Alice, "it is not in the
absence of knowledge. It is true, I was not present,
and Brother C. has not divulged any thing that
transpired: but I am just as positive in my own
mind in regard to the nature of what he heard from
Mrs. Frothingham as if I had been present on the
spot. And now I am willing to test the correctness

13

of what I have said.   Brother C. had to be informed that things were not thus and so when she was young, and that the world was getting crazy, and that the Church was running at the bidding of pride and popularity, and a number of things she tells Simon.   And I will venture to say that Brother C. had to listen to a lecture in regard to the duty of ministers' wives and a mean thrust at their extravagance.   And if papa saw fit to ask for any money for the minister or for church purposes I know he did not succeed."

Such was the accuracy of Alice's sayings, as well as the half-comical style in which they were delivered, that I actually broke out in laughter, in which my wife saw fit to join.   In justice to the daughter I confessed that she was correct in every particular, and that she had come out triumphantly.

In the midst of the merriment the father came in and smilingly inquired, "Well, Alice, what note have you struck now?"

"Pa, I have said nothing naughty; I was only showing Brother C. how well I understood the nature of the entertainment they gave you to-day at Brother Frothingham's."

"I don't consider that as a great exploit," replied the father; "any one knowing the party could do that.   So, Miss Alice, you need not flatter yourself as possessing any extra amount of mental penetration."

"I certainly don't, pa," said Alice; "it was a very easy matter indeed, and I told my mother so. But I wonder if this state of things is to last forever. How much longer must men and women of piety, liberality, and intelligence, be insulted in our social meetings by the coarse vulgarity of those ignorant, penurious mortals, who have no more public spirit than a couple of owls? Only think of the slighting manner in which they speak of our good Brother Sterling, and of Mary, the best and dearest creature on earth! I tell you, pa, the whole church is getting utterly sick of the everlasting slang and cant of those two stingy souls. They destroy our social meetings by their unkind and ungodly personality, and they abuse persons the latchet of whose shoes they are not worthy to stoop and unloose!"

" My daughter," said the father, " all you say is strictly true, and it is not in my heart to blame you. Your language may seem severe to Brother and Sister C.; but let them remember that we have had to carry this grievous burden for many years, and for my part I don't see how we are to be relieved."

" Sister Alice," said I, " our other visits, and especially the one at Brother Sterling's, were enough to compensate us a thousand times for any little reverses at another point."

My first week on L—— charge gave me very clear insight of its workings. With the exception of the Frothinghams I found the membership to be friendly, kind, and liberal, according to their ability. But far above all, in my estimation of that society, stood the man with the ruffled shirt. During my two years' stay on the charge I found him at all times and places the same amiable, dignified, devoted and benevolent man. Unless unavoidably detained he was present at all the meetings, and it was evident from his words and actions that he esteemed the service of the sanctuary far above every thing on earth. During an itinerant life of forty years I have seen hundreds of good and true men officially connected with the Church, and the names of many remain fresh upon the pages of my memory; but in all my sojournings I have not seen one equal in all perfections to Gordon Sterling. For two years I saw him much, and the more I stayed in his society the clearer and brighter to me shone his moral excellencies.

During my stay among them several things occurred worthy of mention. Mary Sterling became the happy bride of a young man of great moral worth and fine talents, the son of a wealthy farmer in an adjoining town. By mutual agreement Mary was to stay at home. Brother Sterling was greatly pleased with the match, and it seemed as if they had all things in common.

Alice Rogers also made the heart of a young itinerant glad by consenting to share his labors and fortune. Rev. Mr. M. has been well known for years as one of the most energetic workers in the Church, and his refined, devoted, and *spirited* wife, has always won a host of genuine friends.

Perhaps the most fortunate occurrence to the charge during my administration was the withdrawal by letter of Brother and Sister Frothingham from the church. They became intolerable, and at last in a quiet way, at their own dwelling, I gave them to understand that the church was much grieved with their perpetual unkind insinuations, and that it was my opinion that the brethren and sisters had a just cause of complaint.

" *Your* opinion, is it?" replied Sister F. " Very likely. I told Simon it wouldn't be a great while before they would soap you over and get you into their worldly ways. When you first came on this charge I thought we had got a man that would amount to something. I told Simon so. Said he, ' Nancy, time will tell.' And, sure enough, time has told, and here you are takin' sides with pride and popilarity. If you had asked more of God's advice and less advice from Gordon Sterling you wouldn't be comin' to our house with such stuff in your mouth."

" Sister Frothingham," said I, " you may abuse me to your heart's content, and I can bear it with but little inconvenience ; but I cannot sit quietly and listen to disrespectful language touching Brother Sterling."

Before Nancy had time to reply Simon said, " Brother C., if you have any idear that we think it any privilege to belong to that proud church you are awfully mistaken. I guess there are other churches in the land, and they aint stuck up with pride either, as they are at L——. Last Sabbath we went to the Red School-house, and there they have the life and power. The way the minister gave these gold-chain Christians a skinning was a caution. My soul was fed under that sermon and—"

" And so was mine," broke in Nancy. " I was

glad to get somewhere where the people enjoyed religion.   I was telling Simon on our way home that it was worth more than all the meetings we had in six months ; and it is the livin' truth."

"And I was just going to tell Brother C.," continued Simon, with an air of threatening triumph, "that a little more of that kind of talk of his'n would just take us over to the Red School-house. We had some talk about it ; didn't we, Nancy?"

"So we did, Simon," was the quick reply ; "and it would serve them just right if we were to leave at once."

"And I have pretty much made up my mind to do just so," said Simon, watching my countenance. "And unless Brother C. backs down pretty middlin' quick he will soon find us members of another church."

"Under ordinary circumstances it is not my business to encourage withdrawals from the church," said I; "but this is a case out of the ordinary line, and I feel it to be my duty as a pastor to say to you that unless you intend to act and speak differently your withdrawal from the society will be a source of joy and gladness to every member of our church and congregation."

This was more than they expected, and for a few moments they remained silent.   But Nancy rallied, and to my great relief she replied :

"Simon, this is enough.   Let us get our letters at once !"

"Brother C.," said Simon, showing a high degree of resentment, "I aint used to such a talk, sir, and

I aint going to stand it! I want you, sir, to give us letters. Let us have them now. Huldah, there is a half sheet of paper—"

"Never mind," said I, interrupting him, "I generally go prepared for an emergency. I have paper and ink; your letters will be ready in less than three minutes."

The letters were handed over, and without ceremony I left the house for the last time. To the church at L——their departure was hailed as would be a deliverance from a common nuisance, while the confidence of respectable outsiders was greatly strengthened in the integrity of the church.

My two years on L—— charge were, upon the whole, the most happy of my life. I never witnessed warmer loves or truer friendships. But the parting day at last arrived, and we had to bid adieu to our many friends. The man with the ruffled shirt "loved us to the end." In every movement he studied our comfort and convenience. Free of charge his men and horses were at our service. Such was the man in every thing that was good that to me, even *me*, his peculiarity of dress became attractive. His ruffle was all right, and the jingle of his golden seals became melodious. Heaven bless him! We parted in silence, and the itinerant with his family turned his face toward his new field of labor.

Throughout the years I have had occasional correspondence with some brethren in L——. Brother Sterling, although quite aged, is yet on the shores of time, full of faith and of the Holy Ghost. Here is a part of a letter I received from him some time ago:

" I am yet climbing up Zion's hill.   I am nearing my heavenly home.   What vast changes have taken place on this charge since 18—, when you were our pastor !   Father and Mother Rogers, as you know, passed away to the better land many years ago, and so have many others that you well knew.   The church is in a flourishing condition and our pastor is greatly beloved.   Mary, her husband and family, are well and happy.   Their son, Gordon, is to graduate next summer at Middletown.   He is a fine young fellow, and will enter the ministry.   Rev. Mr. M. and Alice have a son who, although quite young, has begun to preach. They say he is very promising.   I am sorry to inform you that Mr. and Mrs. Frothingham are out of the church.   You will remember that when you were with us they took letters and joined the society that worshiped at the Red School-house.   But their extreme love of money made them very unpopular in their new relation.   Some years ago, in some pork transaction, his dishonesty became so manifest that he was arrested, and he had to pay quite a sum to save himself from prison ; and his wife being an assistant in the fraud they were both expelled from the church.   Our love to Mrs. C.   We hear grand news of your children, and we congratulate the parents.   Albert and Mary unite with me in sending their warmest regards.

" Yours in Christ,

"GORDON STERLING."

Since that day I have had much experience with all kinds of temperaments and dispositions in the

Church of Christ. I have seen pride arrayed " in purple and fine linen," and I have seen it also in the cheapest calico. I have seen humility in extreme simplicity of apparel, and I have seen the same humility in rich attire. A fashionable garment or bonnet is no proof of pride, and the reverse is no proof of humility. The persons *may* be proud or they *may* be humble ; but it is wholly unsafe to judge them by their dress alone. And if there are any of my young brethren in the ministry who, like myself once, are disposed to measure an individual's religion by the cut of a coat or the style of a hat, let them remember my sad mistake in regard to *the man with the ruffled shirt*, and wait for further developments.

JOHN'S WIFE'S BROTHER.

A THANKSGIVING STORY.

CHAPTER I.

NEIGHBORS AT VARIANCE.

IN a farming portion of Connecticut, known in that town as The Flats, there lived, twenty-eight years ago, two families which, as the term is used, were well-to-do. Their respective farms were models of culture and productiveness. The residences were fine, the out-houses commodious, the carriages of the most modern style, and the horses among the most valuable in the town. These families lived within a half a mile of each other and their land joined. The owners were David Brainard and Richard Brown. Unfortunately, these two men were very much alike in their mental temperament. We say unfortunately, because their disposition was of an unfavorable cast. They were proud, jealous, and retaliating; especially so toward each other. This antagonism had existed for many years and was gathering strength by age. It began with a line fence, over which they went to law, and ever since then they were known as decided foes. Brainard had a wife and one daughter. Katie was mild

and lovely, just entering her eighteenth year. Brown
had a wife and five children. Emma, the oldest,
was married, and lived some six miles away. John
also had married, in his twenty-third year, and was
employed as a book-keeper in New York. Fred
was in his twenty-first year, a diligent worker on
the farm. There were also at home Mary and Alice,
one eighteen and the other sixteen. To the credit
of these wives and children it may be said that
they were much more sensible in their behavior
than were the husbands and fathers. We may as
well say here that Fred Brown and Katie Brainard
were often seen together, that they cherished for
each other feelings which simple friendship could not
explain, and that, finally, at a favorable opportunity
the young man revealed to the maiden the real sentiment of his heart.

"Fred," said the young lady, "I thank you for
your love, and in return you have mine. It is as
full and pure as your own. But in view of the feelings of your father and mine we must look for opposition."

"Katie, I have looked that matter straight in the
face," said Fred. "I am ready to bear joyfully all
the opposition from my own father, and I would
most gladly, if I could, bear your share of trouble."

"I will gladly bear my own, dear Fred," was her
reply. "Let us hope that some good providence
will bring about a happy change in these two angry
men."

The pure-hearted twain were there and then be-
trothed, and they sought their respective homes.

Before long Brown saw unmistakable evidences of his son's partiality for Katie Brainard, and one day he was summoned into the parental presence.

"Well, sir," said the father, "I am compelled to believe that you pay special attention to the daughter of my inveterate enemy. What have you to say for yourself?"

"It is even so, father," said Fred. "We are exceedingly fond of each other; and in this, I think, we show much better sense than our fathers do."

"Your language is shameful, sir!" responded the father. "I am not here to argue. I command you to pay no more attention to Dave Brainard's girl."

"I cannot obey your command," said Fred. "We are engaged. I am fully prepared to take the consequences. I have been a hard worker on this farm for years, and in a few months I shall be of age. If in consequence of my disobedience to your command in this matter you wish me to leave, just say the word, and I shall be in the employ of some other man before sundown."

The father saw that his son was terribly in earnest, and was perfectly astonished to see that quiet boy so aroused. He well knew that Fred's services were indispensable, and yet how could he bear to have his command disregarded? He came to the conclusion that he would try and retain Fred and some of his own dignity at the same time.

"It is of no use to stay here any longer," he said, in a much altered tone. "No, I don't wish you to leave. What put that in your head? You may harness the horses and go to the mill after feed."

Thus terminated the interview, and it looked as if Fred was ahead.

Let us now go to the Brainard mansion and witness an interview of the same nature, but of a much milder type. This one daughter had much influence over her father. She was the pride of his eye and the great treasure of his heart.

"Katie," said he, "are you not aware that in accepting the attention of Fred Brown you are showing your father great disrespect?"

"My dear papa, I would not do such a thing for the world!" said Katie. "Has Fred Brown ever in his life treated you in an unbecoming manner?"

"No, Katie," said Brainard ; "but you well know that his father is my enemy."

"Yes," said the daughter; "but Fred is very sorry that his father treats you so. Does not that make a difference, papa?"

"Well, I think it does," said the father, slowly. "But are you sure of that, Katie?"

"Perfectly sure!" said the daughter, with emphasis.

"Still," said the father, "in view of the circumstances I think you had better drop this thing."

"O, papa, I don't think that you really mean that!" said the girl, with a tear in her eye. "Is there a finer or a more promising young man in all this region of country? Have you any thing against him personally? Is there a single blot upon his moral character? Is he not splendid in form and features? And we have pledged to each other our undying love! Now, can my good papa, that I love so dearly, in view of all this tell his only Katie to 'drop the thing'?"

"No, he can't!" said the father, wiping away a tear. "I am not going to punish two pure hearts for the meanness of old Dick Brown."

The girl rushed into her father's arms and gave him half a dozen kisses in a very short time.

CHAPTER II.

THE REBELLION AND A REVIVAL.

LINCOLN had been made President, and the Rebellion was already a terrible reality. The loyal North was in a blaze of patriotic excitement. Drums beat, cannon roared, and banners waved in the breezes. Regiments were formed and volunteers by the thousands rallied under the flappings of the stars and stripes. Fred Brown felt that he could willingly die in so grand a conflict. The conviction in regard to his duty in this emergency came upon him so heavily that he could find no peace. At last, alone with his God, he fell on his knees and consecrated himself to the service of his country. In words that burned he told the family what he had determined, and hoped that they would consent. Their approbation was given amid copious tears. The parting was bitter, both at home and at Brainard's.

"Brave Fred!" cried Katie, through her tears. "Go, with my prayers and blessing! I believe we shall meet again on The Flats, but if not, Fred, I am yours forever." The lovers parted.

Fred became a member of a regiment organized and completed in a distant city, and within a few weeks of his departure from home he was on the field. He was ever faithful in his correspondence. In all his letters he declared that it was his firm purpose to remain in the army until the Rebellion would be crushed and peace fully restored. He believed that it would be of no benefit for him to come home on a leave of absence; told them to wait patiently, and at the end of the war he would come to stay.

The two farmers continued in their antagonism until the fall of the year 1863. In the church near by there was a very deep religious feeling. A noted revivalist was just commencing his labors there, and his ministry was "quick and powerful." Among the first to embrace religion was Katie Brainard, and she immediately asked the prayers of the church for her dear father. Through her importunity she prevailed upon him to go with her one evening to the meeting. The minister preached on the forgiving spirit of Christ as contrasted with the vindictive temper manifested in so many. The sermon produced a most wonderful effect. Brainard saw himself as in a mirror, and to him the sight was dreadful. Under a deep feeling he bowed in prayer, made a humble public confession, and asked the forgiveness of all those he had misused. No one present doubted his sincerity.

The next day he hastened to the home of his neighbor and made his humble penitential statement:

"Brown, for years I have treated you shamefully. Last night the Lord, by his servant, showed me the depth of my wicked heart; I fell on my knees to ask forgiveness, and now I ask your pardon also. Brown, give me your hand." And he reached out his own.

"Not to-day," said Brown. "This is rather sudden. I'll think the matter over."

"Yes, do!" said Brainard. "And may the Lord lead you into the right way. I am glad that I have done my duty. I would rejoice to see you at meeting. Good morning, Brown, and may God bless you!"

After Brainard left, Brown could hardly believe that it was a reality. Already he felt condemned in view of the manner he had just treated his neighbor. The more he thought of the matter the worse he felt. He remained in a state of mental misery during that night and the following day. The next evening he found his way to the sanctuary. The evangelist seemed to be inspired, and closed his discourse by inviting all who were "weary and heavy laden" to come forward. A large number came, and among them was seen the trembling form of Richard Brown. After a season of prayer the seekers were requested to speak, and he was the first one to rise.

"My friends," said Brown, "I have lived a godless life. I have set a bad example before my children. I have often been unkind and revengeful. Neighbor Brainard and myself have been enemies for years. Yesterday, like a Christian, he came to my house, with tears in his eyes and love in his heart, and begged my pardon just as if the fault was all on one side. He reached out his hand and I wickedly refused to take it. I have been in perfect misery ever since. I view myself as a guilty sinner before God. I have been conceited and self-righteous. I have treated Brainard spitefully for twenty years. Before this congregation I ask his forgiveness, and if that hand is offered to me once more O how quickly I shall grasp it!"

Here the tall form of David Brainard was seen marching down the aisle, and in a few moments two friendly hands were gladly joined and all hardness buried deep at the foot of the cross.

The meetings were a grand success. Brainard and Brown became active members in the same church, and were noted for their unity and harmony in every measure pertaining to the society.

The spring of 1865 arrived, and, although the Rebellion was drawing near to its inglorious end, the battles were sanguinary and closely contested. Among these was the memorable conflict of Five Forks. The carnage was fearful among both our officers and men. The first account of it appeared without many particulars. Later came a partial list of the slain, and among these was found the name of *Fred Brown!* This news was crushing, and tears freely flowed over the sad fate of one so dearly loved. In a few days a letter came from his colonel, to this effect :

"MR. BROWN, DEAR SIR: Already you have heard the sorrowful news of the death of your son

14

at Five Forks.   Fred Brown was one of the bravest
of the brave.   By the desperate force of the enemy's
charge our ranks were scattered and our regiment
divided.   Your son throughout the day was in the
thickest of the fight.   The burial of our dead, on
the second day, was attended to after dark, by the
light of lanterns, and without much order ; so there
is no hope of securing his remains.   Your son was
a true Christian and a thorough soldier.

" Your obedient servant,

" CHARLES D———."

This news from the seat of war overwhelmed the
Brown family in sorrow, and not less deep was the
grief of one, at least, at the residence of David
Brainard.   In solitude Katie poured out her feelings before her heavenly Father.   But a wise Providence has so ordered that time will assuage the
keen pangs of bereavement and heal in a measure
the crushed and wounded spirit.   It was so here,
and gradually a calm resignation took the place of
excessive grief.

Richard Brown, notwithstanding the crookedness
of his former temper, had been fond of his children,
and on Thanksgiving of each year had given them
a most cordial welcome.

" Well, my dear," said the husband, " we have
abundant reason for thanksgiving this year, although
sadly afflicted."

" Let us at least try on that day to be cheerful, for the sake of the children," said Mrs.
Brown.

"Wisely said," was the reply. "I have thought it would be well to invite our pastor."

"I am glad you have thought of it," said his wife; "what say you to my asking Katie?"

"There is no one that I would rather welcome," said Mr. Brown; "she is one of the Lord's bright jewels."

Just then Mary came in and said, "Papa, here is a letter from John." It was soon opened and read aloud:

NEW YORK, November —, 1865.

"DEAR FOLKS AT HOME: Of course we are coming! We would not miss it for a big pile. To us it is the grandest day in all the year. How I love that dear old mansion! Little Freddie is talking about it continually. By the way, you have often heard my wife speak of her brother at the South. He has been with us a few days, and a grand good fellow he is. Although for years among the rebels he is Union to the back-bone. We cannot miss our Thanksgiving, and of course Jennie will not leave her brother; and so she has concluded to bring him along. I cannot tell exactly at what time we shall arrive. You need not meet us at the depot; we can easily find conveyance. I think we shall be in time for the service. Love to all, from

"JOHN AND JOHN'S WIFE."

"The dear boy!" said his mother. "I am glad that he is recovering his old cheerfulness. Yes, Jennie often spoke of her brother in Virginia, and we shall be right glad to see him."

"If he is any thing like his sister," said Mary, "he will be good company."

"If he had been of Jennie's temperament," said Alice, "he would not be a bachelor at forty-five. I put him down as cold and unsociable."

"I think you will find yourself mistaken," said Mary.

"We shall see," said Alice. "If he is an icicle we shall put him under Katie Brainard's warm sunbeams, and if he don't melt then he is a hopeless case."

CHAPTER III.

THANKSGIVING AT THE BROWN MANSION.

THE Thanksgiving of 1865 at last arrived, when a saved nation poured forth its grateful offering at the shrine of the King of kings. The service at the church was to be at eleven, and at the Brown mansion there were high expectations for the appearance of the New Yorkers. They came, and were received with joy and welcome. John's wife, as usual, was in high spirits, while her countenance beamed with life and intelligence; and her brother, contrary to Alice's prediction, proved at once that he could be highly agreeable. He was tall, straight, and, from his appearance, might be past forty. He wore a full beard thickly sprinkled with gray.

"Blessed old home!" cried John, in perfect delight. "Thou art more dear to me than any spot

in the wide, wide world!" And he gave his mother
and sisters a second edition of his very demonstrative kisses. "We have passed through deep afflic-
tion," he continued, while tears filled his eyes; "but
on this day we will be cheerful, and thank God for
restored peace and a thousand other blessings."

At the church the congregation was very large,
and the sermon by Rev. Mr. Powell was a fine production and exceedingly appropriate. The termina-
tion of the war and the preserved Union were dwelt
upon in sentences touching and sublime. John's
wife's brother was deeply interested, and even affected. The services closed, and the people, after
indulging in hearty greetings, departed to their
various happy homes.

Rev. Mr. Powell and his wife, with Katie Brainard, in harmony with a previous arrangement, went
home with the Brown family, and a goodly number
was seated in the large parlor.

Soon the conversation became general and animated. The parents thought they had never seen
John's wife so happy, and on that account they were
delighted. She was brilliant and witty beyond herself; and yet, at times, a certain moisture in her
eyes showed that she was not indifferent to the deep
sorrow that rested on the family.

"Brother," said John, "you don't wonder—do
you?—at the flow of spirit Jennie and myself show
on this occasion. It is not every New Yorker from
the country that can return on Thanksgiving to a
home like this."

"I don't wonder at all," said the gentleman from

the South. "If ever I should become settled in life I would like to find a quiet rest on a farm in this part of the country."

"And I would advise you to hurry up," said John. "You are getting old, and your chances are not improving."

"John Brown, my brother is *not* old!" said Jennie, with some spirit. "He is younger than he looks. If it were not for that horrid gray beard he would pass for a young man, and some New England young lady would fall in love with him."

"If I thought there was any hope for me in that line," said the brother, "I would get rid of my gray beard at once. That would be but a very short job."

"Upon my word, mother," said Jennie, with her eyes sparkling, "I believe this brother of mine has been deceiving us with a false beard! I will see, sir, about that matter!" She ran up to him, sat on his lap, and with one motion of the hand removed the massive beard, and there sat before them, in more than his former beauty, Fred Brown, whom they had long mourned as dead!

The scene then beggared description; compared with the reality all language must be tame. There was one united spontaneous cry of perfect joy, with a rush toward him of father, mother, and sisters, who, for a time, overwhelmed him with their warm embraces. It was a scene of blissful confusion. They were intoxicated with delight. Katie wept out her joy leaning on the bosom of Mrs. Powell. Of course John and his wife, who had planned the

whole, were not moved in the same manner as were
the rest. But Jennie was perfectly delighted, and
in a rich warbling voice she sang:

> "And we'll all feel gay
> When Johnnie comes marching home."

"Well," said John, when comparative silence had
been restored, "perhaps this company would be
glad to know how my wife's brother happens to be
here, creating such an uproar at our Thanksgiving,
after his death and burial at Five Forks. Will he
please explain?"

"I can assure you, upon the most positive evidence, that I was neither killed nor buried," said
Fred. "It is not strange, however, that my name
appeared among the slain, for on the afternoon of
the second day, until sunset, I was in the thickest
of the fight. The last charge of the enemy was
terrific beyond any thing I had witnessed. In some
way which I cannot explain, instead of having re-
treated with our men I found myself in a fighting
attitude in the midst of the rebels. It is a wonder
that I was not instantly shot or pierced through by
half a dozen bayonets. A Confederate soldier close
by said, in a kind voice:

"'Better drop that musket, or you will be a dead
Yank in less than ten seconds.'

"I realized the situation, threw down my gun,
and was made a prisoner, and, as far as I know, the
only prisoner from our regiment. Our officers, being
confident that no prisoners had been taken, and, not
finding me among the wounded, concluded that I

was among the slain who had been hurriedly buried after dark.

"With others I was conveyed to a prison in the far South, where we remained for months without the least facility for correspondence. At last the Rebellion was crushed, and after a tedious journey we found ourselves at the military head-quarters in Petersburg, Va. I reported myself as well as I could, and learned that my name was among the slain. The officers gave me papers and a free conveyance to Washington. Here I was informed that my regiment had been mustered out some two weeks before. My statements were found to be correct. The pay-rolls were examined and I received my back pay for eight months. I might have sent a word home, but I felt a strong desire to surprise you in person. I went to New York. John and Jennie were almost crazy with delight, and you see they have not got over it yet. For this bit of deception you must hold these New Yorkers responsible. Jennie insists, and that correctly, that I am her brother from the South. I am highly proud of such a sister. Is not this a grand day to come home on?"

"Our cup is full, and running over!" said the happy father. "The Lord has given us beauty for ashes and joy for mourning."

"We have met together on many a joyous occasion," said the pastor, "but this is the happiest day of my life."

Dinner was announced. Fred took the happy and blushing Katie to the table, and all were seated.

Rev. Mr. Powell asked a blessing suited to the occasion, and a merrier company was never seen at a Thanksgiving dinner.

It soon became known in the neighborhood that the gentleman seen at church, and said to be John's wife's brother, was Fred Brown in disguise. The news ran like wild-fire. Early in the afternoon, by special invitation, David Brainard and his wife had the pleasure of grasping the hand of the returned soldier. In the evening the house was grandly illuminated, and the band from the neighboring village, accompanied by hundreds, assembled in front of the mansion and made the air vocal with shouts and melody.

On the following Christmas morning, at the residence of the bride, Fred Brown and Katie Brainard were united in holy matrimony. Amid the good wishes of a hundred guests the happy pair left for Baltimore, where the bride had near relatives. On their return, at the earnest request of Mr. and Mrs. Brainard, Fred remained with them, and in time became the manager of the large farm. He is at present in the vigor of noble manhood, surrounded by a charming wife and lovely children. The mother delights to tell the younger ones the story of that wonderful Thanksgiving day when, twenty-five years ago, at their Grandpa Brown's, the company was thrown into raptures by the return from the South of *John's wife's brother.*

THE CONSPIRACY.

A STORY OF THE MEDES AND PERSIANS.

CHAPTER I.

AN AGED PRIME MINISTER.

ON that fatal night of Belshazzar's impious feast, when the God of Israel was blasphemed by a wicked sovereign in the presence of a thousand of his lords, and when high and low officials were engaged in drunken revelry, the legions of the Persian prince on the bed of the drained Euphrates found their way into the great metropolis of Chaldea. On that night Belshazzar was slain, and with him, as such, passed away the Assyrian Empire.

When Cyrus had sufficiently regulated his affairs at Babylon he took a journey to Persia. On his way thither he went through Media to visit his uncle, King Darius. After a brief stay in Persia he returned to Babylon in company with his uncle, where together they formed a scheme of government for the whole empire.

The fame of Daniel, as one who had served under so many kings, was extensive. And since the night of the fatal feast, when he explained to the frightened potentate the mysterious handwriting on the wall, he was held in greater reverence than ever.

"This Daniel," said Cyrus to Darius the Mede, "was brought from the land of Judah, a royal captive, about the commencement of Nebuchadnezzar's reign. He was soon elevated to posts of honor which he filled with wonderful skill and wisdom; and of all the persons within my knowledge I consider this Hebrew sage by far the safest man to appoint as chief president."

"My brother's son speaketh wisely," answered Darius. "But why may we not have a short interview with this wonderful man?"

"Nothing would please me better," said the prince. "I will have him here without delay."

The ex-minister soon made his appearance. The interview was long. At last the king asked:

"Is Daniel willing to serve the king in this capacity, and thus shed honor upon the united empire of the Medes and Persians?"

"For the short period I may tarry among mortals my life will be consecrated to your service."

"Then, Daniel," said the king, "by our united power and authority thou art appointed chief of the presidents. We consider well thine age, and give thee full liberty to procure assistance. But let the oversight be purely thine. Thou art now released, and may the gods prosper thee."

One year had passed away, and closeted together were Ingron and Fragon, the two presidents under Daniel.

"It ill becometh the wisdom of the king to place over our heads this exacting old Hebrew," said Ingron. "The time for action has arrived. He must be removed. But why come not the princes?"

The door opened and four persons walked into the apartment.

"Now we are ready," continued Ingron. "We might have brought together more of the princes, but we have made a wise selection. What availeth to us the dignity of our office, as long as we must move at the bidding of this old man, petted and spoiled at the tables of the kings of Chaldea? To this we can no longer submit. He must be removed from office. In this movement are ye ready to assist your superiors?"

"Ready, O most excellent Ingron!" was the united response of the four princes.

"But we must have a cause of complaint," said Bimrack.

"True," said President Fragon, "and a cause must be found. For this very purpose have we admitted you into our secret council."

The interview was long and earnest. Many methods were considered, and schemes introduced worthy of their depraved authors.

"When and where shall be the place of our next meeting?" asked Bimrack.

"In one week let us meet at the garden of the castle, where the air will be balmy and the heat more moderate," was the reply. "There we shall not be interrupted, as we have been repeatedly at this time.

In order to be secure we shall enter the garden at a late hour of the night." Further arrangements were made and the company separated.

The day following this interview the tall bending form of Fragon was seen hastening toward the office ôf the Hebrew premier. He knocked, and was admitted with due respect.

" And is my friend, the worthy first president, to be seen this morning?"

" My worthy master is in another apartment," answered a youth in attendance.

" I wish to be shown into his presence."

The young man led the way, and Fragon, with a countenance clothed in smiles and a heart overflowing with malice, was conducted into the presence of Daniel.

" I had the impression that my lord, the president, was alone," said Fragon, " and I ask his forgiveness for this interruption."

" Thou art welcome at all times," said the first president. " This is Apgomer, an old friend and a companion of my youthful days."

" And one of thine own nation?" asked Fragon.

" Nay, my friend is a native Chaldean, as were his parents before him," was the answer.

" Then together ye have witnessed the glory and power of the kings of Babylon," said Fragon. " Upon the whole, have we not reason to pronounce Nebuchadnezzar the greatest and most illustrious of all kings?"

" I think this is true as far as the kings of Chaldea are concerned," said Daniel. " Of other kings

I am not prepared to speak. If my worthy friend, Fragon, is ready to pronounce the kings of Media and Persia inferior to the king of Babylon he is at liberty to do so."

" Nay, may the gods forbid that I should cherish such a thought!" said Fragon, somewhat alarmed.

" It was under Nebuchadnezzar that our temple in Jerusalem was destroyed and our people led into captivity," said Daniel. "I received much kindness at his hands, but I was not blind to his many faults."

" Thou speakest of thy captive countrymen," said Fragon. "I fear that many of them are in needy circumstances. This ought not to be. Gold and silver in rich abundance flow into our treasuries. Why not, therefore, direct a certain yearly sum for the special benefit of this worthy people?"

" I am not aware that as a class they are in needy circumstances," was the reply. "There may be many individual cases of want, and, as far as they come to my knowledge, I am not slow to relieve them from my own private means. Such a step as thou recommendest can never meet my approbation unless first proposed by the king."

" I fear our excellent first president is over-cautious," said Fragon. "But this is a matter I would not urge. My chief object to-day is to ask another favor. We have heard so much of the superior style of Chaldean book-keeping, and in order to learn and adopt your system we have ventured, after hesitating long, to ask permission to look over some of thy office-books. We shall retain them but for a short time."

"The books are at thy disposal," said Daniel, "and thou mayest return them at thy convenience."

"Thou art ever kind and obliging," said Fragon. "May the gods be the sure support of our most excellent first president;" and the conspirator left.

"May the gods curse him!" muttered the foiled Fragon, when he had reached the street. "The fortress is strong, but it *shall* be taken!"

"What thinketh my good friend Apgomer of President Fragon?" asked Daniel, with a smile.

"His words were kind," was the answer; "but I am not so well convinced of his sincerity."

"Apgomer," said Daniel, "that man is my deadly enemy. Every word he said was conceived in malice. First, he endeavored to have me speak of Nebuchadnezzar as superior to the kings of Media and Persia. He then with lying hypocrisy proposed that I should take the nation's money and give it to the Hebrews; and under a pretense of adopting a new mode of book-keeping they ask for the parchments in the hope of finding mistakes."

"O, the depravity of their hearts!" cried his aged friend. "But their search will be vain."

The night was calm and beautiful. The bright, full orb poured its silvery rays on the bosom of the deep-flowing Euphrates. The garden had been thronged with thousands of merry hearts who had gone thither to enjoy the grandeur of the moonlight scenes. But the hours had quickly fled, and the moonbeams now fell on the perfect stillness of the extensive inclosure.

The faithful keeper was about to close the massive doors, when six men stood before him and demanded admittance.

"At this late hour ye cannot be admitted!" was the stern reply. "In harmony with our rules the people have all departed. Return to your lodgings at once."

"Thou art a brave fellow, and an honor to thy post," answered Ingron. "But look thou here! Thou standest in the presence of two of the chief presidents and four of the princes of the province. Gaze on these stars!"

"I humbly beg the forgiveness of my lords, the presidents!" cried the keeper. "I had no—"

"Thou art a worthy keeper," interrupted Fragon. "The night is sultry, and we wish for an hour to enjoy the loveliness of the scene." And the six entered the garden.

The conference was long and the conspirators desperate and determined. But with all their ingenuity and depth of malice they could find no way by which to bring about their cruel design. The books had been examined, and no mistakes could be found. They were about to give up in despair, for that night, when Bimrack said:

"I know of but one measure with which we can ensnare the old Hebrew. It must be something concerning the law of his God. Let us form a decree, and prevail upon the king to sign it, that no person within the province of Babylon shall offer any prayer to any god but to the king alone for the space of thirty days, and that in case of a violation the offender shall be thrown into the lions' den. This puts all on an equal footing, and it will shield us from suspicion. It pours homage at the feet of Darius. Let us come upon him suddenly. It will flatter his vanity and he will sign the writing. There is no human power that can keep the old foreigner from the worship of his God. We must expect to meet some difficulties. The king must be deceived. We must unitedly affirm that this movement has the sanction of the first president. He will deny it. But the positive testimony of six men will outweigh his denial."

With this the company was in ecstasy, and Bimrack was highly complimented for the ingenuity of his scheme. They renewed their oath of fidelity to each other and were ready for their departure.

"Hark!" said Scramo. "Heard ye not that voice? I fear that we are not alone in this garden!"

"We heard no voice," was the reply; "it is only thy imagination. What did the voice resemble?"

" It resembled a human groan," was the reply.

A search was made, but too late. A door gently opened on the garden-wall and a venerable Chaldean was safely lodged in his little chamber.

The work of shaping this law and giving reasons for its enactment was given to Scramo. They agreed to meet the next night, at the residence of Ingron, to complete the arrangements, and they left the garden of the castle.

The next morning at an early hour Apgomer sought his friend Daniel, and revealed to him all the wicked plottings to which he had secretly listened on the night before.

15

"Let them proceed in their scheme of wickedness," said the holy man. "The God in whom I trust shall vindicate the honor of his own law. I could easily frustrate all their malicious designs. But the cause of Jehovah shall gather more strength from a display of his power in preserving his servant from harm. The life of Daniel will be as safe in the lions' den as in the midst of his friends at home. Let not Apgomer be troubled, and let our knowledge of this plot be revealed to no one until the proper time."

------·------

CHAPTER II.

ROYALTY DECEIVED.

AGAIN the great city of Babylon was all excitement, and expectation was raised to its highest pitch. The long-expected day had at last arrived, and the grand entry of Darius, the Mede, was momentarily expected by an enthusiastic, curious throng. The new king was regarded by the Babylonians generally in a favorable light. Such had been the profligacy and tyranny of their late sovereign that any change was hailed with delight, and, moreover, the mildness of Darius toward them on a previous visit, when accompanied by Cyrus the Persian, had greatly won their regards. Thousands of the people had gone without the walls to meet him, and tens of thousands were seen thronging the public ground in the vicinity of the royal palace. The monarch's triumphant train appeared in the distance, the shining spears and bright armor of his guard glittering in the clear sunbeams, and soon, amid enthusiastic shouts, they passed in through the massive portals.

The king was not a man of strong moral worth and true decision of character. He was rather weak in mind, and easily flattered. Nevertheless he was a person of tender feelings, and cruelty was no part of his nature. He was greatly elated with the warm reception he received at the hands of the Babylonians, and now or never was the time for the foul conspirators to try their power. They soon entered the palace.

"Welcome into the presence of your sovereign!" said the king, in a very pleasant mood. "Let the full desires of your hearts be made known to the king, and with pleasure he will grant your every request."

"O king, live forever!" said Scramo. "Thou art a mighty ruler. Thy dominions are well-nigh unbounded. Thy rich possessions are found in every clime. The name of Darius falls on the ears of the kings of the earth, and they stand in awe. Now thou knowest, O king, that the provinces are well united, and may the gods forbid that they should be otherwise. There are a few, however, within this province who of late have given us reason to believe that they do not consider the commands of the king as absolute, and that in certain cases they may be disregarded without any danger. This is a poisonous plant that must be crushed in the bud. We have had this subject under our most serious consideration. We have thought over it with throbbing hearts. Some measure of a startling nature must be resorted to that will impress upon the minds of the inhabitants the matchless greatness of our new sovereign, and convince all that when he commands he must be obeyed. Therefore, O king, with thy supreme glory and the good of the nation at heart, thy servants, the three presidents and the princes, have enacted this law, and it is now presented to thee for thy royal signature and seal." And the parchment was handed to the king with a trembling hand.

After reading it the monarch said: "If in your superior wisdom ye have judged that this law is demanded I cannot see why I should refuse to give it countenance."

"The measure will be hailed with joy, O king, among all thy loyal subjects," said Fragon; "and let those who dare disobey suffer the consequence. From this day the name of King Darius will be a terror to evil doers, and if he has any enemies they will be put to shame."

"It is surely a peculiar enactment," said the king, as he took the pen in his hand. "I fail to see its strong points, but at this stage of my reign I am not prepared to oppose a measure that is the offspring of the combined wisdom of my realm. If my Persian nephew were present I would deem it advisable to have his opinion, but as he is off in the wars I cannot avail myself of that."

So the king's name was given to the fatal parchment and, moreover, it was sealed with the seal of the Medes and Persians.

" The thing is done," said Darius. " Is there any thing more ?"

" We will no more trespass on thy time, O king," said Bimrack ; " but will now return to our respective stations to carry out the pleasure of our illustrious sovereign."

The conspirators, with bounding hearts, made their way in haste to the residence of President Ingron, and swore to stand together in the malicious falsehood.

The next day the streets of Babylon rang with the proclamation of the new law. At first it was thought by many to be a mischievous hoax. But too soon it was known to be a reality.

Now, when Daniel knew that the writing was signed, he laid aside his parchments, closed his eyes for a moment in silent devotion, then rose and entered his little chamber where for so many years three times a day he had bowed before his God (a dear spot that to the aged premier!), slowly moved toward an open window, and with his face toward Jerusalem was soon engaged in humble prayer.

While thus engaged he heard a voice close by his side : " We beg pardon for this intrusion. We will not disturb our most excellent first president while he makes his petitions to his God."

The Hebrew turned his head to see the receding forms of the two presidents as they hastened to the street below, and so he continued his supplications to the God of his fathers.

Again the conspirators were seen in the presence of the sovereign. " It is our painful duty, O king," said the speaker, "to inform thee that Daniel, who is of the captivity of· Judah, regardeth not thee nor the law thou hast signed, but maketh his petition to his God three times a day."

"Daniel!" replied the king, "I know of no Daniel but my worthy first president, whom ye say assisted in making the law."

"This same Daniel, O king, is the guilty one," said Fragon.

"What!" cried the king, rising suddenly; "Daniel, noted for his wisdom? Ye have been wrongly informed. Beware how ye thus accuse the best man in Babylon!"

"We are eye-witnesses of his guilt, O king," was the reply. "He daily makes his petitions to his God."

"*His God!*   Who can—but—if—say ye not that Daniel was concerned in framing this law?"

"He was, O king!"

"To me it seemeth strange!" said Darius. "If I find that in this matter I have been deceived I swear by the gods I will pour vengeance upon your guilty heads. I must see the first president and learn more of this matter ere I take another step."

"Thou hast nothing to learn from him, O king, contrary to the words of thy servants," said Fragon. "What would avail his denial against the direct testimony of six competent witnesses? The law is supreme and must be executed, or the kingdom of the Medes and Persians will be a by-word of derision."

"Ye may now depart," said the king. "I cannot

give my consent to—of this we can speak hereafter. To-morrow call on the king and ye shall then learn his pleasure." And the conspirators left with anything but pleasurable emotions, while Darius at once sent for Daniel.

"Thou standest before the king, O Daniel, accused of violating a law, chiefly of thine own making, by offering daily petitions to thy God. What meaneth all this?"

"I readily see that the king has been greatly deceived in this matter," said the premier. "Thy servant had nothing to do in framing a law repulsive to his soul and an insult to his God. This enactment came from mine enemies for the purpose of my overthrow. For over four-score years I have offered prayers to my God. When a little lad in the land of Judah I was taught by a beloved mother to lisp the name of Jehovah. From that time to this, O king, at morning, noon, and eventide, I have regularly offered my petitions. And is Daniel to be frightened from his duty now in his old age? Nay, O king! Sooner would I die a thousand deaths than prove a traitor to the God of my fathers."

"Daniel!" cried the king, "I will cut these lying wretches to pieces. If thou sayest, this very hour the words shall go forth."

"Nay, O king!" was the reply. "The decree has gone forth. Let the law have its course, and be assured that not a hair of thy servant's head shall be injured. No weapon formed against me shall prosper. That same God who preserved alive the three companions of my youth in the midst of a burning, fiery furnace can easily tame the lions and make them as harmless as the lambs of the flock."

The king was affected even to tears, and said, "This experiment must not take place. I know the writing is signed. My heart is sad! My soul is sick. But vengeance will come in due time! Daniel, thou mayest now depart."

"When the proper hour arrives the king shall learn from other lips than mine the deep iniquity of these foul conspirators. Let Jehovah use his own measures for the vindication of his own law." And the first president left the royal presence.

On that night Darius the Mede laid his head on his pillow with the full purpose of delivering Daniel.

Early on the morrow the conspirators in force appeared again before the king.

"Ye are punctual," said the monarch, with a meaning glance. "Since ye left me yesterday I have had a long interview with the first president, and from his venerable lips I learned that he had no voice in framing this law that he has violated. Now, notwithstanding your testimonies, which, in point of law must outweigh the declaration of one man, I freely declare to you my conviction that ye are a band of unprincipled liars, fully bent on the destruction of this Daniel."

At this plain royal truth the conspirators turned pale. But Fragon, quickly recovering his self-possession, replied:

"Then my lord the king can better believe a man that defies his power, by boasting of his determination to violate this decree at least three times a day, than he can his faithful servants who honor his laws and who desire to bring the guilty to punishment. Let not the king be deceived by the smooth tongue of this old Israelite, who, by the eloquence of his lips, can give to truth the color of falsehood and to deception the appearance of sincerity. Remember, O king, that the decree has gone forth and that it cannot be recalled. It is well understood in the city that the first president sets thy power at defiance, and thy decision is watched for by tens of thousands, and if this Daniel escapes punishment we may as well burn up our statute-books. The question now to be settled is not, How came this law to be enacted? but, seeing that it is enacted, Will the king of the Medes and Persians put it in force? Shall it be told in the streets of this proud city that the king has changed his mind, and is sorry for what he has done, because one of his favorites has violated the law?"

The interview was long and severe, and all the weight of their hellish ingenuity was brought to bear on the mind of the king. They failed to convince him that Daniel's words were false; yet partly from a false view of consistency, but chiefly from the advice of the first president, he gave his signature to the death-warrant of the aged premier.

The news soon spread through all Babylon, and the hour of the prophet's doom was well understood. No man in the city was better known or more loved than was the former prime minister of

Nebuchadnezzar. The poor and needy had found ready relief at his open door. The little children, even, claimed the aged man as their particular friend. The mothers broke out in loud weeping, and the universal sympathy was with the condemned.

———◆———

CHAPTER III.

RETRIBUTION.

THE day arrived, and in the vicinity of the first president's residence stood groups of men and women with sad countenances busily engaged in low conversation. These gatherings gradually increased into one solid mass. It was a solemn throng. The stillness was broken by the appearance of several platoons of soldiers, who formed a square in front of the dwelling. The door at last opened and two uniformed officers marched out. Next appeared the sheriff, with the aged prisoner leaning on his arm.

The procession was soon on its way toward the dreadful spot, while the weeping of hundreds broke on the air. They speedily reached the end of their journey, where thousands had already gathered in order to take a last sad look at their distinguished fellow-citizen.

Daniel ascended some steps near by, and by the permission of the king, who was present, proceeded in a few words to address the vast throng :

"Babylonians! Here in the presence of the God of my fathers, whom I worship, in the presence of my king, whom I respect, in the presence of this throng, whose tears flow for my sorrow, and in the presence of my accusers, who thirst for my blood, I solemnly declare that, as first president of the kingdom, I never was consulted in regard to the making of this law that is about to consign your aged servant to the lions. In honor to my king, who now laments the sad fate of his unworthy servant, let me testify that, in order to persuade him to sign a decree which had never entered his heart, the most malicious falsehoods were poured into his ears by those whose only object was the overthrow of Daniel. For violating this law I ask no forgiveness. Babylonians, I say no more. Accept my thanks for your tears. May Jehovah grant you great prosperity when your aged friend shall have passed away!"

Then turning to those whose painful duty it was to lead him to the den he smilingly said:

"Now I am ready; conduct me thither."

The prisoner was seized by strong hands and consigned to his fate, while the throng dispersed in sorrowful silence.

How sad was that night for royalty! Filled with remorse for having signed the fatal decree the king passed the night in agony. With a heavy heart and a throbbing brow he paced the length of his royal bed-chamber, and thus did he converse in his wretched seclusion:

"How he justified the king almost with his last

sentence! Why did I sign that silly and cruel decree, by which the brightest jewel of my kingdom is forever lost? How the multitude sympathized with the noble prisoner! How beloved in their estimation was the aged Daniel! What think they by this time of *my* prudence and wisdom? Will his God indeed deliver him? Is he not already torn by the hungry lions? If he is not, no thanks to me. Will not the people inwardly curse me? What will my nephew, Cyrus, think of my power of discernment?"

He threw himself upon his couch in the hope of drowning his mental agony in slumber; but the precious boon was not granted. He tossed about on his downy bed the very picture of wretchedness. After a long while he fell into a doze and thought himself at the den of lions gazing on the bleeding, mangled form of the first president. Terror-struck he leaped from his couch and found himself in his bedchamber. Another long soliloquy followed. Again he strove to find repose in sleep, but no sooner were his eyes closed than the imaginary roaring of lions would startle and terrify the wretched potentate.

Let us for a while leave the unhappy monarch and take a view of the hero of the lions' den. At first he calmly walked to and fro, then he fell upon his knees, and with uplifted eyes offered prayer to the God of heaven. A number of young lions, quite unused to such a sight, looked on in silent wonder. They then ran together to the other end of the den, where the old lion of all, the "lord of the manor," and his aged companion, the old lioness, the mistress of the establishment, were enjoying a comfortable sleep. A roar from one of the youngsters served to awake the aged couple. Another young fellow put his head close to that of his sire. I am of the opinion from what followed that the young chap told the old folks of something wonderful to be seen at the other end of the den.

The old lion arose and slowly led the way. Close by his heels followed the old lioness. Next in order came the rest of the family. They soon arrived in sight of the strange visitor. The leader paused for a moment, but made up his mind that there was nothing to fear. Daniel reached out his hand and spoke. So with eyes half closed the old lion slowly came up to the prophet and fondly licked his hand. After having conquered his embarrassment he uttered a low growl and looked toward the rest of the company as much as to say, " Come this way; don't be afraid, the gentleman will not hurt you." They slowly and silently gathered around the man of God, and each one appeared to be particularly pleased to be permitted in some way to come in contact with his person. And when the darkness of night gathered around them the old lion answered for his soft pillow, the old lioness lay at his feet, the young lions stretched themselves on either side to keep him warm, and soon the prophet of Jehovah was fast asleep.

Early the next morning the king ordered his chariot, and with a number of his lords he was soon on his way toward the den of lions. He also sent word for Daniel's accusers to be present. The royal

chariot, as it moved through the principal thorough-
fares of the metropolis, attracted much notice.   Its
destination was soon understood.   And as there was
a faint hope in the minds of thousands that the God
of Daniel would interpose they were early at the
den.

The monarch in trembling accents ordered the
heavy door to be opened.   This was quickly done.
Then in a tone of lamentation he cried with a loud
voice, "O Daniel, servant of the Most High, is
thy God whom thou servest able to deliver thee
from the lions?"

O, the breathless silence which followed ! A thousand hearts trembled with deep emotion.   But presently a voice as clear as a lute and as sweet as an
angel's harp ascended from the depth and fell upon
the ears of the throng :

"O—king—live—forever!"

It was enough ! Gladsome shouts broke forth from
a thousand tongues.   The sorrow was turned to joy,
and the name of the God of Daniel was greatly
praised.

In a few moments the Hebrew sage stood again
before the rejoicing throng.

An aged man was seen at this moment urging his
way through the crowd as if endeavoring to find
admittance into the presence of the king. His venerable appearance and pleasant countenance served
to make him room.   The throng parted, and soon
he was by the side of Daniel, who stood near the
king.

"This is my good friend Apgomer, O king," said

Daniel, "one of the companions of my early days. He hath words to communicate to the king in the presence of this throng, that will give thee to understand clearly that this law was prepared on purpose to ensnare thy servant."

"Let Fragon and Ingron, with the four princes, stand in this direction!" said the king, with an angry expression of countenance.

The conspirators with pale faces obeyed.

"Now, Daniel," said the king, "thy friend may give his testimony in a clear and loud voice."

"O king, live forever!" began Apgomer. "These six men who now stand before thee are wicked and deceitful. With lying words did they go to the king. I listened to their midnight plotting. On the night of the fourth day of the eighth month, at the castle garden, these men did meet. I stood behind their bower. Their words of malice fell on my ears. There the law was first spoken of, and for the very purpose of destroying the first president."

"Believe not this man, O king!" said the pale and trembling Fragon. "He prepareth lying words before thee!"

At this moment a young man whose countenance denoted passion rushed to the side of Apgomer, and without an apology began:

"Let not Apgomer be called a liar! As well may the gods lie! Thy servant, O king, is the keeper of the garden. Apgomer on that night was an inmate of my house, which house is within the garden-walls. Those six men at a late hour demanded admission. Not knowing who they were I ordered them away. They gave me to understand that I stood in the presence of the two presidents and four princes. They were admitted and did not leave until after midnight. I have no knowledge of their errand. But be assured, O king, that Apgomer never uttered a falsehood!"

"It is enough! It is enough!" cried the king. " Seize the guilty wretches! Let the cowardly liars meet the doom they had prepared for my servant Daniel! Up, and throw them to the lions!"

No sooner were the words spoken than a score of willing hands seized the trembling forms of the conspirators, and amid the curses of an indignant throng they were thrown into the depth of the den, to meet a far different fate from that of the man of God.

Daniel was taken into the royal chariot, seated by the side of the sovereign, and the grand train moved forward amid the triumphant shouts of delighted thousands.

SUNNY MEMORIES OF CONFERENCE CHUMS.

CHAPTER I.

WE DWELL TOGETHER IN UNITY.

IT was in the summer of 185—. The Conference met at one of our flourishing villages in northern New York. I always looked forward to these seasons with pleasant and even excitable anticipations. I was then, if not now, a *one-horse* preacher serving a *one-horse* charge. But wait a moment, dear reader. Before we proceed an inch further permit me to explain what I mean by the term one-horse. If I don't I fear that you will form a wrong opinion as to the nature of that " charge," and also in regard to the value I now place upon my then preaching abilities. I do not use the term in its *slang* meaning; and if you thought that I intended to speak lightly either of my own talents or the good people I then served you were grandly mistaken. I simply meant that at that time, and, indeed, at almost all other times, I served charges that had a number of preaching appointments, and were of an importance that demanded, in addition to the regular minister sent from Conference, an "assistant" in the shape of an itinerant *horse.* Now

16

you understand' why I called myself a one-horse preacher and the circuit a one-horse charge. I am sorry that those indispensable assistants were not always provided for by the brethren in the " allowance ;" but I am happy to say that mine were never permitted to suffer. I could easily write creditable memorials of these faithful helpers which would be interesting to the reader, and especially to my fellow one-horse brethren. But I must pass along. If John Wesley's views in regard to certain passages in the eighth chapter of the Epistle to the Romans are correct, then in the resurrection of the brutes there will be seen a glorious array of itinerant Methodist horses anointed with the oil of gladness above their fellows, while their joyful neighing shall echo on the sides of celestial mountains.

Yes, I know I am moving rather slowly, as far as the story is concerned. It is a way we get into, and it is almost impossible for us ministers to break loose from our old ways. This shows the great importance of forming good and correct habits while we are young. But I am gliding slowly and imperceptibly into my subject.

On arriving at the seat of the Conference I was directed by the preacher in charge to the residence of Mr. W., a prominent citizen of the village, where, as he said, I would find a number of congenial spirits. It so proved. I was most cordially received by the family, and to my great joy I found that I was to share the society of four other ministers whom I greatly admired and loved. We had often met before, and soon our hearts were knit together in sweet Christian fellowship.   I shall always look back to those few days in their social relation as forming one of the happiest periods in my earthly pilgrimage; and I am very certain that this is the experience of those four brethren, for we have often spoken of it in our subsequent meetings; and many a good, hearty, healthy Methodist laugh we have had over the remembrance of that most delightful week.   Up stairs, aside from several commodious lodging-rooms, we had a large sitting-room richly furnished, where we could meet at any time to enjoy each other's society.   Here we would often discuss points of interest connected with the Conference; but our greatest enjoyment flowed from the relating of incidents connected with our itinerant lives.   These were numerous, and all of them worthy to be preserved and remembered.   I have a few of them, and these were taken down at the time, or soon after, for the purpose, I presume, of preparing them for the press; but they were lost for years, and the other day, in looking over a pile of old manuscript, I came across the following, which will give the reader some idea of our mutual entertainment.   I see they are numbered, and bear such headings as at that time impressed my mind.   Number 1 is headed,

"How I Happened to get into a ' First-class Station.'"

"I don't say, mind you," said Brother L., "but that as a rule you will find ' first-class preachers' on ' first-class stations,' but there are very many exceptions, and it is not always safe to judge of a minister's real strength by the appointments he fills. These things in multitudes of instances have turned upon a mere *accident*. In the great mind of Deity it may not bear that construction, but as things go among us that is just the word. Here *I* am. It is well known to you that for fourteen years I continually served charges that were any thing but popular, and that for the last ten years I have been sent to some of the strongest stations in the Conference. Do you suppose from this that it took place from any improvement or change in *me?* Nothing of the kind. I tell you again, in my case it was purely accidental. You may object to my using that word. I don't quite like it myself, and yet it is as good as any I can think of just now. I don't know that I can better explain this than by calling your attention to my own history and experience.

"I had served two years at Logtown, to the fair satisfaction of the brethren and the members of my congregation, and had gone to Conference under the tearful benediction of many dear friends. I cheerfully looked forward for another charge of moderate pretensions. I had given up all idea of ever serving a good station, because I had for so many years served inferior charges, and I knew that no first-class appointment would be likely to ask for a person who had always traveled *circuits*. When they come to a deadlock in the cabinet, you know, the Bishop comes to the rescue, settles the point, and says to the astonished presiding elders,

'What I have written, I have written.' So it was at this time. Until about one hour before the meeting of the last session of the Conference my name had stood for Pacific Charge, with which I was well satisfied. While the Bishop and the elders were just finishing up, a line was received from B—— Station, signed by a brother whose will it was not healthy to oppose, saying that Brother F. must not be sent to B——, that he could not be received, and that the thing was exceedingly unfortunate. What was to be done? ' Brethren,' said the Bishop, ' I will make short work of this. Brother L. will go to B——, and Brother F. will go to Pacific.' 'Bishop!' cried the presiding elder in whose district was B——. (so I was informed), ' that will not answer ! B—— is a " first-class station." Brother L. is a good man and a fair preacher, but he is not of that class that will answer for B——.' ' Time will show,' answered the Bishop as he closed his portfolio and started for the Conference-room. There were many astonished countenances when my name was read out for B——; and no one was more astonished than myself.

" With much fear and trembling, after having been in the Conference for fourteen years, I started for my first station, and that one of the best. Contrary to my expectations, the brethren gave me a cordial welcome. On my first Sabbath I had great liberty, and at once I found favor in the sight of the people. In addition to a liberal salary they gave me a magnificent donation, and at the close of the year they unitedly asked for my return. I did return, and my second year was also a success. From that time to this I have filled excellent stations, and you would be astonished to see the invitations I have had from official members of ' first-class appointments,' brethren who would have scorned the idea a few years ago. But am I a better preacher than I was when I served Logtown, Smoky Hollow, Hard Scrabble, Snake Hill, and Pumpkinville? Of course not. I never hear the term ' first-class station' without smiling, and I invariably think of the simple accident that sent your unworthy brother to be a pastor of such a church.''

Brother L., being the only "first-class station" preacher in the company, the rest of us being "one-horse," and naturally cherishing—well—a pretty fair opinion of our respective abilities, we were greatly pleased with his remarks, knowing that in him we had a friend whose sympathy and fellow-feeling we might safely depend upon.

Number 2 is headed,

" JACK AND POPPET.''

" I am comparatively young among you Americans,'' said Brother M., who was a genial Welshman. " In my own experience in this country there have been no incidents that would add any interest to this occasion, and so you will please excuse me.''

" No excuse, Brother M.,'' said Brother L. " Give us something from Wales, of any sort that you may deem best ;'' and in this he was joined by the others.

"Well," said Brother M., "I will give you a specimen of the manner in which the late Rev. Mr. Richard of Abergwaen used to administer reproof, when needed, at church meetings. He always made use of figures, and his favorite was the horse.

" At one time a certain society was much grieved with one of its official members, who insisted on having his own way in regard to every church measure, and who, if it was not granted, would show bad temper and utterly refuse to co-operate with his brethren. In every thing he would be a leader or nothing. He was a man of ability and means, and when all would submit to his dictation he would be liberal. But he was so selfish and obstinate that it was very hard to get along with him. Mr. Richard was aware of this, and at one of their church meetings, when this obstinate man was present, among other remarks he brought in his favorite figure in this fashion :

"' Yes, Jack is a good horse, but not as good as Poppet. Poppet is easily managed and willing to work at any time and at any place. Jack is a strong, powerful horse ; but sometimes he is obstinate and ugly, and often acts the worst when he is most needed. Jack can draw splendidly, you understand, but he must have his own way or he will not draw a pound. Jack must be the leader or nothing. Put him between the thills, or in the middle, and he will not move an inch. Coaxing and threatening will be useless. But let him be the foremost horse, and he will show wonderful energy. Sometimes if he doesn't get his own way he will fall into a violent fit of kicking, to the great danger of all who are near him. You will understand that Jack in many respects is a good horse, but he has these tricks. If these were taken out of him he would be a valuable beast, but it is hard to take a trick out of an old horse. He is not like Poppet. Poppet is ever willing and ready. He is not as strong as Jack, but is perfectly reliable. He will work faithfully at all times and in any sphere. You may put him in the shaft, or in the middle, or foremost, and he will pull steadily. You may put sacks of grain on his back to carry to the mill, and he will move along most willingly. Two or three of the children may get on his back at once, and with the greatest pleasure he will take them to school. Ah, every body admires Poppet ! As for Jack, although a good horse in his way, he is not to be trusted. It is not best to venture to put a sack on *his* back to go to mill, nor the children to carry to school. It would be a very dangerous experiment. Better far to depend on Poppet.'

" And in this way, without referring to names nor directly to individuals, Mr. Richard would administer reproof that almost always produced a favorable effect. I have already found that in America, as well as Wales, we have some Jacks ; but, thank Heaven, compared with our noble Poppets they are very few."

Number 3 is headed,

"An Affecting Incident."

" Yes," said Brother S., with that deep solemnity which was his on peculiar occasions, "We are to 'weep with those that weep.' Every Methodist minister has mingled in scenes of bereavement, to administer comfort to the disconsolate. It was in the early part of my ministry, and at the commencement of the conference year on a new charge. On a certain Tuesday, after a hard morning's study, I thought I would devote a part of the afternoon to visiting my parishioners and forming their acquaintance. In my congregation on the Sabbath previous I had noticed a lady in dark habiliments which I naturally took as an evidence of bereavement, especially as the expression of her countenance suggested deep inward sorrow. I first called at the house of Brother Stebbins, who was one of my stewards. Sister Stebbins received me cordially. She was ready and fluent in her conversation, and mingled her sentences with such a degree of wit and pleasantry as to make me feel perfectly at home. If she had a fault at all it was an over-readiness to indulge too freely in hilarity.

" ' Sister Stebbins,' I said, ' I noticed in the congregation on the Sabbath, in the third seat from the altar, in the middle pews, a lady in black. She seemed to be in deep grief. Who was she, and where does she live ?'

" ' O,' answered Sister Stebbins, ' that was Sister Thomas. She lives on this street, the third house below ; on this side.'

" ' I should judge from her sorrowful appearance,' said I, ' that she has lately passed through scenes of bereavement.'

" I was pained at her reply, which seemed to me

unsympathetic and trifling; and so, with as much earnestness in my manner as would become a stranger, I kindly replied :

"'When you meet with a like bereavement you will judge poor Sister Thomas with more tenderness.'

"Sister S. simply answered, 'Pardon me, Brother S., but I will assure you I am not a hard-hearted woman;' and the subject was dropped.

" I parted with Sister S. and slowly walked toward the mansion of Sister Thomas. She answered my call in person, remarking,

"'Brother S., I am glad to see you. I knew you would call. My mind was just resting on some consolatory passages in your Sabbath sermon.'

"'I am thankful,' said I, 'that any thing in my humble discourse has served to cheer you in the day of adversity.'

"'Thank you,' she replied, in a tremulous voice; 'of course you have heard of it. Some think I go too far; but he was the idol of my heart. If not with me in the street he was the first to welcome me home. I miss him at morning, noon, and night.'

"'And how old was this dear object of your affection?' I asked.

"'He had just completed his fifth year,' was the reply.

"'And what was the nature of his sickness?' I inquired, brushing away a tear.

"'At first it was a cold,' she said, 'but it ended in a fever. He knew me to the very last. I was not aware that he was so near going. I knelt by his little bed, but he heeded me not. ' Fido !' said I, '*dear* Fido, don't you know me?' He opened his eyes, *gently wagged his tail* and died!'

" Fortunately my hat was within easy reach and the door was not closed. The next moment the new parson was found making rapid strides toward the parsonage, and I know that I heard the voice of Sister Stebbins in laughter as I passed her door. From that day I have had but little taste for *dog*-matic theology."

Of course Brother S. preserved a grave countenance throughout, and even at the close, when the rest of us roared, he looked more solemn than ever. If we thought that he had given us an overdrawn picture we really pardoned him, as he had given so telling a burlesque ŏn a weak form of sentimentality.

Number 4 is headed,

THE SOOTHING EFFECTS OF BREAD AND MILK POULTICE.

"You see," said Brother J., " in those days I was bashful and modest. Well, you may laugh as much as you please. I suppose you think that those are rather doubtful terms when applied to me, but it is true. Perhaps you did not know me then. Years have worked a great change. Since that time I have mingled much in society, and I am not as I used to be. I tell you again, brethren, without the least joking, that there was a time when I was both bashful and modest.

"It was at a ministerial association in O———. I was sent to 'chum it' with my dear Brother R., at a certain house not far from the church. We took an early supper, and having in another place eaten a late dinner I scarcely took any thing for tea. That evening I preached, there were lengthy exercises after the sermon, and the meeting closed at a late hour. In company with my good Brother R. I reached my lodging-place under the unmistakable impression that I was very hungry. I hoped that the good lady of the house would have asked, ' Brother J., you have been laboring hard, wouldn't you like a bit of something to eat ?' She certainly ought to have asked me, and my brief answer was all ready. But she didn't, and my hunger was momentarily growing more alarming. You see, at home I had been in the habit of having milk every night. *' Bad habit ?'* I don't believe a word of it. I have used it—well, from a *very* early period, and it agrees with me splendidly. But I am digressing. At that moment things looked dark, and a night of keen hunger stared me in the face. *' Why didn't I ask ?'* There ! now comes in the proof of my bashfulness. Ask ? No, indeed, and I fully made up my mind to suffer.

" ' Brother J.,' asked Brother R., ' What is the matter with you ?'

" ' O, nothing serious,' I replied, ' I am a little tired. The meeting, you know, was very lengthy.' And I looked toward my hostess, hoping that this would fetch her ; but it didn't.

" By the way, on the week previous Brother R.

had met with an accident by which his leg below
the knee was badly bruised, and at this time he was
quite lame and complained of pain.

"'And what do you do for it, Brother R.?' asked
the lady.

"'At night I poultice it thoroughly with bread
and milk,' answered Brother R., 'and if it will not
trouble you too much I will ask you to make me
some, and I will put it on when we get up stairs.'

"'Don't talk about trouble,' answered the little
woman, jumping up, 'I will have it ready in a little
while.'

"There, boys! Aye, then did I see that my re-
demption was drawing nigh. I could actually feel
the aspect of my countenance changing, while men-
tally I exultingly cried, 'I am saved! I am saved!'

"'In a case like this,' said Brother R., 'bread
and milk poultice is capital.'

"'There can be nothing better,' said I in an elevated tone, 'if it is only applied in sufficient quan-
tity.'

"'That's so,' said the lady, and I will make a
good lot.'

"And so she did, for I keenly watched the quan-
tity as well as the quality. It was all right—nice
white bread, pure milk, and a clean shining tin
basin, and, better than all, 'a good lot' of it.

"'Will you need any assistance, Brother R.?'
asked the lady.

"'Brother J. will lend a helping hand when we get
up stairs,' was the answer.

"'With the greatest pleasure,' I replied.

" After prayers we went to our chamber, Brother R. leading the way, bearing in his hand the sovereign remedy, while in eager expectation I followed on. When I revealed to my good friend the exact situation, and the fortunate way of escape, he fell into a fit of laughter. Well, he treated me with the utmost generosity. The poultice was divided on the most equitable terms. Our slumber was tranquil and peaceful. Brother R. kept the secret at least until after we left O——. Since that event I have increased faith in the soothing effects of bread and milk poultice."

Those dear chums are yet in the work doing vigorous service for the Master. A little humorous indulgence now and then when released from the severity of their labors does not in the least injure their spirituality. Laughter is a gift from the Lord. It may be abused, I know, like many other blessings; but in thousands of instances it is a healing balm for both body and mind. I know that at Conference as well as other places we are to watch over our spirits and retain, yea, increase our devotional feelings. But in order to do this must every thing in the shape of social mirth be banished? I do not thus understand Christianity nor the laws of our being. Let all act freely, in harmony with the disposition and temperament which God has given them, subject to the wholesome regulations of our holy Christianity. I will not find fault with my serious brother who hardly ever smiles. If that is the result of his natural disposition I suppose he cannot help it.   But I trust that he will have the good sense to know that his perpetual solemnity is no proof that he better answers the end of his creation than does his brother who obeys the promptings of his more jubilant nature and indulges in a good, hearty laugh.   Be it remembered that the wisest of men has said, " There is a time to laugh and a time to weep."   A Christian minister, I trust, will easily understand this, and act accordingly. He will not be very apt to weep at a Fourth of July celebration or laugh at a funeral.

"I TOOK YOU WITH GUILE."

I VENTURE to say that, in this year of grace, 1890, no portion of our world under the hallowed influence of our holy Christianity presents a more intelligent class of people, touching the fundamental doctrines of the Gospel, than does that small section of the British Isle known as the Principality of Wales. It is readily admitted that, as far as knowledge in the arts and sciences is concerned, they are far behind their English neighbors; but that in theology and in deep attachment for religious worship they excel. This state of things, however, is comparatively of a recent date. One hundred and twenty years ago gross darkness covered the people, and the masses in Wales were exceedingly ignorant touching the most common truths of the Christian religion. It is true that on Sabbath morning they had a brief service in the parish church, often conducted by unregenerated and immoral curates. Few attended these services, and less took any interest in them. The Lord's day was given to ungodly diversions, drinking, carousing, and often ending in fighting.

The wonderful awakening under the preaching of

Whitefield reached Wales, and in many localities the people by the hundreds, with tears of penitence, turned to the Lord. Several men of talent, clergymen of the Established Church, who had mourned for years over the desolation of Zion, joined in the movement, and finally, by the force of circumstances, identified themselves with the newly-formed Whitefield Methodist societies, and earnestly labored in the face of the most bitter persecution.

At that early day there arose from among the converts many men possessing strong natural talents, and, in the absence of regular clergymen, they were commissioned by the churches to go forth as lay preachers to call sinners to flee from the wrath to come.

Among these exhorters, whose hearts burned with love to God and with intense desire for the salvation of their fellow-men, was one Thomas Hughes. He had been a rough, swearing, drinking man. His education was limited, but he had a strong mind, a ready command of language, and a very fair knowledge of the Bible and its doctrines. His conversion was very clear. The thorough change was evident to all, and his unadorned ministry was highly acceptable to the common people.

In many places these preachers, lay and ordained, were persecuted most violently. Indeed, there were vicinities where they could not stand up to preach without endangering their lives. Such a spot was Towyn y fferi, on the shore, between Llandudno and Conway, in North Wales.

For a long time Thomas Hughes had felt a strong

17

spirit-drawing toward the wicked and desperate inhabitants of this place, who from Sabbath to Sabbath assembled by the hundreds on the shore to
engage in their unholy diversions. He had never
been there, but their daring ungodliness was well
known far and near. Hughes had a dear friend—a
confidential bosom friend—by the name of Morris
Jones. They were often together, and Jones generally accompanied Hughes to his appointments,
and often assisted in the preliminaries.

"Morris," said Hughes one day, "for weeks I
have been impressed that it is my duty to preach
Jesus to that ungodly throng at Towyn y fferi.
They are rushing toward hell, and there is no one
to plead with them."

"I understand," said Morris, "that there is a
gang there of forty roughs, headed by a fighting
bully by the name of Dick Morgan, that are pledged
to roughly handle any preacher that will dare come
among them and open his mouth."

"Morris," was the answer, "let us take them with
guile. I am determined to visit their play-ground
on some Sabbath day, and that soon, if God wills,
and preach to them ' Jesus Christ and him crucified.'
I have matured a plan in my own mind which I
think will succeed. I have prayed over it, and I
am pretty well convinced that, by God's help, we
can manage those roughs, and perhaps save them.
Morris, will you stand by me?"

"That I will, Tom," was the ready answer.
"Proceed in your own way, and may God bless
you!"

Word was sent to Towyn y fferi that in one week from the following Sabbath there would be preaching on the shore play-ground, but no mention was made of the preacher or where he would hail from. The roughs were delighted in view of their anticipated sport, and promised to themselves a day of rare enjoyment.

The day arrived and the ground was covered by hundreds. There were many among them who had come in hopes of hearing the Gospel preached. They felt no ill-will toward any preacher that desired to make the people better. They knew that Towyn bore a hard name, and they were sorry for it. There were many more who, although wild and ungodly, would not molest the man of God. But the majority were in sympathy with the gang. They did not intend to permit any dissenting ranters to interfere with their Sunday sports, and it gave them pleasure to know that the expected preacher would be roughly handled.

Our two friends, Hughes and Jones, were early on the ground. They mingled freely with the gang and laid themselves down on the grass. There was nothing in their exterior that in the least resembled clergymen, and no one took any particular notice of them.

Time was passing, The people were anxiously looking for the appearance of the preacher and getting somewhat uneasy.

After further waiting Dick Morgan said : " Boys, the shouter has not dared to show his sanctimonious Methodist face. His courage failed him. He has escaped a good shaking and a nice cold salt bath. But, confound the fellow, he has robbed us of our expected fun. He would have been here before this time if he was coming. So let us begin some other sport."

Here Hughes jumped up from his prostrate position and, in a manner quite unclerical, said:

"Well, my lads, as Morgan has said, there is no sign of a clergyman. I shouldn't wonder if the fellow heard we were going to give him a rough one. But don't let us be cheated out of preaching. I have come a long distance. Let one of you stand on that stone and give us a preach! Why not? [Great laughter.] Let one of us occupy the pulpit, and the rest will sing. I tell you, lads, it will be a grand play, especially on Sunday."

"Bravo!" cried the bully, with an oath. "Three cheers for the stranger! [Given with a will.] Ha, ha! Here is fun after all. Step on that stone and fire away, stranger!"

"I ought to have a book," said Hughes.

"Here is a book for you," said Morris Jones, "if you only promise to preach for us."

"Well," said Hughes, "if you will only be civil I'll try. Don't you laugh at me if I fail."

"I'll make them civil," said Morgan; "and if any one laughs at you or disturbs you in any manner I'll break his head with one of these stones."

Hughes then stood on the stone and said: "I believe that praying comes first, does it not?"

"Yes; pray," said Morgan, "and I will throw in an amen now and then to make it lively.

I declare, this is the strangest kind of performance I ever heard of! Somehow it doesn't look so funny to me as it did a minute ago. But hurry up and rush it through! Go on, stranger."

"Let us pray," said Hughes, with a countenance of indescribable solemnity. The prayer welled up from the depth of an honest heart earnestly longing for the salvation of those around him. The roughs listened to the prayer with great attention, and although, so far, they thought it was simply an imitation, they felt a solemnity creeping over them which they could not explain, and the bully did not see fit to produce the promised amens. The prayer closed, and it was loudly complimented by a great many. One cried out at the top of his voice:

"I'll bet a crown there is not a parson in North Wales that can beat that prayer!"

Mr. Hughes was just about to announce his text, when Morgan cried out, "Not quite so fast, stranger! Singing comes next."

"O yes," was the reply; "I had forgotten." He then gave out one verse:

> "Come, Holy Spirit, heavenly Dove,
> With all thy quickening powers."

Morris Jones started a familiar tune, in which many united. Mr. Hughes then called their attention to these words of St. Paul: "This is a faithful saying, and worthy of all acceptation, that Christ Jesus came into the world to save sinners; of whom I am chief." He first gave a very graphic account of the apostle's early history, how he gave countenance to the killing of Stephen and took charge of the garments of those who stoned him, and how after this he became a bitter persecutor of the infant Church, casting men and women into prison. Then he spoke of his wonderful conversion and his subsequent laborious life in the cause of God. The preacher, as he proceeded, felt an unusual degree of inspiration. He gathered spiritual power as he went on. The people looked upon him with awe and wonder as, with a tongue of fire, he spoke of the wonderful change produced in the human heart by the Gospel of Christ. Tears began to flow from the eyes of many, and before the sermon was half through the audience was under his complete control. When it was perfectly safe he gave them to understand that he was, indeed, the humble, unworthy servant of Christ, who had sent his appointment to Towyn y fferi, and that he had chosen that method in order to get a quiet hearing. Before closing he said: "Three years ago I was a poor miserable slave of the devil, a wicked, swearing, drinking wretch, fearing not God nor regarding man. What money I earned, the most of it went for drink, while my wife was broken-hearted and my children in rags. This was my condition when a most powerful revival of religion broke out in our village. I was persuaded to attend the meetings. I was led to see myself a guilty sinner against God. I fell on my knees and cried to God for mercy. After some days of weeping under a deep sense of guilt, God saw fit to pour the balm of his love into my wounded heart, and I was enabled to rejoice in hope of the glory of God. I was received into the Church, and since then, my friends, I have tried to live a Christian life. I became a sober, industrious man. My wife is now happy and cheerful and my children are well dressed. That is what the Gospel has done for poor Tom Hughes, and I am very anxious for others to feel its saving power. I thank you for your candid attention. I greatly desire the salvation of your souls. After the meeting closes you may treat me as you deem best. If Dick Morgan thinks that I deserve a shaking and a cold bath I will try to bear the ordeal with Christian patience. I hope, however, he will not find it necessary. Let us now pray."

The closing prayer was wonderfully affecting. The speaker pleaded with God in sentences the most pathetic, while scores in the assembly were strangely moved.

That rough gang was wonderfully tamed. The bully was the first one to give the preacher the friendly hand after he came down from his stone pulpit. With a moisture in his eyes he asked Mr. Hughes to come again, with the full assurance that he would receive a respectful treatment. He went again and again. A powerful revival followed his labors and a large number embraced religion. Among these was Dick Morgan, with many of his former gang. They became respectable members of society and pillars in the Church of Christ.

THE GREAT REVIVAL AT TONVILLE.

CHAPTER I.

FOUR MINISTERS.

NO, Tonville is not the name by which you can find it on the map. Story-writers are granted a very liberal privilege in this line, and it is not always that it is used with prudence. They often offend eyes and ears with outlandish names. Tonville is expressive in meaning and melodious in sound. The first part of the word has no reference to any kind or amount of weight. Two thousand pounds has nothing to do with it. In Webster's we find a little noun of three letters, with its signification, that will satisfy the reader as to the meaning of Tonville. It is now a flourishing village with a population of six thousand. At the time of our story of course it was not as large as it is to-day; but even then it was one of the most beautiful places of its size in the Empire State. Its citizens were proud of it, and claimed that their advantages were not inferior to those of the cities. They had a first-class academy, under the supervision of Professor Strong, a gradu-ate of Harvard; a musical conservatory, directed by Professor Peters, of Germany; an opera-house capable of seating fifteen hundred, and a dancing academy over which Professor Hopper presided. Many of Tonville's private residences were of a very superior order. Strangers visiting the village would linger long to admire their beautiful proportions. Flower-gardens abounded, which in their season bloomed like Eden. It had its extensive lawns, a square, and an ornamental park. It could boast of a very competent band, which on summer evenings sent forth sweet melody, on the wings of the gentle breezes, to delight the listening hundreds. Tonville had six splendid churches, four of which were considered orthodox. Two hotels of modern construction graced the village, the "Union" and the "American," where choice ales, wines, and liquors were dealt out with the most finished politeness at bar-rooms rendered doubly tempting by glittering splendor. From these drinking-rooms there were ready entrances into commodious billiard parlors, which were often thronged until late hours of the night. The village had also a number of elegant saloons doing thriving business. And, not to be outdone by larger places, it furnished a number of low groggeries, where those could be accommodated who were no longer smiled upon at the Union and American, and who were offensive to the young bloods at the fashionable saloons. Such, and very much more, was Tonville.

From an evangelical point of view, vital piety and genuine spirituality at this time in Tonville were very low. Even in the churches there were many that were "lovers of pleasure more than lovers of God."

Heaven's order had been seriously reversed. Instead of Christians by consecrated holy lives attracting the world toward Jesus, the world, with its multiform charms, was bringing church members to its own level. While in the prayer-meetings of the various churches a few faithful souls, with their beloved pastors, were struggling to keep up the spiritual interest of Zion, scores of their brethren and sisters at the same hours could be seen at parties, comic exhibitions, the theater, and the dance. Let it not be supposed that this state of things was owing to a lack of energy and spirituality on the part of the pastors. They were indeed men of God, who without fear declared all his counsel. But the worldliness of their communicants was more than a match for their best efforts. It is no wonder that they were measurably cast down, and often found "weeping between the porch and the altar."

One morning Rev. Thomas Alvord, of the Baptist Church, while in his study thinking over the desolation of Zion, came to the conclusion that something would have to be done; and under that impression he started for the Methodist parsonage to see the Rev. John Lloyd. He found him in a state of mind very much like his own. After a little conversation they walked together to consult with the Rev. Dr. Spicer, of the Presbyterian Church, in regard to Tonville's moral and religious dearth. They found the doctor's feelings in perfect harmony with their own, and he was much more than willing to enter into any measure which, under God, would wake up the churches from their spiritual lethargy.

" Let us ask Brother Latimer to come in and join us in this conversation," said Dr. Spicer.

"I would be delighted to have him with us," said Mr. Lloyd; " I regard him very highly. But as an Episcopal clergyman I fear that he will hardly be willing to unite with us."

" He may not feel free to join personally in the measures that we may propose,'' said Dr. Spicer, " but I am sure that we shall have his sympathy and prayers. He greatly laments the lack of spirituality among his own members, and will gladly welcome any movement that will bring the churches nearer to God. His house is close by, and I would be glad to have him invited.''

" By all means let us ask him,'' said Mr. Alvord; and Dr. Spicer started for the residence of Rev. William Latimer, the eloquent rector of St. Mark's Episcopal Church.

Mr. Latimer was a finished gentleman, a polished scholar, a fine pulpit orator, and withal a devoted Christian. Among his brethren he was known as what is termed " low church." He firmly believed that the form, liturgy, and manner of worship in the Episcopal Church were more in harmony with those of the apostolic age than any other form of church worship. Yet he was free to confess that all evangelical societies who worshiped the Father in spirit and in truth formed the one holy catholic Church of Christ on earth. His profound respect for the views and offices of his superiors moderated his utterances on these points in the pulpit. But in social conversation among his parishioners he would without hesitation speak of other ministers with great respect and acknowledge the validity of their ordination. This liberality had much displeased a few influential members of his congregation; but the majority of his flock were in harmony with his views, and he was very popular among the masses. At this time he had been the rector of St. Mark's for about two years.

Dr. Spicer soon returned, accompanied by Mr. Latimer, who was cordially received by the other two.

"Brother Latimer bids us God-speed," said Dr. Spicer.

"I am thankful for this mark of your confidence," said the rector. "I deeply sympathize with the object you have in view. For prudential reasons, however, I must be much out of sight. Proceed, brethren, and let me be a listener. I may have a word to say before we part."

After an earnest prayer, Brother Alvord, as the originator of the gathering, said that for a long time he had been greatly troubled in his mind in view of the low state of religion in his own church. A large number of his members never attended the weekly prayer-meeting, and on very trivial excuses neglected the public service on the Sabbath. They were prompt at all worldly gatherings, and some of them attended dances and theaters. They were not backward in those features of church work that required no particular devotion, but they would not deny themselves, take up the cross, and follow Christ. And while such was the moral condition of so many of the members of his church, what could he expect from an unbelieving world?

Brother Lloyd and Brother Spicer followed much in the same strain. The question was asked, "What shall be done?" The conclusion at which they arrived was that, under the circumstances, it was desirable to hold union revival meetings, and that all in the village who favored such a movement be invited to meet at the Baptist church on the following Tuesday evening and express their views as to the best method of proceeding.

Now, as the meeting was about to close, the Rev. Mr. Latimer rose and said: "In a great measure your experience is also mine. I mourn over the worldliness of a large number of the members of my church. They are absorbed in worldly amusements, and when in pastoral visiting I touch upon personal religion they have no relish for the subject, and for relief they quickly run to some secular theme. Some are so given up to the world that the solemnities of Lent, even, are disregarded. Others, who observe this fast as a matter of form, crowd their worldly pleasures to its very threshold and rush into them again at its close with a new relish. My heart is sick, and with Jeremiah I am ready to cry, ' O that my head were waters and mine eyes fountains of tears! ' In view of the candor with which you have told your experience on this point it gives me relief to let you know the feelings of my own heart. I trust that your anticipated meeting may be blessed of God ; and, although I cannot be with you in the front, be assured that my influence will be in your favor, and I shall be glad to know that my people attend the meetings." Here the interview closed.

To the great delight of the pastors the meeting at the Baptist church was largely attended. The deliberations in regard to having a series of meetings showed a strong desire to secure the services of the talented evangelist, Rev. A. B. E., D.D. A resolution to that effect was carried without a dissenting voice.

The answer to the committee's letter was as follows:

"DEAR BRETHREN: I can give you three weeks in January. I am glad that there is a hearty union of the churches. Commence the work at once. 'Prepare ye the way of the Lord, make his paths straight.' Let there be a union prayer-meeting four or five times a week until I come. A great work is in progress in W——, and over three hundred have embraced religion. To God be all the glory!

"Your servant in Christ, A. B. E."

This letter was read at the next union meeting, and gave great satisfaction. From that time a prayer-meeting was held almost nightly, and the interest was on the increase.

On the Sabbath preceding the coming of Mr. E. the ministers preached sermons particularly suited to the occasion. But what created the most stir was the one preached by Mr. Latimer at St. Mark's; especially the closing part of it. His text was Luke ix, 49, 50. "And John answered and said, 'Master, we saw one casting out devils in thy name; and we forbade him, because he followeth not with us.' And Jesus said unto him, 'Forbid him not: for he that is not against us is for us.'"

The scope of the eloquent discourse was against religious bigotry. While it is perfectly right for us to have our strong preferences in regard to the various branches of the Christian Church we should never cherish that spirit that says, "Come not near to me, for I am holier than thou." In closing he said: "Beloved brethren, while we dearly' cherish our own beloved Zion, and gladly believe that the church of our choice in its mode of worship is nearer the apostolic standard than any other, let us bid God-speed to all branches of the church militant which in the name of the Lord Jesus 'cast out devils.' With a sad heart I am obliged to confess that in this village worldly hilarity, carnal mirth and unsanctified amusement have such a hold upon the affections of scores, if not hundreds, of church members that vital piety and genuine spirituality are confined to a very small number. Few indeed are those who can sincerely say, 'A day in thy courts is better than a thousand.' Multitudes whose names are found among the communicants are under the influence of worldly fashionable devils, who have taken away all of their devotion. I am ready to welcome to our midst any brethren, whether they follow with us or not, who in the name of the Lord Jesus Christ cast out devils. It is announced that a celebrated revivalist is about to commence his labors among us—a man noted for his piety, moderation, and order. If there is any value in history he certainly puts to flight evil spirits. He follows not with us. Shall we therefore forbid him ? Nay, brethren ! If Mr. E., under God, can arouse this village to a sense of its awful condition, let all who love our Lord Jesus Christ give him a hearty welcome. I have properly weighed these words before giving them utterance. I am fully prepared to defend them and stand by them. May God deliver the Church from satanic influence !"

CHAPTER II.

HOW IT LOOKED TO MARY.

COLONEL DUNBAR was a wealthy banker, and his residence was one of the finest in Tonville. He was friendly, cordial, highly intelligent, and looked upon as a very valuable citizen. He was a regular attendant at the Episcopal church, but not a member. He had high regards for Christianity, and was considered by many a religious man. In his contributions he was liberal, not only for the church which he attended, but his generosity reached the others also. His wife's parents, who had departed this life, were " high church " Episcopalians, and their daughter, now Mrs. Dunbar, from her early childhood had very naturally imbibed the views of her father and mother. She was a kind-hearted, intelligent lady, noted for her " high church " convictions. In early youth she had been confirmed, and her zeal for that interesting branch of the church militant was very positive, if not always "according to knowledge." With this exclusiveness her husband had no sympathy, and oftentimes in his pleasant way he would express his opinion in plain terms.

Mrs. Dunbar, was a leader in gay circles. She frequented the theaters, and was generally present at all the fashionable dancing-parties. Her husband would go to these gatherings, not because they yielded him any satisfaction, but as company to his wife. He often thought it strange that Mrs. Dunbar and so many of her fellow church members should be leaders in worldly gayeties; but such was his regard for her feelings that never as yet had he called her attention to the subject. In the common acceptation of the term she was an excellent lady, and amid all her gay and often deceitful surroundings there was in her a refreshing degree of sincerity. Sometimes, when disputing with her friends, and expressing herself in the most positive style and in the strongest terms, she would unexpectedly surrender, and in the most frank manner admit that she had seen her mistake. They had one child; a daughter. She was fair in person, had a strong, vigorous mind and ready utterance. Mary Dunbar from her early childhood had been a lover of study. Her advantages had been superior, and now, at twenty, she was a ripe scholar. With her parents, she was a regular attendant at church, but was not a communicant. More to please others than from her own inclination she would attend theaters and

18

dancing-parties.   To her mother's astonishment she
would often beg for the luxury of staying at home.
She was the pride of her parents, and in the village
she was a universal favorite.   By common consent
she was considered the most beautiful young lady
in Tonville.   She was perfectly free from vanity,
conceit, or haughtiness.   Her smiles were bestowed
upon the deserving poor as well as the rich.   In
company she would be attired in simple elegance,
while others displayed their tastes by "superfluity
of apparel."

Colonel Dunbar's parents also resided in Tonville, with whom a widowed daughter, Mrs. Sin-
clair, stayed, devoting herself to the comfort of the
somewhat aged couple.   These parents, with the
daughter, were faithful members of the Methodist
church.   Mary Dunbar was passionately fond of her
grandparents and her Aunt Martha, and no face
brought more sunshine into the home of the venerable twain than that of their smiling grandchild.
Grandma Dunbar, in her own sweet, impressive
manner had often spoken to Mary on the subject
of religion, and of the great importance of personal,
experimental piety.   The young lady, with tears in
her eyes, would kiss her grandmother, thank her for
her good advice, and secretly wish that her mother's
religion was of the like stamp.

It was the afternoon of the Sabbath on which
Mr. Latimer had given his stirring sermon on
sectarian bigotry. Colonel Dunbar, his wife, and
daughter, were seated in the parlor.   Hitherto the
subject of the morning discourse had not been

touched upon, although it was fresh and uppermost in the minds of all. Perhaps they had only been waiting for a convenient time. It was evident that the father and daughter were delighted with what they had heard, and there were unmistakable signs that the mother was highly dipleased. The conversation was opened by Mrs. Dunbar, in whose mind had accumulated a rich abundance of " high church " sentiments which longed for permission to be heard.

" Well," said she, " the walls of our church echoed this morning to strange sentences, I must say."

" I honor them for their echo, my dear," said the colonel. " Any sensible walls would have done the same. I think the sentiments found an echo in the hearts of the people."

" They found no echo in my heart," was the reply.

" And so much the worse for your heart," said the husband, with a very pleasant smile. " I always liked Mr. Latimer's preaching, but to-day more than ever."

" We have had ministers at St. Mark's that did not trouble themselves about their parishioners' amusements," said Mrs. Dunbar. " They left that to our sense of propriety and attended to their own legitimate business. We then went to church and enjoyed the sermon, but now we often come home and feel sore from an unjust chastisement administered by one who would deprive us of our few entertainments."

"But if Mr. Latimer fully believes that these entertainments are destroying the spirituality of his church is it not his duty, as a faithful watchman, to warn his flock against their pernicious influence?" asked her husband in a kind voice.

"At least he ought to do it in a different way," said the wife. "It was altogether too much in the vein of the sects. If it were not for his gown a stranger coming in would have easily taken him for a Methodist minister."

"I agree with you there, my dear," said Colonel Dunbar, smiling, "and the mistake of the stranger would have been as complimentary to Mr. Latimer as to the Methodist ministry."

"His sermons lack in that smooth, graceful, dignified, and melodious oratory becoming the pulpits of the Church," said Mrs. Dunbar; "and, worse than that, there was in the last part of his sermon a shameful lowering of our standard to the level of the sects."

"Not so, my dear," said the husband; "he lowered no standard. He only said that the one great Church of Christ on earth was composed of all true believers, of whatever names or denominations."

"Very well," said the wife; "and is not that putting the Church on a level with the sects?"

"Yes, it is," was the answer; "but it is not lowering the Church's standard. It is simply acknowledging that God's favorites are not confined to any particular communion."

"Christ has but one Church, and of that Church

I am a member," said Mrs. Dunbar. "In her you will find the only true ordination. And for an Episcopal rector from the pulpit of the church to put her on a level with these sects is a shame!"

"I am happy to believe that my dear wife is far more charitable than her words, at least, would indicate," said the father.

"Charity has nothing to do with it," said the wife. "No charity can alter facts. The sects are outside of the true Church, and all the charity in the universe cannot make it otherwise."

"So thought Peter once," was the reply; "but the vision gave him to understand that what God had cleansed he was not to call common or unclean. Let us be careful, my dear, that we do not look with disdain upon those whom God has purified, 'because they follow not with us.'"

"That sounds well enough," said the wife, in a more reflective mood. "But I say again that Mr. Latimer, in putting us on a level with the sects, did not act the part of a true churchman."

"My dear mamma," said Mary, "I think the *members* of the church, at least, are complimented by being put on a level with the 'sects,' as you call them."

"That is a strange idea, surely," said the mother. "Mary, what do you mean?"

"I mean," said the daughter, in a quiet tone, "that the members of the sects, at least in Tonville, lead far more exemplary Christian lives than do the members of our own church. I have watched this point for years, and that is my conviction."

"I am perfectly astonished to hear such language from you, my daughter," said Mrs. Dunbar. "It is wholly uncalled for. What is there in the conduct of our church members to which you can object?"

"I would not purposely hurt your feelings for the world, my dear mamma," said the daughter. "I have had, and do have, much serious thought on the subject of religion, and when I take exception to the behavior of members of our church it is not in a sneering, cold, fault-finding spirit. You ask me to what I object in the conduct of our church members. I answer, it · is that which almost crushes our good pastor and his most excellent wife: a constant running of the members into all the frivolities and vanities of an unbelieving and wicked world. Theaters, operas, card-tables, and dances—these are the favorite objects of a large number of his flock, while hardly ever a word is heard of vital piety and experimental religion. Mamma, just think over the members of our church, and how many can you find that lead a life of religious consecration; that take up the cross and follow in the footsteps of the humble Nazarene? The most prominent of our members are leaders in masquerades and fashionable dancing-parties. This is true, in a measure, of members of other churches, but not to such an extent. Among them I find a large number of faithful, devoted souls who are deeply grieved over the backslidings of the rest. And that is the reason why I think our church complimented by being put on a level with the sects."

The parents listened in perfect astonishment. They had never heard her express herself in that wise before. The mother looked reflective, and in the eyes of the father there was a moisture which denoted a degree of inward emotion.

" Mary,'' asked the mother, " do you think it wrong for members of the church to attend theaters and dances ?''

" If I should answer that question directly, dear mamma,'' said Mary, " I am afraid it would sound almost disrespectful. I will only refer you to the solemn questions and answers in our baptismal service, and which are ratified by the candidates at confirmation. There they promise to ' renounce the devil and all his works, the vain pomp and glory of the world, all the carnal desires of the flesh, to keep God's holy will and commandments, and walk in the same all the days of their lives.' I have heard those solemn promises from the lips of young ladies at the baptismal altar, and then at confirmation, who in the week following, in the society of irreligious persons, were seen waltzing until three o'clock in the morning. The next night they were at the theater and the next at another dance. Confirmation, with its solemn promises, a theater, and two dancing-parties in one week! If church members are to rush into all the amusements of an ungodly world where does the self-denial come in? Where is the cross that is to be taken up? And where is the crucifixion of the world to us and ours to the world? Is it any wonder that Mr. Latimer is crushed in spirit, and is glad to welcome some one to this wicked village who will give it a tremendous shaking and ' cast out devils ' ? "

" Why, Mary," said the mother, while a peculiar trembling came over her, " from the way you speak I should think that you would never be seen again either at a dance or in a theater."

" Mamma," was the reply, " I have not enjoyed a dance for years. I knew that you wished me to attend them, and to please my mother I went. If left to my own free choice I would never attend another ball or be seen in a theater. Dancing is frivolous and the theater demoralizing."

" Mary, you actually frighten me ! " said the mother, gazing at her daughter with a puzzled look. " What would society think of you ? What would your young associates say—the Nelsons, the De-longs, the Chathams, the Dunlaps, the Armitages, and others ? You certainly ought to reflect before taking such a step."

" Reflect ! " said Mary. " It is reflection that has brought this about. I am not indifferent to the opinion of my friends. But if I am to fall in their estimation because I see fit to abandon ball-rooms and theaters, I am fully prepared to make the sac-rifice."

" Those are noble sentiments, and worthy of my own dear Mary," said the father, with much feel-ing. " Dear as you have been to me always, you stand higher in my estimation at this moment than ever before."

" Mary," said the mother in a subdued tone, " if you thought that, as a member of the church, I was leading an unbecoming life, why did you not tell me so long ago?"

" Mamma, dear, would it become a child to reprove her parent? And even to-day I hope that I have not been disrespectful to my good mother," said Mary.

" Have you not been conversed with of late in regard to the matter?" asked her mother.

" My dear grandmother, with earnest affection, has often spoken to me on the subject of religion," said Mary. " To her kind admonition more than anything else I am indebted for my present feelings. Mr. Latimer also has often spoken to me on the same subject, but I think he never advised me in regard to theaters and dances."

" That is certainly a wonder," said the mother.

" I think I can see two reasons why he did not mention those things while conversing with Mary," said the father. " First, his chief object was to bring her to embrace experimental religion, and then he would show the dangers that would beset her. Secondly, there would be something like absurdity in advising a young lady not a member of his church to shun those fashionable amusements to which so many of his own members were so deeply attached. Does it not so appear to you?"

Without replying the mother again addressed her daughter: " Mary, if you shut yourself up from society I fear you will be despondent and gloomy, and it may possibly injure your health."

" I have not the least intention of absenting myself from society. I intend to greatly enlarge the circle," said Mary. "Society, in the good sense of the term, does not mean an exclusive set that dreads to come in contact with common people. For one, I long to get loose from the gilded but oppressive chains of what is termed fashionable society and imitate more fully the Saviour of the world, who 'went about doing good.' I pant for that inward peace and spirit-rest that flow from fellowship with God through our Lord Jesus Christ. Now, without any particular forethought, I have revealed to my dear parents the secret feelings and desires of my heart. What others can do is not for me to say, but, as for myself, I can never be a humble self-denying Christian and at the same time a worshiper at the shrine of worldly pleasure."

"Mary, dear," said the father in tremulous accents, "I am sure your mother will never ask you to join in any company or amusement not in harmony with your religious convictions."

Mrs. Dunbar's countenance manifested a peculiar expression. In that mother's heart there was a struggle. The solemn words of her daughter had reached not only her ears but her inmost conscience. The awful truth flashed upon her mind that throughout the years she, a mother and a member of the church, as far as her example was concerned had been leading her child into the broad road that leads to death. After what her husband had said she remained silent for a few moments, then rushed up to her daughter, fell weeping upon her bosom, and broke out in sobbing accents: "O my dear child, your wonderful words have opened my blind eyes! I accept them as a revelation from Heaven. Instead of giving my daughter a good Christian example, and leading her to the Saviour, I have encouraged her in the ways of sin and vanity. I will do so no more, God being my helper! I have wickedly despised the truth and disliked our godly pastor. May God forgive me! No, my dear child, as your father has said, I will no longer lay a straw in your way. I will follow your example and try to be a good Christian. I ask both of you to forgive me and—"

"O mamma, mamma," interrupted Mary, "don't ask forgiveness at my hand! I cannot bear it. It shocks me. You have only done what you considered proper."

"Yes; but what right had I to consider the life I led as right and proper?" said the mother. "I have led a worldly life. I have had a name to live while dead. I have prided myself on the superiority of the Church to the sects, and looked down upon the purest Christians in Tonville 'because they follow not with us.' Even your godly grandmother I have considered as outside of the true Church. I pray the Lord to lead me in the right way. O Mary, darling, you have led your mother to the foot of the cross." And as a fitting conclusion she warmly embraced her daughter and fondly kissed her husband.

CHAPTER III.

A PARTY AND THE REVIVAL.

THE evening union prayer-meetings had now been held constantly for nearly two weeks. From the first the faithful devoted souls in all the churches had entered into the work with a firm faith that the Jehovah whom they sought would "suddenly come to his temple." The hills were being lowered, the valleys elevated, and the way of the Lord prepared. As these meetings progressed the interest increased, and nightly the attendance had become more encouraging. On the Sabbath evening before the appearance of the evangelist the prayer-meeting at the Methodist church was a season of "refreshing from the presence of the Lord." "A sound of a going" was heard "in the tops of the mulberry-trees," and the army of God was already shouting for the battle.

It was Monday evening, and there was a small party of young people at the residence of Thomas Armitage, who was a wealthy merchant, and had been in trade at Tonville for thirty years. He was an official member of the Presbyterian church, and was a man of great influence in the community. His wife, much younger than himself, was of a lively temperament, fond of company, and, with her husband, a member of the church. She would give liberally for any worthy object that needed money. She was careful that the poor were not neglected at "Christmas-times." She would plan festivals, manage sociables, engineer surprise parties, encourage concerts, go to church, take the sacrament, give dancing-parties, play cards, and go to the theater. Deacon Armitage was a devout, humble Christian, and silently grieved over his wife's extreme worldliness. They had two children, George and Grace. The brother was twenty-five and the sister five years younger. It might be supposed that these children would have naturally followed in the footsteps of the mother, and rush into all the fashionable amusements of the day. But it was otherwise. Although not Christians they were rather inclined to follow the example of their pious father. The young company were together in the commodious parlors.

"Well," said Robert Nelson, in a trifling tone, "they say that our Tonville dominies gave us dancing characters 'Hail Columbia' yesterday morning. If I had known that they were to fire off such big guns I would have gone to meeting myself."

"It was well that you stayed at home," said Arthur Delong. "The preaching was unusually interesting, and the people listened as they had never listened before ; and if in any of the churches they had seen you I fear that such a strange occurrence would have diverted their minds from the preacher's discourse."

This produced some merriment which Nelson did not quite enjoy. He soon rallied, however, and said :

"The reverend gentlemen have taken upon their hands too big a job. I would advise them to drop it and turn their attention to repentance and faith, which would be far more legitimate to their calling than to undertake to regulate dances and theaters."

"And I think that Mr. Robert Nelson has taken upon his hands too big a job; and I would advise him to drop it and pay his attention to corn, wheat, oats, barley, and flour-sacks—which would be far more legitimate to his calling than to regulate ministers and churches," said Emma Thornton, a lively lass of eighteen, who could say what she pleased without giving offense. "Our ministers are men of brains, and are supposed to know their duty. If they wish to advise their own members in regard to theaters, dances, and playing cards, is it any of Mr. Nelson's business?"

"Come, Em, don't be too hard on a fellow," said Nelson. "But even with their own members I fear that their task is a hopeless one, for, as far as I can see, 'pilgrims and sojourners' love to dance, play cards, and go to theaters, as well as we poor guilty wretches who are going to the bad."

"Thank you, Mr. Nelson, for your timely and fearless reproof," said Emma; "and it is to be hoped that we shall profit by the same."

"Reproof, indeed!" said Nelson. "Far from it. I think that you do perfectly right in acting out your independence, and not to go at the bidding of any set of men, whether priests or deacons. Rather say I compliment you."

"I am really sorry to hear your explanation," said Miss Thornton. "As a reproof your words had decided merit. As a compliment they are ludicrous. 'Independence,' indeed! What kind of independence is that which tramples upon the feelings of a faithful pastor, causes sorrow to the best members of the society, and violates church covenants and sacred vows? Is this the independence that you wish to compliment?"

"I trust that Miss Thornton does not accuse herself or any of her friends of any of those things she mentioned," said Mr. Nelson, feeling rather uneasy.

"I have no accusation against my friends," said Emma. "But in regard to my own behavior as a church member I plead guilty. I have grieved my minister, I have wounded the feelings of my brethren, and I have in spirit violated my church covenant. Let no person that has any regard for my feelings compliment me on this wicked independence. Last Saturday I would have not spoken in this way. The solemn truths to which I listened yesterday at the Baptist church opened my eyes, and I saw where I stood ; and your flippant remarks touching our ministers have in a measure loosened my tongue."

"I declare!" said Miss Julia Chattam, with a displeased look. "This sounds more like a prayer-meeting than an evening party."

"If Julia remembers how a prayer-meeting sounds she must have a vigorous memory," said her brother, with a calm smile.

"Fred, don't be hateful," said Julia. "You don't often go yourself.   I simply meant that the conversation had taken a religious turn, which you know is not becoming."

"I don't know any thing of the kind," said Fred. "I began to enjoy it very much. Our parties greatly stand in need of a new departure in the line of conversation.   Why should it be considered unbecoming, in a company chiefly made up of church members, to have an occasional exchange of views in regard to religious matters? Yesterday I did not hear Dr. Spicer, my own minister. I went to St. Mark's, and there I heard a discourse which I shall never forget.   As a professor of religion I felt ashamed of myself. For years I have been one of Nelson's 'independents.' I must lead a new life or leave the church. If there had been a prayer-meeting to-night I would have gone."

"Fred Chattam, what has come over you?" cried his sister.   Then turning to Mary Dunbar, she said, "Mary, don't you think that my brother and Emma are getting insane on this subject?"

"I am not an expert on the subject of insanity," was the answer, "and my opinion would be of no value."

"But we must have it," said Julia, while several others joined in the request.

"Well," said Mary, calmly, "it is my opinion that the language of Mr. Chattam and Miss Thornton indicates a very healthy state of mind and perfect moral sanity. They have spoken words of truth and soberness. I am no Christian. I often have

serious feelings, but I am well convinced that if I
should follow the Saviour he would never lead me
to dances, card-tables, and theaters."

" Worse and worse!" said Julia, while the rest of
the company were much astonished. " I certainly
thought, Mary, that you were safe against this con-
tagion, but you have taken it badly. I am sure
your mother will not encourage you in this nonsense."

" My mother will not encourage me in any nonsense," said Mary, smiling ; " but we view this matter alike. Since yesterday morning a great change
has taken place in our family. We have given up
forever theaters, dances, and card-tables. This may
modify Mr. Nelson's view in regard to the hopeless-
ness of our minister's task."

" I take it all back, Miss Dunbar," said Nelson.
" I think the ' big job ' will be accomplished."

Julia looked a little bewildered and somewhat
vexed. She turned to William Dunlap; a young
lawyer, not a member of the church, and said, " Mr.
Dunlap, what think you of these things ? Do you
think there is any harm in Christians dancing, playing cards, and attending theaters?"

" The theater, upon the whole, has a corrupting
influence," said the young lawyer; " and if I had a
sister for whom the play had great attractions I
should look upon it as a great calamity. In regard
to cards, the young man that never touches them,
even for amusement, is to be congratulated. In
regard to dancing, it is a worldly amusement entirely
destitute of any beneficial moral effects. As an
19

answer to your question I will say that in my opin-ion those persons, members of the church, who indulge in those things, are hurting themselves, and giving strong grounds to those who are without to think that they may as well be in the world as in the church."

"Well, now I'll give up!" said Miss Chattam. "I have never heard such things in all my life, and I don't feel comfortable. I shall have to think these things over. I am not sure but that I also feel some of the symptoms of this epidemic. Well, let it come. When I shall see things in that light I shall be as honest as the rest of you. Mrs. Armitage, why don't *you* say something? Here you have heard these astonishing things and you have not said a word. I hope we have not hurt your feelings."

"Far from that, my dear," said Mrs. Armitage; "I have been very much pleased with the conver-sation. I was prepared to be interested from what I heard yesterday from Dr. Spicer. He seemed to be divinely inspired. He brought us to the bar of our own consciences, and, for one, I felt condemned. There were but few dry eyes in the house, and we made a new consecration. I have set a bad example before my children, but fortunately they had a de-voted Christian father. To-morrow morning Mr. E. commences his labors, and I hope to attend all the meetings. Now, Julia, dear, let us have some music —something with 'the ring' in it."

Here the smiling countenance of Deacon Ar-mitage appeared, who was warmly greeted by the young people.

"What shall we sing, Mrs. Armitage?" asked Julia.

"Sing Mr. Armitage's favorite," was the answer, "'Jesus, I my cross have taken.'"

The deacon was well pleased, and had an impression that the selection was not in harmony with former usages. The whole of the grand hymn was sung in an impressive style by well-trained voices.

"May Heaven bless you, my dear young people," said the good man, "and may you be delivered from the deceitful charms of an ungodly world!"

They tarried together for some time longer, and then left for their respective homes, each wondering at the strange turn the little party had taken.

The evangelist was made acquainted with the exact state of things at Tonville down to the morning of the first day of his labor. The committee from time to time had cheered his heart with the promising features of the union prayer-meeting. On the Monday evening of his arrival at the village, like Barnabas at Antioch, "when he saw the grace of God he was glad." The meeting on Tuesday morning at the session-room of the Presbyterian church was largely attended. The man of God had come to them "in the fullness of the blessing of the gospel of peace." His countenance beamed with love and an assurance of victory. His words were accompanied with power. The Scriptures were read, then the affecting hymn was sung, "Just as I am, without one plea."

He then engaged in a most earnest supplicating

prayer. Others followed. There was an ardent desire for the baptism of the Holy Ghost, a panting after the living God, a holy breathing after divine power. There were humiliations, secret confessions, new consecrations, and a clinging to the cross. At half-past ten the service commenced in the audience-room, where a large congregation had assembled. The hour was devoted to impressive remarks on the third chapter in the book of Malachi. The evangelist gave it a spiritual meaning throughout. " Tithes and offerings " had to be brought in. " Brethren," said he, " I know that you desire a revival. But do you desire it above every thing in the universe? Can you think of any thing that you would rather have than a revival of religion and the salvation of your children and friends? Bring yourselves to the test. Can you think of any sum of money that you would prefer to a revival? Suppose a bag of gold containing ten thousand dollars was placed before you, with the positive assurance that you could choose between that bag of gold and a glorious revival of God's work in Tonville. Could you get but one, which would you take?." Just then, under the burning words of the evangelist, the secret response of all the members present seemed to be, " Lord, give us the revival ! " He spoke for an hour, while bosoms heaved, hearts throbbed, and eyes wept.

In the afternoon he preached from these words: " Old things have passed away." He showed the radical change which genuine conversion produced. The picture which he drew of those church members whose sole delight was in worldly pleasures was terribly graphic, while scores in the audience as in a mirror beheld their own images. " In these meetings," said the speaker, " before we can have confidence to approach the sinner we must redeem the members of our churches from the corrupting influence of unholy amusements. My brethren here in the ministry on last Sabbath opened fire all along the line, and already the breastworks of the enemy are giving way. Some who were ' at ease in Zion' are waking up to a sense of their duty, and when church prodigals shall return then sinners will be converted to God. I am glad to witness indications that already there are those who are in haste to confess their wanderings."

When this most impressive sermon closed a hymn was sung with a will by the large audience, and the evangelist said that there would now be an experience meeting, especially for those in the church who were willing to confess their departure from God and renew their consecration.

In an instant Mrs. Armitage was on her feet. " For many years, as you well know, I have been a member of this church, but in my outward life I have been on a level with the world. I have had no taste for spiritual things. I have neglected prayer-meetings and patronized dances and theaters. I have set a bad example before my children ; I have grieved my husband ; I have caused sorrow to my pastor and the church. I ask forgiveness. ' Show pity, Lord ! O Lord, forgive !' "

No sooner had Mrs. Armitage sat down than the

voice of Mrs. Dunbar was heard, and it sent a thrill through the vast assembly. "Last Saturday, if some one had told me that on Tuesday afternoon I would be found in the Presbyterian church making confessions and asking forgiveness, I would have indignantly laughed him to scorn. I am a member of another communion. I prided myself on my church relation and led a life of gayety. I was prominent in fashionable dances and I attended theaters. I had no taste for devotion. Last Sabbath afternoon, while listening in perfect astonishment to the religious views of my own daughter, who is not a church member, my blind eyes were opened to see my awful condition. I trust that I have found forgiveness of the Lord, and I feel that I am indeed 'a new creature.' My bigotry is all gone. To me you are all members of the one great Church of God, and I now look upon these ministers as the regularly ordained embassadors of the King of kings."

These words, from such a source, produced a wonderful effect. Tears freely flowed, while the sanctuary was filled with the divine presence. Then followed testimonies of the same nature from Fred Chattam, Emma Thornton, and many others from all the churches, until it was time to close the meeting.

"There may be those here," said Mr. E., "that feel their need of a Saviour and a spiritual home, who have hitherto stood aloof from membership in the Church of Christ. If there are any such let them stand up."

Colonel Dunbar and his daughter rose to their feet, and so did George Armitage and his sister Grace, together with half a dozen others.

The evening meeting was very full, while the ministry was quick and powerful, and there was a large number of anxious seekers bowing at the mercy-seat.

CHAPTER IV.

THE "RETREAT" LOSES A CUSTOMER.

"IT seems to me like an utter impossibility," said Mrs. Brougham, who had called upon her friend, Mrs. Major Pugh. " I never heard of any thing so ridiculous in all my life. I *will* not believe it! There is some great mistake somewhere. Mrs. Colonel Dunbar would never so disgrace herself or the church to which she belongs. Dear me! what are we coming to, I should like to know? A member of *the Church* making confessions in a Presbyterian meeting-house! The woman must have lost her senses."

" Please drop in for a few minutes on your return, Mrs. Brougham," said Mrs. Pugh, with a smile, " and give me your opinion in regard to Mrs. Dunbar's mental condition."

" I will surely do that," said Mrs. Brougham ; and she left for the fine mansion of her erring sister.

Mrs. Dunbar was at home and alone. Mrs. Brougham was received with great cordiality and prevailed upon to remove her wraps. The visitor was ill at ease. She had dreaded the interview, and feeling that the sooner the subject was introduced the better, she came to the conclusion to begin at once.

" Mrs. Dunbar," she said, " I have heard that you attended what they call a ' revival meeting' at the Presbyterian meeting-house yesterday, and that you there made humble confessions. I can hardly believe such a report unless I hear it from your own lips."

" My dear Mrs. Brougham," said Mrs. Dunbar, with a calm smile, " I know exactly how it must have shocked your sense of propriety, and yet you have heard nothing but the exact truth."

" Your life has been all correct," said Mrs· Brougham, " and for Mrs. Colonel Dunbar, a member of the only church in the place, to go to a revival meeting of the sects and there make confessions is, I really believe, a disgrace to herself as well as to the Church."

" Mrs. Brougham," was the answer, " I know Mrs. Colonel Dunbar better than does any person in Tonville, and I know that her behavior as a member of the church has been a disgrace to the cause of Christ. Let me give you a brief sketch of this lady's life, and I will do her no injustice." She then, in her most graphic manner, went over her history from the days of her youth to that moment, including the interview in the parlor on Sabbath afternoon, while Mrs. Brougham listened in utter astonishment. In closing, Mrs. Dunbar remarked, " There is for you a brief history of Mrs.

Colonel Dunbar, without a single element of genuine Christian character; a ' lover of pleasure more than a lover of God.' I have humbled myself before the Lord in deep penitence, and he has poured into my heart the balm of consolation. I am very happy. I now ' renounce the devil and all his works, the vain pomp and vanity of the world.' I will endeavor to ' keep God's holy will and commandments, and walk in the same all the days of my life.' "

At the close Mrs. Brougham was deeply affected, but not demonstrative. Her words were few, and she seemed to be in deep reflection. When about to leave she said : " Mrs. Dunbar, I am glad that I came here. I have had some wonderful revelations. I hardly know what to think of them. I will candidly consider them over and see you again. If your views are correct in regard to yourself it leaves me in a sad condition. I feel a heaviness resting upon me, and I must hurry home." They kissed each other and Mrs. Brougham left.

" Well," said Mrs. Major Pugh, "you have kept your promise. Now let me hear your opinion in regard to Mrs. Dunbar's mental condition. Is she really insane ? "

" Don't let us talk any more nonsense, my dear," said Mrs. Brougham ; " I never saw her appear more lovely or heard her conversing more intelligently. She has met with a most wonderful change, and that through the instrumentality of Mary. Now, if all this is so, what must *I* think of myself? I must go home and think this matter over. Mrs. Dunbar is very happy and I am very miserable." And Mrs. Brougham burst into tears.

" Only commit your ways to the Lord," said Mrs. Pugh, who was a devoted member of the Baptist church, " and, if I am not mistaken, you will soon be as happy as Mrs. Colonel Dunbar."

Mrs. Brougham, with feelings that she could not well explain, left for her fine mansion.

———

The " Retreat " was one of Tonville's fashionable saloons, duly licensed to sell ales, wines, and spirituous liquors. This ornamented den was owned and kept by one Nicholas Tracy, whose Christian name was usually reduced to smaller dimensions and pronounced " Nick." He had been brought up on a farm about two miles out of the village. His mother died when he was quite young. He was an only child, and his morals were very far from being worthy of imitation. He married while young and brought his bride to his father's house. In about two years after this his father died, and a very handsome property fell into his possession. The village saloon had much more attraction for him than had his good farm, and, contrary to his wife's wishes, he exchanged it for some village property including a fine residence and the adjoining " Retreat." The saloon was soon rebuilt on a fashionable scale, and was one of the finest in the village. Tracy had become fleshy, and presented all the features of a hard drinker. He was coarse and vulgar, and prided himself on the slang phrases with which he ridiculed the churches.

It was on Wednesday afternoon, and there were sitting in the bar-room of Tracy's saloon four young men finely dressed and fair in their personal appearance. It was evident that they were in the habit of drinking, but as yet they had not become indifferent to their costumes. John Delancy was about twenty-six years of age. His father, a successful merchant, had died, leaving the business to his son. This young Delancy still carried on, but spent much of his time at the Retreat, trusting the trade to his clerks. He had a mother and a sister, with whom he stayed. The others present at this time were John Dexter, a brother of Mrs. Tracy, William Thompson, a son of a wealthy tanner, and Thomas Brown, the son of a rich brewer.

"Well, boys," said Tracy, leaning on the bar from the inside, giving a fine exhibition of costly rings and expensive sleeve-buttons, "they say that the religious circus at the Presbyterian church opened finely yesterday and last night. I once thought it wasn't going to be much of a show, but I hear they have a rush. There are three home clowns, and one imported, for whose services they must shell out a big sum. The small performers are numerous, and they say George Armitage has entered the ring."

To this there was a loud "ha, ha!" from Dexter and Brown, while Delancy looked indignant and Thompson rather serious.

"To me it is no great wonder that they have roped in George," continued Tracy. "I never thought much of him anyway. He has no independence. He is too much under the old man's thumb. I trade with him some, but he never darkens my saloon-door."

"It may be possible that Armitage has no particular fancy for the articles you keep for sale," said Delancy.

"But why can't he come in and take a social glass like the rest of you?" asked "Nick," elevating his voice and looking exceedingly spiteful. "Answer me that, John Delancy."

"Perhaps I cannot tell you all the whys," said Delancy, "but I think I can furnish you with a few. In the first place, he thinks that the practice of drinking is wrong, and very dangerous. Again, the class that visit your saloon do not compose the society in which he desires to mingle. Again, he possesses a large share of good sound sense, and that is in the way. Again, if he should visit this saloon he would lose the respect of the best citizens of our village. Do you want another why?"

"Yes, go on and finish your speech as long as you are about it," said Nick, looking angry.

"And lastly," said Delancy, looking the saloon-keeper in the eye, "Armitage has no respect for Nick Tracy. He looks upon him as a low, swearing, vulgar fellow, fearing not God nor regarding man."

"Delancy," said Tracy, with quivering lips, and paleness which forced itself to the surface of his bloated face, "I rather suspect that under a pretense of speaking for George you have been piling up your own opinions."

"You have rightly judged," said Delancy. "The

language you have used in regard to the religious meeting at the Presbyterian church, conducted by persons of the highest respectability, stamps you as a low, vulgar wretch, and I so pronounce you. I have a mother and a sister who are deeply interested in those meetings, and they must not be insulted in my presence."

"Neither am I to be insulted!" said Tracy, in a loud, angry tone. "I don't want you here, so I would advise you to join the howling at the Presbyterian church."

"The only good advice I ever heard from your lips, and I will take it under my serious consideration," said Delancy, as he rose. "Whether I shall seek a place among Christians or not, I will never trouble *you* again."

"Perhaps I was a little rough on the church people," said Tracy. "I call it back. Come, boys, let us all drink at my expense;" and he put five glasses on the bar.

"No more drink for me!" said Delancy; and he left the saloon.

There was much talk after Delancy's departure, and Thompson quietly slipped away.

On this day John Delancy was perfectly sober. Nothing of an intoxicating nature had touched his lips. After leaving the saloon he slowly walked out of the village so as to have time and place for reflection; and thus he mused: "For years I have poured my money into the polluted treasury of that vulgar wretch! And worse than that; I have measurably wrecked my noble manhood and caused grief to the best of mothers and the most loving of sisters. I have left Nick's Retreat forever! Shall I seek another saloon, or abandon them all? O my God! I almost hear the voice of my sainted father crying from the skies, ' John, abandon them all and take the pledge!' Father, I'll do it! In the name of God *I'll do it!* "

Dr. Spicer was in his study, and in a very happy state of mind as he thought over the wonderful things already accomplished in connection with the revival services. "This is the Lord's doing," said he, "and it is marvelous in our eyes." His wife came in and informed him that John Delancy was below and wished to see him on particular business.

The doctor went down, met the young man with a smile, and conducted him to his study.

"Doctor," said Delancy, without any hesitation, "I ask of you as a favor to write out a strong total abstinence pledge, which I will sign in your presence relying on God for help to keep it as long as I live. I am perfectly sober. I have not touched a drop of liquor this day. I have neglected my business, grieved my mother, afflicted my sister, and measurably destroyed my moral and intellectual powers. I think there is in me yet a remnant that is worth saving. Now, please write the pledge, and let it be strong and thorough."

The doctor took the young man by the hand and with tears of joy in his eyes said, " John, since yesterday afternoon you have been remembered in our prayers, and we accept this as the work of the Holy

Ghost in answer to our humble petitions. Here is a temperance pledge, John."

"No," said the young man ; " I would rather have it in your own hand-writing. It will seem stronger."

The pledge was written. It was as strong as language could render it. John took the pen, and, after carefully reading the paper, he wrote his name in a large, clear, beautiful hand.

"Dr. Spicer," said he, "it is done! My fetters are broken and I am free! But I am not a Christian. My mother and Jennie are Christians, and I believe in the power of prayer. Now, I will kneel down right here while you pray the Lord to keep me from breaking the pledge."

They knelt. They prayed ; and there was joy in the presence of the angels of God. The young man promised to attend the meetings, and left.

In about fifteen minutes after the departure of John, his sister Jennie called and asked Mrs. Spicer to call her husband and accompany him to the parlor, where she wished to speak to them both in regard to her brother. Mrs. Spicer slightly smiled, but the young lady did not notice it. The pastor and his wife were soon in the parlor.

"My dear pastor!" cried the young woman, " I have been so distressed all day on account of my dear brother that I could no longer stay in the house. In many respects he is an excellent young man, but for a long time he has been gradually gliding into a drinking habit, and I am afraid it will prove his ruin. He is often found at Tracy's den, in company with low characters, and I think he is there now.   Dr. Spicer, John has great confidence in you, and he never mentions your name but with great respect.   I came here to beg of you to seek a personal interview with him and try to persuade him to give up his tippling.''

"Jennie, your request is a very reasonable one," said the doctor.   "In the meanwhile remember him at the throne of grace, and God will answer your prayers. For your encouragement I will say that not over half an hour ago a young man of this town who has been in the habit of drinking came voluntarily into my study and under deep feeling asked me to write for him the strongest temperance pledge that I possibly could.   He was perfectly sober.   I wrote it and he signed it.   He then kneeled down and asked me to pray with him."

"O, I would give all the world, if I had it, if my dear John would only do the same!" cried Jennie. "Perhaps it would not be right for you to tell me who that young man is."

"Perfectly right, Jennie," said the doctor.   "I think you are acquainted with him.   Here is the pledge, and you can read it."

She glanced at the familiar signature, and with joyful sobbing fell on her knees and bowed her head on Mrs. Spicer's lap.   "I thank thee, O Father," she cried, "for answering the prayers of thy children in behalf of my erring brother!"

"John is not far from the kingdom of Heaven, my dear," said the minister's wife, fondly kissing her young sister, who was one of the most devoted and spiritual in the church.

Miss Delancy went home, told her mother the glad news, and together they wept for joy.

When John came from the store to supper the mother and daughter could not keep back. It was the most happy hour they had experienced in many a day.

"Yes, Jennie," said John, "to-night I will gladly go with you to meeting."

CHAPTER V.

AN ANGRY MISS AND A WORD FROM ENGLAND.

MISS EDITH WINTHROP was an ardent worshiper at the shrine of worldly pleasure. Encouraged by her wealthy parents her mind was greatly taken up with the fashionable amusements of the day. The family attended the Episcopal church, but were not communicants. For Mary Dunbar, until her recent change, she had entertained much respect, although she had been often displeased with the banker's daughter's seeming lack of interest in those gayeties which so absorbed her own mind. In regard to religious doctrines she had no settled views. Indeed, there lurked in her heart a great deal of infidelity. Those points in theology that seemed to her distasteful she threw aside, and accepted only those features that did not particularly interfere with her worldly taste. She was brilliant and attractive, amiable in her smiles and sarcastic in her frowns. She was respected for

her position in society.   She was feared on account
of her eloquent severity.   But to no one outside of
the circle of her relatives was Edith Winthrop an
object of intense affection.   The revival she detested
with all the warmth of her strong nature, and what
she heard of it from day to day filled her proud
heart with indignation.   Such was the young lady
to whom Mary Dunbar, in Mr. Winthrop's parlor,
under a deep sense of duty, introduced the subject
of personal religion.

"Mary, your anxiety for me is entirely uncalled
for," said Miss Edith, with a smile meant for reproof, "and, at the hazard of offending you, I must
say that it borders closely on the ludicrous."

"Edith," said Mary, wholly undisturbed, "I thoroughly weighed this matter before I started from
home.   I knew that in all probability you would
not relish the subject, and that you would manifest
your disapprobation in strong terms.   For all this
I am fully prepared, and let no fear of offending
me interfere with your freedom of speech.   I think
I am in a frame of mind that is not to be easily
disturbed."

"That is exceedingly fortunate," said Miss Winthrop, "for I am bound to use language that may
be called severe.   While I can laugh at the foolish-
ness of your errand I am still glad to meet you, for
it gives me an excellent opportunity to let you
know how utterly I detest these religious antics in
our village that are called a 'revival.'   A revival it
is, sure enough!   A revival of confusion, disturb-
ance, animal excitement, and fanaticism.   If this

were confined to that class that has been credulous
and superstitious it would not be so bad. But it is
forcing itself into genteel society and aristocratic
circles. Our best families are being drawn into it,
and it looks as if the whole village were under the
influence of this moral mania. Wherever I go this
is talked of. The topic commands respect in quarters
where it ought to be despised ; and here is one of
our own set transformed into a home missionary in
the interest of religious fanatics, while her father
and mother, and a score of others who have moved
in the most cultivated circles, are regular attendants
at this excitable gathering !   I am indignant." And
Miss Winthrop ended her paragraph.

" Edith," said Mary, " with your present mode of
living do you feel as if you were prepared to die
and meet your God in peace ? "

" Upon my word," said the lady, in a gay, sneering tone, " you seem to be splendidly adapted for
your mission ! A Methodist minister could not have
put the question in better form or with purer in-
tonations. I am very well satisfied with my mode
of living, and the God I expect to meet is not that
angry being that you hear about in these revival
meetings."

" Or that we read of in the Bible," said Mary.

" Yes, you may have it so, if you like," said
Edith. " Any thing in the Bible about God that
sounds to me as unreasonable I cast aside."

" I was not aware that you were skeptical," said
Mary. "I really wish you would attend these
meetings."

"Your wish is vain," was the answer. "I detest the very thought of them. I can hardly respect those that speak well of such excitable demonstrations. They have broken up our set, and it looks now as if we could not get enough together to form a respectable dance. To the utmost of my ability I have labored to keep our young people away from these meetings, and I will do all I can to win back those that have been stolen from us. In a great measure I hold Mr. Latimer responsible for the havoc this thing has made in his own church. His sermon, lately delivered, gave it encouragement. By this time perhaps he sees his mistake."

"I can assure you, Edith," said Mary, "that no one in Tonville rejoices more over this revival than does Mr. Latimer."

"Then I say he disgraces his calling, and should not be permitted to preach in an Episcopal pulpit," was the reply. "He is eloquent enough, and often too much so; but he is altogether too religious to suit polite circles. In the church service such sentences are all right, but to thrust them on people in the parlor is not in good taste. He is not a bit like dear Mr. Smoothly. 'Rejoices over the revival,' does he? Ha, ha! Now that *is* rich! His rejoicing will turn to something else when he sees the members of his flock joining the three sects."

"I am very confident," said Mary, "that no one will leave St. Mark's. I think also that a number that have embraced religion at these meetings will seek their spiritual home in our church."

"So much the worse for St. Mark's," said Miss

Winthrop, with a sneer. "A nice lot of Episcopalians they would make! No, I say. Let them go to where they legitimately belong. I don't fancy the shop in which they have been manufactured."

"Edith," said Mary, "I find you in a more disagreeable mood than I expected. I think it will not be wise for me to remain here any longer. I hope to see you again when you will be more favorably disposed toward your friends than you are to-day. I am deeply interested in your spiritual welfare. I will remember you in my prayers."

"That you may do, and welcome, if it will give you any satisfaction, as long as you confine your prayers to your own room," said Edith; "but let no prayer, private or public, be offered for me at those meetings. In regard to seeing me again on this subject, please let that be postponed until I send you a special request."

"It shall be even so, Edith," said Mary, and she left for home with a heavy heart.

The revival had gone on with increasing interest and power from the very first. The women of the Church, in the fear of the Lord and with genuine Christian modesty, had accomplished a mighty work by their personal interviews with those who had not embraced religion. Saloons were abandoned, dances proved failures, and the academy for dancing was well-nigh deserted. There was a solemnity over the whole village. Thompson had followed the example of Delancy and had signed the pledge, while both had embraced religion. Emma Thornton was thoroughly restored from her wanderings. Fred

Chattam was fully engaged in the work and had much influence among the young people, and Julia had found "the pearl of great price." The youths by the score had bowed at the altar of prayer. The windows of heaven were opened and blessings were poured forth in abundance. Tonville was flooded by divine influences. Among ministers and members there was complete harmony, and nothing of an unpleasant nature had transpired during the services.

The closing exercises of the protracted meeting were in the afternoon, and were confined chiefly to experience. The testimonies were very striking and numerous. The most affecting was that of Thomas England, who for many years had been a slave to intemperance. He was a man of strong native talent and much acquired ability. The reader will better know his history from his own testimony, delivered before an audience of eight hundred people. He had come forward at an early stage of the meeting with deep penitence, and his conversion was clear and positive. Hitherto he had said but little. Now the time had come when the redeemed man considered it his duty to declare publicly what Christ had done for him. He rose and in a clear voice said:

"I feel more like shrinking from publicity and hiding my head in shame than to stand before you and speak. Here you see the wreck of one who was once considered a respectable member of society and a worthy citizen of Tonville. Under the conviction that possibly I yma say a word that will magnify the grace of God, that has saved a poor guilty wretch, I take up my cross. To many of you the history of Tom England is well known. I was well brought up, liberally educated, and was graduated with honor. I studied law and was admitted to the bar. Twenty-five years ago I came to Tonville with a fair young wife and a bright little boy two years old—our little Charlie." [Here the speaker's emotions almost mastered him.] "I had some means; I bought a house and office and became established as a lawyer. I secured a flattering reputation in my profession, and I had a large practice. Early in life I formed the habit of drinking, but for some years, by an effort, I so conducted myself as to be called a moderate drinker; but the habit grew upon me. I neglected my business, wronged my clients, and finally I was pronounced a drunkard. About ten years ago my wife, who had faithfully stood by me notwithstanding my degradation and the abuse she often suffered when I was maddened by rum, sickened and died. This left me alone with Charlie and a sister of mine, who took charge of my sick wife. After this I became worse than ever, and when drunk I was exceedingly abusive, even to my boy, one of the finest lads that ever breathed. He would bear my abuse with much patience, and often, with tears in his eyes, he would beg of me, by the memory of his mother, to stop drinking. O that noble boy! Now, saved from my drunkenness and partially restored to my right mind, I appreciate his worth as I never did before, and it almost breaks my heart to think of it. One day, about nine years ago, when deeply under the influence of liquor, I violently struck that precious son, who never gave me an unkind word, and ordered him to leave my premises. In about an hour after I struck him he came to me calmly and said, 'Father, I forgive you. I am going. Good-bye.' I have never seen him since. We heard that he went to sea, and we heard also that his ship was lost. O my noble Charlie! Well, I sank deeper and deeper in degradation, and for years I have been wandering about, doing chores around taverns to pay for my rum. By the earnest entreaty of kind ladies of this village, who did not despise even poor Tom England, I was persuaded to attend these meetings. Amid all my moral pollution I was not an infidel, and the wonderful words of that man of God, accompanied by the power of the Holy Ghost, reached the depth of my depraved heart. I bowed before the Lord in an agony of penitence, and he has forgiven me the iniquity of my sins. I ask the forgiveness of all whom I have wronged. Charlie with his parting breath said he forgave me. O how I would fall on his neck and tell him how sorry I am! Dear Charlie! I hope to meet him in heaven."

Thomas England sat down. The man, the circumstances, and the undescribable pathos of his remarks, rendered them thrilling. The audience was in tears, and in silence for a few moments the people gave way to their feelings. Soon, however, their attention was called to a well-dressed, fine-looking gentleman of youthful appearance, who rose in the farthest part of the church from the pulpit, left his pew, slowly walked to the front and faced the congregation. Like hundreds of others he was deeply affected, and was making every effort to master his feelings. Soon he spoke, while every eye was fastened upon him.

" Pardon me for making myself thus conspicuous. I have but little to say, but that little I want you all to hear and understand. That is the reason why I have chosen this spot. I am a stranger, having just arrived in this village, and, learning of this meeting, I most gladly came in. My feelings are wonderfully affected by the thrilling remarks of the gentleman that spoke last. His story brought vividly to my mind the scenes of other days and years. My father also through strong drink fell from a respectable position to the depths of intemperance. My dear mother died chiefly of a broken heart, and I was often pointed at as the drunkard's boy. My father, when not under the influence of the cup, was kind and affectionate, and he loved his son, but when drunk he was completely changed. After the death of my mother I ventured into the wide world. I committed my ways to the Lord and went into a foreign land. I united with the Church of Christ. I found favor in the sight of the people. Providence smiled upon me wonderfully and I procured abundance of the things of the present life. I thought I would return to my native land and visit the scenes . of my childhood. This is the most happy day of my life!"

He rushed to the seat where England sat and

cried in a loud voice: "*Father! Charlie has come home!*" He fell upon his parent's neck and both wept aloud. The scene was "unspeakable and full of glory."

After a most impressive admonition to the young converts and those restored from their backsliding, the meeting closed with singing the familiar hymn:

> "Blest be the tie that binds
> Our hearts in Christian love."

The benediction was pronounced, and the revival meeting proper was at an end.

About two hundred and fifty professed conversion. Besides this a large number of church members had been saved from dead formality and brought into the enjoyment of vital godliness. Many of the converts were from distant localities, and these united with the churches in their immediate vicinity. In the village seventy united with the Presbyterians, fifty with the Baptists, forty-five with the Methodists, and at the next confirmation thirty-one with the Episcopalians. Among these were Colonel Dunbar and his daughter. On that occasion St. Mark's was crowded and the interest was intense.

CHAPTER VI.

A SEVERE ORDEAL, AND HOW IT ENDED.

NICHOLAS TRACY grew more blasphemous and eloquent in his curses as he saw himself abandoned by his former customers. His profanity was so terrible as to almost alarm common swearers. He was continually under the influence of liquor, and his saloon presented a neglected appearance. Tracy had a fast, spirited horse, in which he took great pride, and with which he often took careless liberties. One day, while quite drunk, he ordered his man to put the horse before the cutter and bring it out. The man was loth to obey, but in order to escape a volley of curses he complied. The fiery steed was soon before the saloon-door.

"Nick," said Dexter, "you are not in a fit condition to-day to drive that horse."

The reply was angry and very profane ; he stepped into the cutter and off he went at a fearful rate.

It is useless to dwell on particulars. In less than a half hour the same horse, with broken harness and without a cutter, was seen trembling with fright in front of the saloon, while in the distance a crowd of people were approaching bearing the bleeding, dead form of Nicholas Tracy, whose profane spirit had passed into the great eternity.

Deep sorrow pervaded the Winthrop mansion. As yet the dark flag of death did not wave over the imposing structure, but one of its inmates was in the grasp of a raging fever that threatened to prove fatal. On a bed in a richly furnished and commodious room, with a flushed countenance and a high pulse lay Edith Winthrop. In the same apartment stood the parents, with sad countenances watching the heavy breathings and constant tossings of their only child. The doctor sat by the side of the bed examining the pulse of the sufferer and evidently calculating the chances.

"Well, doctor," said the father, in a deep, earnest tone, "can you give us one encouraging word?"

"I have more hopes than I had four days ago," said Doctor Sprague. "She has more vitality at this hour than I could have reasonably expected under the circumstances. The fever is yet high, but I think it will turn in twenty-four hours. I now have strong hopes that her firm constitution will carry her safely through."

The parents wept for joy.

"O Mary, dear, my words were cruel?" cried the sick one in feverish delirium. "O Mary, will you forgive me? I was very wicked!"

"Poor child! She is dreadfully troubled about something she said to Mary Dunbar," said the mother.

"I presume it is the result of a dream, Mrs. Winthrop," said the doctor.

"I think not," said the mother, "for it has troubled her for two weeks."

"I take it all back, dear Mary!" said Edith again. "Mr. Latimer is all right. O, what made me so wicked? Mary, put your hand on my head! There!"

Twenty-four hours soon passed away, and the doctor, faithful to his charge, sat again by the side of the sick-bed. The fever had just turned, and the sufferer, much exhausted, seemed to fall into a sleep.

"We have arrived at a critical point," said the

doctor, in a very low voice. "Miss Winthrop is very weak, but I trust by God's blessing she will rally."

Her slumber gradually became more natural, with a slight improvement of the pulse.

"I am very happy to inform you," said the physician again, "that your daughter is saved. I know she is in the hands of the very best of nurses. In the course of an hour she will wake up. You may speak just a word to her and then retire to rejoice together. I will call again in the morning."

The sick daughter awoke and looked about in intelligent astonishment. In a weak voice she asked, "Miss Williams, what is the matter?"

"You have been very sick, my dear, for three weeks," said the nurse; "the fever has just left you. You are very weak, but you are going to get well. The doctor says you must not talk. Take this medicine, my darling."

The parents spoke to her a few endearing words and left for another part of the house.

In about ten days from this time, when Edith could converse without embarrassment, she expressed to Miss Williams a wish to see her mother alone for a half hour. In a few minutes the smiling mother was in the room, and Miss Williams left.

"Mamma, dear," said Edith, "in my fever did I mention any names?"

"Only two, my darling," said the mother. "You seemed to regret that you had not used Mary Dunbar kindly, and you appeared to be troubled in regard to what you had said about Mr. Latimer.

The doctor thought that your words were but the result of a dream."

" The doctor was mistaken, mamma," said Edith. " I was greatly troubled in regard to that before I was taken sick. I never told you, and you knew nothing about it. Mary Dunbar, the dear girl, in all the sincerity of her good, pure heart, called on me one day with the intention of conversing with me on the subject of religion. I resented it with bitter and cruel words, and spoke of their religious meetings in the most contemptuous language I could use. I also spoke unkindly of Mr. Latimer. I was actually angry. She bore it all with the most perfect patience and said she hoped to see me again. I told her, as far as that was concerned, that she had better postpone her visit until I should send her a special request. ' It shall be even so, Edith,' she said, and went away with a heavy heart. Many weeks ago I felt deeply condemned in view of the rough treatment one of the best girls in Tonville received at my hand. I could hardly look her in the face as, with thirty others, she stood to be confirmed, all of whom were brought into the church by means of that revival which I had denounced in such harsh terms. While feeling thus condemned, and preparing to make proper confession, I was taken sick, and the same thing has troubled me during my fever. Now, mamma, dear, I have told you all. God, in mercy, has spared my hitherto almost useless life, and from hence I hope to be a better girl. I shall never feel comfortable until I have an interview with Mary Dunbar. I am too weak to write. Will you, with your own hand, pen a few lines saying that to-morrow morning, about ten o'clock, I shall be very glad to see her?"

"With all my heart, darling! And it will please Mary as well as yourself," said the mother.

The interview was had. There were confessions and pledges of undying love and friendship. Edith's recovery was rapid. She was "transformed by the renewing of her mind." Not many weeks after her restoration to health she was baptized by Mr. Latimer and afterward confirmed by the bishop.

Thomas England accompanied his son to New York, where the young man, at a very high salary, was employed in the office of a German steam-ship company. The father was employed in the same place, leading a consistent Christian life.

The churches in Tonville still reap the benefit of that great revival. They have an abiding spirituality and freedom from religious bigotry. Mr. Latimer is yet at St. Mark's, a zealous Episcopalian, but always ready to bid God-speed to all that cast out devils in the name of Jesus.

THE END.

www.ingramcontent.com/pod-product-compliance
Lightning Source LLC
Chambersburg PA
CBHW031024120726
47905CB00007B/2032